# JAMES PATTERSON

# BEACH ROAD

### AND PETER DE JONGE

**headline**

First published in Great Britain in 2006 by
HEADLINE PUBLISHING GROUP

First published in paperback in Great Britain in 2007 by
HEADLINE PUBLISHING GROUP

This edition published in 2010
by HEADLINE PUBLISHING GROUP

2

Cataloging in Publication Data is available from the British Library

ISBN 978 0 7553 4952 4

Typeset in Palatino Light by Palimpsest Book Production Limited,
Falkirk, Stirlingshire

Printed and bound in Great Britain by Clays Ltd, St Ives plc

Headline's policy is to use papers that are natural, renewable and recyclable
products and made from wood grown in sustainable forests. The logging
and manufacturing processes are expected to conform to the environmental
regulations of the country of origin.

HEADLINE PUBLISHING GROUP
An Hachette UK Company
338 Euston Road
London NW1 3BH

www.headline.co.uk
www.hachette.co.uk

# BEACH
# ROAD

For Daina, Matthew, Joseph and Porter. Love, Peter.

And as always, for Jack and Susie. Love, Jim.

*I* n the summer of 2003 there were three brutal and
tragic murders in East Hampton, a wealthy beach
community on Long Island, and two related murders in
New York City. These were the subject of countless news
stories, both in New York and nationally.

But the horror of the murders paled in comparison to
the tension and social upheaval in the Hamptons leading
up to and during the murder trial.

This is the story of what happened, and it is told from
several points of view. Keep in mind that people often lie,
especially in the current age, and that the full extent of
their lies can be almost beyond our comprehension.

The players, in order of appearance:

> Nikki Robinson, a seventeen-year-old part-time
> housemaid in East Hampton, Long Island
> Tom Dunleavy, a former professional athlete,
> now a defense attorney in the Hamptons
> Dante Halleyville, accused of four of the

*murders, one of the most talented schoolboy athletes in the country*

*Katherine Costello, another important defense lawyer in the murder trial*

*Loco, a drug dealer who supplied the Hamptons*

*Detective Connie P. Raiborne, a streetwise Brooklyn detective*

*Marie Scott, Dante's grandmother and his mentor in all ways*

*This is their story.*

# PROLOGUE

---

# SOMEBODY ELSE'S SUMMERHOUSE

# Chapter One

## Nikki Robinson

Seventeen and criminally cute, Nikki Robinson sulks through the sultry afternoon trying to keep from staring at her useless shocking-pink cell phone. She hasn't heard from Feifer in three days and is getting the awful feeling she's already been dumped and just hasn't been told yet.

So when Nikki's cell rings while she's waiting in line to pay for her drink at Kwik Mart, her heart goes off with it. She grabs for the phone so fast her best friend, Rowena, behind the counter flashes her a disapproving look that says, 'Chill, girl.'

Rowena is all about maintaining dignity under

romantic duress, and as usual, she's right. It's only Maidstone Interiors calling about a cleaning job for Nikki out in Montauk.

Nikki has been working for Maidstone all summer and likes it okay, but the thing about Maidstone is that she never knows where they're going to send her.

It takes Nikki forty minutes to drive from Kings Highway in Bridgehampton to Montauk, and another five to find the hilly neighborhood perched just above Route 27 where all the streets are named for dead presidents – and not the recent ones, the ones who have been dead awhile.

Forty-one Monroe is neither a mansion nor a dump, but somewhere in between, and as soon as she gets through the door, she sees it's nothing catastrophic and was probably rented by a couple, maybe a small family.

Besides the steady money, what Nikki likes best about this job is that she's alone. She may be cleaning white folks' houses, but at least they aren't standing over her shoulder, watching and supervising her every move. Plus she can dress how she wants, and so she pulls off her jeans and T-shirt, revealing a skimpy two-piece bathing suit underneath. She puts on her headphones and some R. Kelly, and gets busy.

Nikki starts with the ground-floor bedroom. She gathers the dirty towels and strips the sheets, balls them up in a giant damp pile and wrestles it down the steep basement staircase. She quickly gets the first load of wash running, then races all the way up to the second floor, and by now her dark skin, which she sometimes loves and sometimes hates, is shimmering.

When she reaches the landing, there's a funky smell in the air, as if someone's been burning incense or, now that she gets a better whiff, smoking reefer.

That's nothing too out of the ordinary. Renters can be stoners too.

But when Nikki swings open the door to the master bedroom, her heart jumps into her mouth, and yet somehow she manages to scream and to think, *The white devil.*

# Chapter Two

## Nikki

Poised on the bed with a long, curved fishing knife in his hand, and wearing nothing but boxers and a twisted grin, is a skinny white guy who looks as though he just got out of prison. His hair is bleached white, and his ghostly pale skin is covered with piercings and tattoos.

But the scariest part, maybe even scarier than the knife, is his eyes. 'I *know* you, Nikki Robinson,' he says. 'I know where you live. I even know where you work.'

For a couple of seconds that feel much longer, those flat, horror-movie eyes freeze Nikki in the doorway and seem to nail her Reeboks to the floor.

Her lungs are useless now too. She can't even get enough air to scream again.

Somehow she breaks the paralyzing spell enough to lift one foot, then the other, and now she's moving, and *screaming,* running for her life toward the bathroom door at the far end of the hall.

Nikki is fast, a hurdler on the Bridgehampton High School varsity team, faster than all but a handful of the boys, and faster than this snaky, beady-eyed intruder too.

She reaches the bathroom door before him, and even though her hands shake, she manages to slam and lock it behind her.

Her chest heaving so hard she can barely hear his footsteps, she leans her head against the door, her terrified reflection looking back at her in the full-length mirror.

Then turning and pressing her back against the door, she desperately scans the room for a way out.

The window leads to a roof. If she can get on the roof, she can find a way down, or if she has to, jump.

And then she sees it. But she sees it too late.

The brass doorknob twists in the light.

Not the doorknob that's pressing into her back, either. A second doorknob on the other side of the sink, attached to another door, a door she didn't know was there because she's never been to this house until now, a door that leads directly from the bedroom.

As she stares in horror, the doorknob stops turning and the door slowly pushes open, and he's in the tiny bathroom with her. The white devil.

There is *nowhere to go, nowhere to go, nowhere to go,* she thinks, her terror bouncing back at her from every mirror.

And now the devil is pressed up against her, breathing in her ear, the razor-sharp blade tracing a line into her neck. When she looks down he pulls her hair back until their eyes meet in the mirror.

'Don't cut me!' she begs in a weak whisper. 'I'll do whatever you want.'

But nothing she says means a thing, and those pitiless eyes laugh at her as he pushes her shoulders and stomach down over the sink and roughly pulls her bikini bottom to her knees.

'I know you'll do whatever. Don't stop looking.'

Nikki looks at him in the glass just as she's been told to and takes a shallow breath. But when he pushes himself inside her, he shoves so hard her head hits the mirror, and it falls into a million pieces. And even though the blade is pressed against her throat, and she knows it's against the rules, she can't keep herself from moaning and begging him to never stop. But it's not till he's finished that Nikki leans into the mirror and says, 'Feif, I love it when you come up with this freaky romantic role-play shit. You *are* the devil.'

It's not until twenty minutes after that, when they're both lounging around on one of the stripped-down beds, that he tells her the smell in the room isn't reefer, it's crack.

And that's how the story begins – with Feif and Nikki, and the crack they smoke that lazy afternoon at somebody else's summerhouse in the Hamptons.

# PART ONE

---

# MURDER ON
# BEACH ROAD

# Chapter Three

## Tom Dunleavy

It's Saturday morning on Labor Day weekend, and I'm rolling down what some might call the prettiest country lane in America – Beach Road, East Hampton.

I'm on my way to meet four of my oldest pals on the planet. The '66 XKE I have been working on for a decade hasn't backfired once, and everywhere I look there's that dazzling Hampton light.

Not only that, I've got my loyal pooch, Wingo, right beside me on the passenger seat, and with the top down, he hardly stinks at all.

*So why don't I feel better about another day in paradise?*

Maybe it's just this neighborhood. Beach Road is

wide and elegant, with one ten-million-dollar house after another, but in a way, it's as ugly as it is beautiful. Every five minutes or so a private rent-a-cop cruises by in a white Jeep. And instead of bearing the names of the residents, the signs in front of the houses belong to the high-tech electronic security companies that have been hired to keep the riffraff out.

*Well, here comes some prime riffraff, fellas, and guess what you can do if you don't like it?*

As I roll west, the houses get even bigger and the lawns deeper and, if possible, greener. Then they disappear completely behind tall, thick hedges.

When that happens, Wingo and I have put the sorry land of the multimillionaire behind us and have crossed, without invitation, into the even chillier kingdom of the billionaire. In the old days, this would be where the robber barons camped out, or the guys who had invented something huge and life-enhancing, like the refrigerator or air-conditioning. Now it's reserved for the occasional A-list Hollywood mogul, or the anonymous mathematicians who sit in front of their computer screens and run the hedge funds. A mile from here, Steven Spielberg slapped together three lots on Georgica Pond, then bought the parcel on the other side so he could own the view too.

Before I get pulled over for rubbing the rich the wrong way, or being a grouch for no good reason, I spot a break in the hedges and rumble up a long, pebbled drive.

Beyond a huge, sprawling manor built in – no, decorated to look like it was built in – the 1920s is a shimmering pack of cars parked on the grass, each one chromed and accessorized.

Just beyond them is the reason they're here, and the reason I'm here too – a brand-new, custom-built, state-of-the-art, official NBA-length-and-width basketball court.

But if there's a Hampton sight more welcome and less expected than a full-size basketball court with an ocean view, it's the dozen or so people hanging out beside it, and they immediately come over to greet us – the guys lavishing attention on my vehicle, the ladies giving it up for my faithful dog, Wing Daddy.

'This baby is pure class,' says a hustler named Artis LaFontaine as he appraises my antique Jag.

'And this baby is pure cute!' says his girl, Mammy, as Wingo gets up on his hind legs to lay a big wet one on her pretty face. 'Can I adopt him?'

The warm way they all greet me feels as terrific as always – and not just because I'm the only white person here.

# Chapter Four

## Tom

I don't have the honor of being the sole Caucasian for long.

In less than five minutes, Robby Walco arrives in his mud-splattered pickup, WALCO & SON, the name of his and his old man's landscaping company, stenciled on the cab.

And then my older brother, Jeff, the football coach at East Hampton High, shows up with Patrick Roche in his school-issued van.

'Where the hell is Feif?' asks Artis. Artis has never actually volunteered what he does for a living, but the hours are highly flexible, and it pays well enough to keep his canary-yellow Ferrari in twenty-two-inch wheels.

'Yeah, where's the white Rodman?' asks a dread-locked dude called Marwan.

Artis LaFontaine and crew can't get enough of Feif, with his bleached-white hair, the piercings and tats – and when he finally rolls in barefoot on his *bicycle*, his high-tops dangling like oversized baby shoes from the handlebars, they practically give him a standing ovation.

'Be careful with this one, fellas,' says Feif, meticulously lowering his kickstand and parking his eight-dollar bike between two hundred-thousand-dollar cars. 'It's a Schwinn.'

I've depended on Jeff my whole life, but all these guys are indispensable to me. Roche, aka Rochie, is the deepest soul I know, not to mention a terrible sculptor, a mediocre poker player, and a truly gifted bartender. Walco is pure, undiluted human earnestness, the kind of guy who will walk up to you and, apropos of nothing, pronounce Guns N' Roses the greatest rock-and-roll band of all time, or Derek Jeter the finest shortstop of his generation. As for Feif, he's just special, and that's immediately obvious to everyone, from the Dominican cashier at the IGA to your grandmother.

This whole place is owned by the movie star T. Smitty Wilson, who bought it five years ago. Wilson wanted to show his fans he was still keeping it real, so after dropping $23 million for a big, Waspy house on four acres, he dropped another half mil on this sick basketball court. He used the same contractor who built Shaq's court in Orlando, and Dr Dre's in Oakland, but he hired Walco & Son to do the landscaping, and that's how we found out about it.

For a month, we had the court to ourselves, but when Wilson invited his celebrity pals out to the country, it got to be even more fun.

First came a handful of actors and pro athletes, mainly from LA and New York. Through them word leaked into the hip-hop crowd. They told their people, and the next thing you know this court was the wildest scene in the Hamptons – *ever* – a nonstop party with athletes and rappers, CEOs and super-models, and just enough gangsters to add some edge.

But as the celebs thinned out, one of the most expensive residential acres on Beach Road was starting to seem like a playground in a South Bronx housing project.

At that point, Wilson made his retreat. For weeks

he barely ventured from the house; then he began to avoid the Hamptons altogether.

Now about the only person you can be sure of not running into at T. Smitty Wilson's Hamptons compound is T. Smitty Wilson.

# Chapter Five

## Tom

Me, Jeff, Fief, Walco, and Rochie are stretching and shooting around one basket when a maroon SUV rumbles up the driveway. Like a lot of cars here, it looks as if it just rolled off a showroom floor, and its arrival is announced well in advance by five hundred watts of teeth-chattering hip-hop.

When the big Caddy lurches to a stop, three doors swing open and four black teens jump out, each sporting brand-new kicks and sweats.

Then, after a dramatic beat or two, the man-child himself, Dante Halleyville, slides out from the front passenger side. It's hard not to gawk at the kid.

Halleyville is the real deal, without a doubt the best high-school player in the country, and at six foot nine, with muscled arms and chest tapering to a tiny waist and long, lean legs, he's built like a basketball god. Dante is already being called the next Michael Jordan. Had he declared himself eligible for this year's NBA draft, he would have been a top-three pick, no question, but he promised his grandmother at least one year of college.

The reason I know all this is that Dante grew up nine miles down the road, in Bridgehampton, and there's a story about him every other day in the local paper, not to mention a weekly column he writes with the sports editor called Dante's Diary. According to the stories, which suggest that Dante is actually a pretty sharp kid, he's leaning toward Louisville – so rumor has it that's the academic institution that leased him the car.

'You fellas want to have a run?' I ask.

'Hell, yeah,' says Dante, offering a charismatic smile that the Nike people are just going to love. 'We'll make it quick and painless for you.'

He slaps my head and bumps my chest, and thirty seconds later the crash of collapsing waves and the squawking of gulls mix with the squeak of sneakers and the sweet *pock* of a bouncing ball.

You might think the older white guys are about to get embarrassed, but we've got some talent too. My big brother, Jeff, is pushing fifty but at six five, two-seventy, he's still pretty much unmovable under the boards, and Walco, Roche, and Feif, all in their early twenties, are good, scrappy athletes who can run forever.

As for me, I'm not as much of a ringer as Dante, and I'm pushing thirty-five – but I can still play a little.

Unless you're a basketball junkie you haven't heard of me, but I was second-team All-America at St John's and in '95 the Minnesota Timberwolves made me the twenty-third pick in the first round of the NBA draft. My pro career was a wash. I blew out my knee before the end of my rookie season, but I'd be lying if I told you I still couldn't hold my own on any playground, whether it's a cratered cement court in the projects or this million-dollar beauty looking straight out at the big blue sea.

# Chapter Six

## Tom

Paradise couldn't be too much better than this.

Seagulls are flapping in the breeze, sailboats are bobbing on the waves, and the green rubberized surface is bathed in dazzling sunshine as I dribble the ball upcourt, cut around my brother's double-wide pick, and snap off a bounce pass to an open Walco under the basket.

Walco is about to lay it in for an easy hoop, when one of Dante's teammates, a tall, wiry kid I will later find out is named Michael Walker, comes flying at him from behind. He blocks the shot and knocks Walco to the court. It's a hard foul, and completely unnecessary in my opinion. A dirty play.

Now the Kings Highway squad is bringing the ball upcourt, and when one of their players goes up for a little jumper, he gets mugged just as bad by Rochie.

Pretty soon, no one stretched out on the grassy hill beside the court is noticing the flapping seagulls or bobbing sailboats because the informal Saturday-morning game has escalated into a war.

But then a beat-up Honda parks beside the court, and Dante's pretty seventeen-year-old cousin, Nikki Robinson, steps out in very short cutoffs. When I see the way Feifer checks her out, I know the Montauk townies still have a chance to win this shoot-out by the sea.

# Chapter Seven

## Tom

Nikki Robinson leans provocatively against the wire fence, and the shameless Feifer immediately takes over the game. He uses his quickness, or stamina, or surprising strength to force three consecutive Kings Highway turnovers.

When Jeff taps in my missed jumper, we're all tied at twenty.

Now Nikki isn't the only one up against the fence. Artis LaFontaine and Mammy and Sly and everyone else on the hill are on their feet, making a lot of noise.

Michael Walker races upcourt with the ball.

With five pretty women paying attention instead of

just one, Feifer swoops on Walker like an eagle bearing down on a rabbit on one of those TV nature shows. He effortlessly strips him of the ball and races the other way for the winning lay-up.

This time, however, he doesn't stop at the rim. He keeps climbing, showing that Montauk boys got *ups* too. When he throws the ball down, Artis, Mammy, and Marwan go crazy on the sidelines, and Nikki Robinson rewards him with a little R-rated dance that seventeen-year-old girls aren't supposed to know how to do.

This provokes Michael Walker to shove Rochie, Feif to shove him back, Dante to shove Feif, and Feif to *really* shove Dante.

Ten seconds later, on the prettiest day of the summer, Feif and Dante are squared off at half-court.

At this point, both sides should jump in and break it up, but neither does. The Kings Highway crew hangs back because they figure the white surfer boy is about to get a whooping and don't want to bail him out. We stand and watch because in a dozen barroom brawls we've never seen Feif lose.

And right now, despite giving up a foot and more than fifty pounds to Dante, Feif's holding his own. But now I really have seen enough. This is bullshit, and I don't want either of them to get hurt.

But as I jump between them, catching glancing blows from both for my trouble, the court falls silent.

There's a high-pitched scream, the blur of people scattering, and then Artis yells, *'Tom, he's got a gun!'*

I turn toward Dante, and he's holding his empty hands up in front of his face. When I turn to Feif, he's doing the same thing.

I am the last person on the court to see that the guy with the gun isn't Dante or Feifer. It's Dante's homeboy Michael Walker. While I was breaking up the fight, he must have run and grabbed it from the car.

I didn't see him or the gun until just now, when he walked back onto the court, lifted it to the side of Feifer's head, and with a sickening *click,* thumbed back the hammer to cock it.

# Chapter Eight

## Dante Halleyville

When Michael puts that gun up beside that boy's head, no one is more freaked than me. *No one!* Not even the bro with the gun to his head – although he looks plenty freaked too. This is my worst nightmare coming true. *Don't pull that trigger, Michael. Don't do it.*

Because of my promise to my grandmother Marie, I've got sixteen months to get through before I go into the NBA, and the only thing that can stop me is some ridiculousness like this. That's why I never go to clubs or even parties where I don't know everyone, because you never know when some fool is going to pull out a gun, and now that's exactly what's happening and it's my best friend doing it, and he thinks he's doing it for me.

And it's not like Michael and I haven't talked about it. Michael wants to watch my back, fine. But he's got to stay between me and trouble, not bring it on.

Thank God for Dunleavy. He doesn't know this, but I've watched him since I was starting out. Till me, he was the only player from around here who amounted to much. I used to track him at St John's and then for that short time with the pros in Minnesota. He never got the big tout, but if he hadn't got hurt, Tom Dunleavy would have done some damage in the League. Trust me. But what Dunleavy does today is better than basketball. It's like that poem we read in school – if you can keep your head screwed on tight, when all around you motherfuckers are freaking.

When Michael puts the gun to the white guy's head, everyone scatters. But Dunleavy stays on the court and talks to Michael calm as can be.

Not fake calm either. Real calm – like whatever is going to happen is going to happen.

I can't say for sure it was like this word for word, but this is what I remember.

'I can tell you're Dante's friend,' Dunleavy says.

'That's obvious. As obvious as the fact that this guy should never have thrown a punch at Dante, not at someone who's about to go to the NBA. He hits Dante, maybe one of his eyes is never the same and the dream is over. So I'm sure there's a part of Dante that would like to see you mess him up right now.

'But since you're Dante's best friend,' he goes on, 'it's not what Dante wants but what he needs. Right? That's why even if Dante was screaming at you to kill this punk, you wouldn't do it. Because it wouldn't help him in the long run. It would hurt him.'

'Exactly,' says Michael, his gun hand shaking now even though he's trying to cover it. 'But this shit ain't over, white boy. Not by a long shot. *This shit ain't over!*'

Somehow, Dunleavy makes it look like it was Michael deciding on his own to put down the gun. He gives Michael a way out so it doesn't look like he's backing down in front of everyone.

Still, the whole thing is messed up, and when I get to my grandmom Marie's place, I'm so stressed I go right to the couch and fall asleep for three hours.

Nothing would ever be the same after that catnap of mine.

# Chapter Nine

## Kate Costello

'Oh, Mary Catherine? Mary Catherine? Has anyone here seen the divine MC?' I call in my sweetest maternal-sounding voice.

When there's no answer, I jump up from my little plasticized lounge chair and search my sister's Montauk backyard with the exaggerated gestures and body language of a soap-opera actress.

'Is it truly possible that no one here has seen this beautiful little girl about yea big, with amazing red hair?' I try again. 'That is so peculiar, because I could swear I saw that same little girl not more than twenty seconds ago. Big green eyes? Amazing red hair?'

That's about all the theatrics my twenty-month-old niece can listen to in silence. She abandons her hiding spot on the deck, behind where my sister, Theresa, and her husband, Hank, are sipping margaritas with their neighbors.

She races across the back lawn, hair and skinny arms flying in every direction, the level of excitement in her face exceeding all recommended levels. Then she throws herself at my lap and fixes me with a grin that communicates as clearly as if she were enunciating every syllable: *I am right here, you silly aunt! See! I am not lost. I was never lost! I was just tricking you!*

The first ten years after I finished college, I rarely came home. Montauk felt small to me, and claustrophobic, and most of all, I didn't want to run into Tom Dunleavy. Well, now I can't go two weeks without holding MC in my arms, and this little suburban backyard with the Weber grill on the deck and the green plastic slide and swing set in the corner is looking cozier all the time.

While MC and I sprawl on the grass, Hank brings me a glass of white wine. 'Promise you'll tell us when you need a break,' he says.

'This *is* my break, Hank.'

Funny how things work out. Theresa has known

Hank since grade school, and everyone in the family, me included, thought she was settling. But seeing how much they enjoy each other and their life out here, and watching their friends casually wander in and out of their yard, I'm beginning to think the joke's on me.

But of course the best part of their life is MC, who, believe it or not, they named after yours truly, the so-called success of the family.

Speaking of my darling namesake, I think she's slunk off again because I can't seem to find her.

'Has anyone seen Mary Catherine? Has anyone here seen that scruffy little street urchin? No? That is just too odd. Bizarre even, because I could have sworn I just saw her a minute ago right under this table. Beautiful red hair? Big green eyes? Oh, Mary Catherine? Mary Catherine?'

So peaceful and nice – for the moment anyway.

# Chapter Ten

## Tom

After all the drama, a night on the couch with Wingo and the Mets won't cut it. I head to Marjorie's, which is not only my favorite bar out here but my favorite bar anywhere in the known universe. The Hamptons have hundreds of heinous joints catering to weekenders, but I'd sooner play bingo at the Elks Club than set one foot in most of them.

Marjorie's definitely skews toward townies, but the owner, Marjorie Seger, welcomes anyone who isn't an ass, no matter how bad their credentials might look on paper, so it doesn't have that bitter us-against-them vibe of a dyed-in-the-wool townie institution, like Wolfie's, say.

Plus, at Wolfie's, I'd never hear the end of it if I ordered a Grey Goose martini, but that's exactly what I want and need, and exactly what I order from Marjorie herself when I grab a stool at the outdoor bar set up on the docks.

Marjorie's big blue eyes light up, and while she puts a glass on ice and washes out her shaker, I listen to the ropes groan and the waves slap against the hulls of the big fishing trawlers tied up thirty feet away. Kind of nice.

I was hoping one or more of my fellow hoopsters would already be here, but they're not. I'll have to content myself with Billy Belnap, who was in my history and English classes at East Hampton High. For fifteen years, he's been one of East Hampton's finest.

Belnap, in uniform and on duty, sits on the stool next to me smoking a cigarette, sipping a Coke. That could mean he is drinking a rum and Coke, or a Jack and Coke, or, unlikely as it may sound, a plain old Coke.

Either way, that's between him and Marjorie, who is now concentrating on my cocktail. And when she places the chilled glass in front of me and pours out the translucent elixir, I stop talking to Billy and give her the respectful silence she deserves till the last drop brings the liquid to the very rim, like the water in one of those two-hundred-thousand-dollar infinity swimming pools.

'I hope you know I adore you,' I say, lowering my head for my first careful sip.

'Keep your affection, Dunleavy,' says Marjorie. 'A couple more of these, you'll be pawing my ass.'

As the Grey Goose does its work, I'm thinking about whether or not I should tell Billy, off the record of course, about the events of the afternoon. For the most part, so little happens to us townies, it seems ungenerous not to share a good tale.

So trying to strike the right balance of modesty and humor, I give it a shot. When I get to the part when Michael Walker puts the gun to Feifer's head, I say, 'I thought for sure I was going to be scrubbing blood off Wilson's million-dollar court.'

Belnap doesn't smile. 'Was Wilson there?' he asks.

'No. I hear he's afraid to set foot down there.'

'I believe that.'

I'm wrapping it up, describing Walker's last face-saving threat, when a scratchy voice barks out of the two-way radio lying next to Belnap's half-full glass. He picks up the radio and listens.

'Three bodies in East Hampton,' says Belnap, draining the rest of his drink in one gulp. 'You coming?'

# Chapter Eleven

## Tom

'Three males, early twenties,' says Belnap as he drives. 'A jogger just called it in.'

I want to ask from where, but the hard way Belnap stares through the windshield and the way the car squeals around corners discourage me from any questions.

I must have lived a sheltered life, because this is my first ride in a squad car. Despite the frantic flashing and wailing, it seems eerily calm inside. Not that I feel calm. Anything but. *Three dead bodies in East Hampton? Outside a car crash, it's unheard of.*

The roads out here are wooded and windy, and the

powerful beams of Belnap's cruiser barely dent the dark. When we finally reach the end of Quonset and burst into the glaring light of Route 27, it feels like coming up from the bottom of a deep, cold lake and breaking through the surface.

A quarter of a mile later, just before the beach, we are braking hard again and turning back into the darkness. It takes a second for my eyes to adjust enough to see we're on Beach Road.

In the dark the hulking houses seem threatening. We're really flying now, hitting eighty-five as we pass the golf course.

A quarter of a mile later, Belnap brakes so hard I come up into my harness, and he swerves between a pair of tall white gates – T. Smitty Wilson's white gates.

'That's right,' says Billy, staring straight ahead. 'Back at the scene of your latest heroics.'

The driveway is empty, and not a single car is parked beside the court, something I haven't seen in months. Even when it's pouring rain, there'd be a crowd partying in their cars. But on Saturday night, Labor Day weekend, the place is as deserted as if it were Christmas Eve.

'This is bad, Tom,' says Belnap, the master of understatement. 'Nobody gets murdered out here. Just doesn't happen.'

# Chapter Twelve

## Tom

It's eerie and creepy too.

Exaggerating the emptiness around the court is all the light that is being pumped in. For night games, eight high-watt halogens have been set on tall, elegant silver poles. They're the same lights used on movie sets, and they're blazing tonight.

A police cruiser and ambulance have beaten us out here.

Belnap makes me stay by the car as he hustles down to where two ambulances are backed into the dunes.

From the hood of his cruiser, I hear an uninterrupted

wail of sirens, and then I see a posse of cop cars race up Beach Road from both sides.

Pairs of headlamps converge at the tall gate at the bottom of the hill and snake their way toward me up the driveway.

The next five minutes bring at least a dozen more cruisers and three more ambulances. In that same ominous rush come the department's two detectives in their black Crown Vics. Plus the K-9 and Forensic units in separate vans.

Then the cop cars stop arriving and the sirens stop wailing, and I can hear the ocean waves again. The whole vibe is as strange and unnatural as a small child's wake.

For the next few minutes, I stay by the car, the one person there not in the crowd ringing the crime scene, and just by looking at the backs, the postures, I can tell that this is far heavier than what the cops are used to, and I can feel the anger. A few years ago a millionaire was murdered in his bed within a mile of here, but that was different. These bodies aren't summer people.

The way the cops are acting, these are three of their own – maybe even cops.

When the volunteer firemen show up, I figure I've

stayed put long enough. After all, I'm not exactly a stranger here. For good or bad, everybody knows Tom Dunleavy.

But halfway to the ambulance, Mickey Harrison, a sergeant who played hoops with me in high school, steps up and puts both hands firmly on my chest.

'Tommy, you don't want to go any closer right now. Trust me.'

It's too late. As he restrains me, the circle breaks, and I glimpse the shapes the cops are scurrying around.

It's dark down here, and at first the shapes make no sense. They're too high, or too short, with no connection to familiar human outlines.

I squint into the shadows, my mind still unable to process the images. Then a cop from Forensics drops into a crouch, and there's a powerful flash from his camera.

It sets off a second flash at the very middle of the scene, and before it fades to black again, I see the white circle of Feifer's bleached hair.

'Oh, Jesus God,' I say, and Mickey Harrison takes my arm at the elbow.

Then, almost immediately, another shock. The bodies aren't lying side by side. They're stacked, one on top of the other, *in a heap.* Feif is in the middle on his back. Robert Walco is lying on top of him face-down, and Rochie is on the bottom turned on his side.

Now there's a voice cutting through the others, maybe Billy Belnap's, but the way I'm suddenly feeling I can't tell for sure. 'You think Dante and his nigger friends could have done this?'

I don't actually hear the response because I'm down on my knees puking into the damp sand.

# Chapter Thirteen

## Kate

'Hey, Mary K, how you doing?' I hear as I arrive at the nightmare scene, the murder scene on a beach I think of as being partly my own since I spent so much time here as a kid.

'Not too good. You?' I say, not even sure who I'm talking at, or why I'm bothering to answer the guy's stupid question.

An hour after a Montauk volunteer fireman hears the call go out on his police scanner, at least two hundred local folk are milling on the beach below the Wilson estate, and I'm one of them. I haven't lived out here for a dozen years, but I guess being a Montauk townie isn't something that ever goes away because I'm as anxious and scared as my former neighbors.

Above where I'm standing, three ambulances are parked in the dunes, surrounded by the entire East Hampton Police Department.

Over the next ten minutes or so, terrible rumors sweep down the hill like mud slides, confirming or correcting or replacing the names of the dead that people have already heard. Desperate parents call children, rejoicing when they answer, panicking when they don't. I think of red-haired Mary Catherine streaking across the lawn earlier today, and of how vulnerable parents become the second their child is born.

We have known for hours that all three of the victims are young males, but the police are withholding the names until they can notify the families.

But the people out on the beach know too many of the cops inside the crime scene tape, and when someone gets a call from his brother-in-law up on the hill, we find out that the dead kids are Walco, Rochie, and Feifer. The news hits all of us like a hand grenade.

In the summer there might be ten thousand people living in Montauk, but the number who live here year-round is probably a tenth of that, and at times like this we're one big family. It's one of the reasons I left, and one of the things I miss the most. Out here, the person who lives next door is not an indifferent stranger, but a genuine neighbor who actually cares about your life and feels your triumphs and tragedies, and because of that, people are sobbing and shrieking and trying to comfort one another.

The three dead boys were ten years younger than me, and I haven't spent much time here lately, yet I still know that Walco's girlfriend is pregnant, and that Rochie's mother is sick with stomach cancer. Long before Feifer became a surfer stud, I was his babysitter, for God's sake. I remember that he wouldn't go to sleep without a bowl of Rice Krispies.

Grief turns to rage as more details of the killings trickle down the hill. All three were shot point-blank between the eyes. All three had rope burns on their wrists. And when the bodies were found, they were piled on top of each other like garbage left at the town dump. We all know enough about these kids to know they weren't angels. We also know they weren't criminals. So what the hell happened here tonight?

I turn away from the row of ten-million-dollar beach houses and back to the ambulances. Among the two dozen cops milling around them is a handful of locals who for one reason or another have been allowed to get close to the crime scene.

As I watch, one of these, a large, heavyset man, drapes an arm over the shoulder of a tall, much thinner man beside him. *Shit,* I think to myself.

Their backs are to me, but I know that the larger man is Jeff Dunleavy, the other his younger brother, Tom, and now I feel a fresh jolt of pain, which I'm ashamed to say has nothing to do with the horrible murder of three sweet-natured Montauk kids.

# Chapter Fourteen

## Tom

The current crop of East Hampton cops has never had to deal with a horrifying, almost scatological crime scene like this, and it sure shows. There are actually too many cops, too many bodies, and too many emotions, which are all way too close to the surface.

Finally, Van Buren, the youngest detective on the force, stakes off a ten-yard square around the bodies and runs lights down from the court so Forensics can dust for prints and scrape for DNA.

I don't want to bother Van Buren, so I approach Police Chief Bobby Flaherty, who I've known forever.

'Has Feif's family been told yet?' I ask.

'I'm sending Rust,' he says, nodding toward a rookie cop who looks as green as I must have forty minutes ago.

'Let me do it, Bobby. Okay? They should hear it from somebody they know.'

'It's not going to help, Tom.'

'I just need a ride back to the marina. To pick up my car.'

The Feifers live by the junior high on a quiet cul-de-sac in one of Montauk's last year-round neighborhoods. It's the kind of place where kids can still play baseball in the street without getting run over, and where families like Feif's chose to raise their kids precisely because they thought they wouldn't have to worry about some unspeakable thing like this ever happening.

Late as it is, the lights are still on in the den of the house, and I creep up near the picture window, quiet as a burglar.

Vic and Allison Feifer and their teenage daughter, Lisa, share the big, comfortable couch, their faces lit by the TV. A bag from Montauk Video hangs from a nearby chair, and maybe they're watching a chick flick because old man Feifer's chin is on his chest, and Ali and Lisa are transfixed, not taking their eyes off the screen even when they dig into the bowl of popcorn on the couch between them.

I know it's never that simple, but they look like such a nice, contented family.

I take in a deep breath; then I ring the doorbell. I watch Lisa spring off the couch in her pink sweats and white furry house slippers.

Lisa yanks the screen door open, eager to return to her movie. She tows me behind her into the den, not even thinking about the unusualness of such a late visit.

But once I'm standing in front of them, my face gives me away. Allison reaches for my arm, and old man Feif, still rousing himself from when I rang the doorbell, staggers to his stocking feet.

'It's about Eric,' I say, forcing the words out. 'I'm real sorry. They found his body tonight, along with Rochie and Walco, at the Wilson estate on Beach Road. He was murdered. I'm so sorry to have to tell you this.'

They're only words, but they might as well be bullets. Before they are out of my mouth, Allison's face has shattered into pieces, and when she looks at her husband, they're both so devastated all they can offer each other is the shell of who they were just five minutes before.

# Chapter Fifteen

## Tom

Ask me how long I spent at Feifer's house, I'd have sworn it was close to an hour. According to my kitchen clock, it was probably less than ten minutes.

Still, it's all I can do to pull a bottle of whiskey off the shelf and carry it out back, where my pal Wingo is waiting. Wingo knows right away I'm messed up. Instead of begging me to take him for a walk, he lays his jaw on my lap and I pet him like there's no tomorrow. For three of my friends, there isn't.

I have a phone in my hand, but I can't remember why. Oh, yeah, *Holly.* She's a woman I've been going out with for the past few weeks. No big thing.

Unfortunately, I don't want to call her. I just want to want to call her, in the same way that I want to pretend she's my girlfriend, even though we both know we're only killing time.

Wingo's a dog, not a pal. My girlfriend isn't really my girlfriend. But the whiskey is the real thing, so I pour out half a glass and gulp it down. Thank God that son of a bitch Dr Jameson still makes house calls.

I'd feel better if I could cry, but I haven't cried since I was ten, when my father died. So I take another long gulp and then another, and then instead of thinking about every horrible thing that's happened today, I find myself thinking about Kate Costello. It's been ten years since we broke up, and I still think about Kate all the time, especially when something important happens, good or bad. Plus, I saw her tonight out on Beach Road. As always, she looked beautiful, and even under the circumstances, seeing her was a jolt.

Once I start regretting how I screwed things up with Kate, it's only a matter of a couple more sips before I revisit *The Moment*. Boston Garden, February 11, 1995. Barely more than a minute to play and the T-wolves are down by twenty–three. A part of the game so meaningless it's called 'garbage time.' I come down on a teammate's ankle, blow out my left knee, and my pro career is over before I hit the famed parquet floor.

That's how it works with me and Dr Jameson. First, I think about losing Kate Costello. Then, I think about losing basketball.

See, first, I had nothing. That was okay because in the beginning everyone has nothing. Then, I found basketball, and through basketball I found Kate. Now, Kate would deny that. Women always do. But you and I, Doc, we're not children. We both know I never would have gotten within ten feet of Kate Costello without basketball. I mean, look at her!

Then, I lost Kate. And then I lost basketball. Bada-bing. Bada-boom.

So here's the question I've been asking myself for ten years: how the hell am I going to get her back without it?

*Doc, you still there?*

# Chapter Sixteen

## Kate

Until this god-awful, god-forsaken morning in early September, the only funeral for a young person I'd ever attended was, I think, Wendell Taylor's. Wendell was a big, lovable bear who played bass for Save the Whales, a local band that made it pretty good and had begun to tour around New England.

Two Thanksgivings ago, Wendell was driving back from a benefit show in Providence. When he fell asleep at the wheel, he was six miles from his bed, and the telephone pole he hit was the only unmovable object for two hundred yards in either direction. It took EMS ninety minutes to cut him out of his van.

That Wendell was such a decent guy and was so thrilled to actually be making a living from his music made the whole thing incredibly sad. Yet somehow his funeral, full of funny and teary testimonials from friends from as far back as kindergarten, made people feel better.

The funeral for Rochie, Feifer, and Walco, which takes place in a squat stone church just east of town, doesn't do anyone a lick of good.

Instead of cathartic tears, there's clenched rage, a lot of it directed at the conspicuously absent owner of the house where the murders took place. To the thousand or so stuffed into that church on Sunday morning, Walco and Feif and Rochie died for some movie star's vanity.

I know it's not quite that simple. From what I hear, Feif, Walco, and Rochie hung out at the court all summer and enjoyed the scene as much as anyone. Still, it would have been nice of Smitty Wilson to show up and pay his respects, don't ya think?

There is one cathartic moment this morning, but it's an ugly one. Before the service begins, Walco's younger brother spots a photographer across the street. Turns out that the *Daily News* is less cynical about Mr Wilson than we are. They think there's enough of a chance of him showing up to send a guy with a tele-photo lens.

Walco's brother and his pals trash his camera pretty bad, and it would have been a lot worse if the police weren't there.

That scene, I come to think later on, that violent altercation, was what some people might call an omen.

# Chapter Seventeen

## Kate

It just kept getting worse and worse the day of the funerals.

*I don't belong here anymore,* I think to myself, and I want to run out of the Walcos' house, but I'm not brave enough.

The line of neighbors waiting to offer their condolences to Mary and Richard Walco starts in the dining room in front of the breakfront, snakes along three living-room walls, then runs past the front door and most of the way down the bedroom hallway. Clutching Mary Catherine's tiny hand for dear life, I thread my way through the heavy-hearted gathering as if the carpet were strewn with mines, and make my way to the end of the line.

All morning I've clung to my niece like a life preserver.

But MC, who thank goodness knows nothing of human misery, has no intention of staying put and breaks out of my grip and zigzags blithely around the room. She finally gloms on to her mom.

When MC scampers off, all the gloom of this dreadful day floods into the space she's left behind.

I steady myself against one yellow-wallpapered wall and wait my turn, trying to will myself into invisibility. It's not a skill I've mastered over the years. Then there's an alarming tap on my shoulder.

I turn. It's Tom.

And as soon as I see him, I realize he is the landmine I was hoping Mary Catherine would protect me from.

Before I can say a word, he moves in for a tentative hug that I don't reciprocate.

'It's awful, Kate,' he mumbles. He looks awful too, as if he hasn't slept in about ten days.

'Terrible,' is what I manage to say. No more than that. Tom doesn't deserve more. Ten years ago he broke my heart, blew it apart, and didn't even seem to care that much. I'd heard the rumor that he was running around on me and partying hard. I hadn't believed the rumor. But in the end I sure did.

'It's still good to see you, Kate.'

'Spare me, Tom.'

I see the hurt in his face and now I feel bad. Mary, mother of God! What is it with me? After five years together, he breaks up with me ON THE PHONE, and now I feel bad.

The whole thing has me so contorted, I want to run out into the street and scream like a crazy person.

But of course I don't. Not good girl Kate Costello. I stand there with a dim-witted little smile plastered on my face, as if we have been enjoying innocuous pleasantries, and finally, he turns away.

Then I take a deep breath, give myself a stern talking-to about the need to get over myself, and wait my turn to offer some consoling words to the thousand-times-more-wretched Mary Walco.

One strange and disturbing thing: I hear virtually the same line half a dozen times while I'm standing there waiting to see Mary – *Somebody's got to get those bastards for this.*

# Chapter Eighteen

## Kate

I offer Walco's mom the little that I can, and then I cast about the room for a red-haired toddler in a black velvet dress.

I see MC in the corner, still with her mom, and then spot my precious pal Macklin Mullen and his handsome grandson Jack over by the makeshift bar. Jack, a lawyer like myself, wanders off as I approach. Okay, fine. I was going to congratulate him on getting married, but whatever.

Mack is sipping a whiskey and leaning heavily on a gnarled blackthorn shillelagh, but when we throw ourselves into each other's arms, his embrace is as warm and vigorous as ever.

'I was fervently hoping that would never end, Katie,' he says when we finally release each other.

'For God's sake, Macklin, cheer me up.'

'I was about to ask you to do the same thing, darling girl. Three boys dead – tragic, pointless, and mystifying. Where you been keeping yourself all this time? I know about your many accomplishments, of course, but I've been waiting to toast you in person. Actually, I've been waiting to get you drunk! Why in Christ have you been such a stranger?'

'The standard explanation includes long hours, parents in Sarasota, and brothers scattered with the wind. The pathetic truth, I'm afraid, is I didn't want to run into Tom Dunleavy. Who, by the way, I just ran into.'

'The truth is always pathetic, isn't it? That's why I avoid it like the plague myself. In any case, now that you've gotten over the dreaded encounter with Dunleavy, why don't you come out here and put the little shit out of business? Not that it would be much of an accomplishment. I hear he bills about a hundred hours a year.'

'Better yet, why don't I just forgive him and move on? It's been almost a decade.'

'Forgive? Move on? Kate Costello, have you forgotten that you're Irish?'

'Macklin, you've made me laugh,' I say, and just then, none other than Mary Catherine wobbles across the room and flings herself at my legs.

'Drivel aside, Mack, this is the true problem for me and Montauk. Of my two favorite people, one is twenty months old, the other eighty-four.'

'But, Kate, we're both just hitting our strides. This shillelagh nonsense is nothing but a corny piece of atmosphere.'

# Chapter Nineteen

## Tom

The next day, to sweat out the funeral, I head to the beach, my four-legged personal trainer, Wingo, nipping at my heels. It's the first Monday after Labor Day, the unofficial start of townie summer, and most of the insufferable New Yorkers are gone.

On a cool, brilliantly sunny day, the greatest stretch of beach in North America is empty.

Running on the damp packed sand close to the water is no more difficult than running on the track behind the high school. To punish myself, though, I stay on the soft stuff that sucks at your feet with every step.

In five minutes, everything that's attached to me hurts – legs, lungs, back, head – so I pick up the pace.

In another five minutes, I can smell the whiskey from last night as the sweat pours off my face. Five minutes after that, my hangover has nearly vanished.

Later that afternoon, Wingo and I are recovering from our midday workout, me on the couch and Wingo asleep at my feet, when a knock on the front door rouses us. It's about four, still plenty of light outside, and a black sedan is parked on the gravel driveway.

At the door is young master Van Buren, the detective who ran the show on the beach the other night.

Barely thirty, he made detective early this summer. Considering his age, it was quite a coup. He leapfrogged half a dozen pretty decent cops with more seniority, including Belnap, and it didn't win him any friends in the station house.

'Tom, I don't need to tell you why I'm here,'he says.

'I'm surprised it took this long.'

Still dehydrated from my run, I grab a beer and offer him something, just to hear him say no.

'Why don't we sit outside while we still can,' I say, and then because of the force with which he rejected my first offer, or because I'm acting like a prick for no good reason, I repeat it. 'Sure I can't get you that beer? It's almost five.'

Van Buren ignores me and takes out a brand-new orange notebook he must have just bought for the occasion at the stationery store in Montauk.

'Tom, people say you did a good job getting that kid to put down his gun the other day. What confuses me is why you didn't call the police.'

I can tell Van Buren doesn't expect an answer. He's simply letting me know that he can be a prick too.

'Obviously, I should have, but I could tell the kid had no intention of using it.'

'That's not what I heard.'

'I was closer. Believe me, he was more scared than Feif.'

'You know what kind of gun it was?'

'I don't know guns, Barney.'

'Can you describe it?'

'I barely looked at it. In fact, I made it a point not to. I tried to pretend that me and Walker were just two people having a conversation. Ignoring the gun made that a lot easier.'

'You know any reason Michael Walker or Dante Halleyville might want to kill Feifer, Walco, or Roche?'

'No. There isn't any.'

'Why's that, Tom?'

'They barely knew each other.'

The young detective purses his lips and shakes his head. 'No one's seen them since the murder.'

'Really.'

'Plus, we got reason to think Dante and Walker were at the scene that night.'

I start shaking my head a little at the news. 'That makes no sense. There's no way they'd go back there after what happened that afternoon.'

'Not if they were smart,' says Van Buren. 'But, Tom, these boys weren't smart. They could be killers.'

# Chapter Twenty

## Tom

Wow! Half an hour after Van Buren leaves with his little orange notebook in hand, Wingo sounds the alarm again. *More company.*

When I look through the front-door window, all I see is torso, which means it's Clarence, and that's not good news either.

Clarence, who drives a cab in town and does some college scouting, has been a close friend since he steered me to St John's fifteen years ago. Because there's as much downtime for a Hampton cabbie as a Montauk lawyer, he comes by my office two or three times a week. The six-foot-six Clarence is also Dante's cousin, and I know from his worried expression that's why he's here. *This cannot be good.*

'I just got a call from him,' says Clarence. 'Boy is scared out of his mind. Thinks they're going to kill him.'

'Who? Who's going to kill him?'

'He's not sure.'

I pull two beers out of the fridge and Clarence takes one.

'Where the hell is he? Van Buren just left here. He says Dante and Walker bolted. It *looks* bad.'

'I know it does, Tom.'

With the sun on the way down, we sit at the counter in the kitchen.

'Van Buren also implied that they were at the murder scene that night.'

'He got a witness?' asks Clarence.

'I can't tell. He was being cute about it. Why the hell would they be going back there after what happened?'

'Dante says he can explain everything. But right now we got to get him to turn himself in. That's why I'm here. He respects you, Tom. You talk to him, he'll listen.'

Clarence stares at me. 'Tom, please? I've never once asked you for a favor.'

'He tell you where they are?'

Clarence shakes his head and looks hurt. 'Wouldn't even give me a number.'

I spread my hands wide. 'What do you want to do, Clarence? Wait here and hope he calls again?'

'He says we should talk to his grandma. Dante says if Marie says it's cool, he'll give us a call.'

# Chapter Twenty-One

# Tom

I can feel right then and there that this is going real bad in a big hurry, and I should not be involved. But I go with Clarence anyway.

We climb into his big yellow Buick station wagon and head west through Amagansett and East Hampton, and just before the start of Bridgehampton's two-block downtown, we turn right at the monument and go north on 114.

Stay on it long enough, the road leads to Sag Harbor, but along the way is the one enduring pocket of poverty left in the Hamptons. It's called Kings Highway but is often referred to as Black Hampton.

One minute you're passing multimillion-dollar estates, the next minute shotgun shacks and trailer homes, old rotting cars on blocks like in the Ozarks or Appalachia.

Dante and his grandmother live off the dirt road leading to the town dump, and when we pull up to her trailer, the woman who comes to the door has Dante's cheekbones and lively brown eyes but none of his height. In fact, she's as compact and round as Dante is long and lean.

'Don't stand out there in the cold,' says Marie.

The sitting room in the trailer is dark and a little grim. The only light comes from a single low-watt table lamp, and the desperation in the close air is a palpable thing. It's hard to imagine that both she and Dante can live in here together.

'We're here to help,' says Clarence, 'and the first step is getting Dante to turn himself in.'

'You're here to help? How is that? Dante and Michael had nothing to do with these crimes,' says Marie. 'NOTHING! Dante is very aware of the chance he has been given, and earned, and what that could mean.'

'I know that,' says Clarence, heartbreak in his voice too. 'But the police don't. The longer he stays out, the worse it looks for him.'

'My grandson could have entered the NBA draft,' says Marie as if she hasn't heard a word Clarence said. 'This home was filled with vultures waving cars and money under his nose, and Dante turned them all down. He told me that when he does go pro, he wants to buy me a new house and a new car. I asked him, what's wrong with this house? What's wrong with my car? I don't need those things.'

Marie fixes us with a hard stare. Her tiny place is immaculate, and you can see the defiant effort to create a semblance of middle-class stability. Barely visible on the wall directly behind her is a formal photograph of Dante, his older brother, and his parents, all dressed up outside the Baptist Memorial Church in Riverhead. In the picture, Dante looks about ten, and I know from Clarence that soon after that picture was taken, Dante's father was stabbed to death on the street and his mother went to jail for the first time. I also know that his brother, who many thought was almost as good a pro prospect as Dante, is serving a two-year sentence in a corrections center upstate.

'Marie,' says Clarence, 'you got to get Dante to give Tom a call. Tom used to be a heck of a ballplayer. Now he's a heck of a lawyer. But he can't help Dante if Dante won't let him.'

Marie stares at me, her face not revealing a thing. 'This neighborhood is full of folks who used to be great ballplayers,' she says.

# Chapter Twenty-Two

## Loco

On a sleepy midweek afternoon in the teeming metropolis that is downtown Montauk, Hugo Lindgren sits at the counter of John's Pancake House, killing time like only a cop can, turning a free cup of coffee into a two-hour paid vacation.

Since Lindgren's all alone at the counter – the only 'customer' in the whole place, in fact – I do the sociable thing and take the stool beside him. Now, how many other drug dealers would make a gesture like that?

'Loco,' he mutters.

As I sit, luminously green-eyed Erin Case comes over bearing a nearly empty pot of coffee.

'Good afternoon, darlin',' says Erin in her still-strong Ulster brogue. 'What can I get you?'

'I'd love a double-vanilla latte decaf, if it's not any trouble.'

'No trouble at all, darlin'. Got it right here,' says Erin, filling my mug with the dregs of the pot in her right hand. 'You said double-vanilla latte decaf, right?'

'Must be my lucky day.'

'Every day's your lucky day, darlin'!'

Pancake John is getting ready to close up shop and flip the sign, so when Erin excuses herself to wipe the maple syrup off the red Naugahyde booths, me and Lindgren shyly return to our so-called coffee. And when Erin stoops under a table to pick up a fallen menu, I slide him my *Newsday*.

'John Paul Newport's column on Hillary,' I say. 'It's hilarious. Kind of thing your lieutenant might get a hoot out of too.'

'Thanks, pal,' says Lindgren.

He cracks the editorial section just enough to see two fat envelopes, then slides over his *New York Post*.

'Crossword's a bear today,' he says, 'but maybe you'll have better luck with it than I did.'

'Coffee's on me, Hugo,' I say, dropping five dollars on the counter as I head to the door.

I don't open my *Post* until I'm safely back in the Big Black Beast stationed in the middle of the empty parking lot.

Then I read the note from Lindgren.

Apparently some sharp-eyed civilian called in a tip to the cops this morning about a wanted fugitive looking a lot like Michael Walker. The suspect was leaving a Brooklyn gym last night, and the name of the establishment now fills the twenty-two letters set aside for nine across. And when I glance at the back-seat, I see Hugo has also left me a little party favor – a brand-new, bright-red Miami Heat basketball cap.

I may have been underestimating Lindgren all these years. I know it's only the *Post* and not the London *Times*, but who would have thought that a corrupt, degenerate excuse for a police officer had the balls or the vocabulary to do the crossword in ink?

# Chapter Twenty-Three

## Loco

On account of the fact that I'm a whole lot brighter and craftier than I look, locating the Bed-Stuy Community Center is a piece of cake. The tricky part is finding a place to park where the Big Black Beast doesn't draw too much attention to itself and I still have a halfway decent view of both entrances. This, after all, is a stakeout. Just not by the cops.

After circling the block a couple times, I double-park half a dozen spaces past the community center. That's right across the street from Carmine's Pizzeria, so it looks as if I'm just sitting there enjoying my Pepsi and slice like any other self-respecting neighborhood goombah.

I thought these boxing clubs were extinct, something out of a black-and-white Cagney flick. These days, tough kids don't scrap. They strap. So mastering the sweet science is only going to get you killed.

But maybe I'm wrong, because the place looks all renovated and spiffy, and folks are going in and out at a pretty good clip. Most of 'em have a strut too.

If nothing else, banging on a heavy bag has got to be good stress management. And right now our man Michael Walker has got to be seriously stressing, what with an APB out for him in fifteen states and an outstanding warrant for triple homicide.

While Walker works out, I blacken the end of the Graycliff Robusto I bought at the Tinder Box in East Hampton. And it looks like I picked it well. It's nice and soft, and lights like a dream.

The bad news is that I'm exactly three puffs into my delightful cigar when Walker slides out the back door in a gray hooded sweatshirt, a big gym bag slung over his bony shoulder.

Now I'm fucked. If I put it out and relight it, the Graycliff will never taste the same. If I take it with me, it's hardly going to be the relaxing experience I had in mind when I dropped fifteen dollars on it.

So making the kind of difficult executive decision that earns me the big bucks, I open the sunroof and place the cigar gently in the ashtray. Then I follow Walker north toward Fulton Street.

Staying half a block back, I see him take a quick left. Just as I round the corner, he looks both ways and ducks into a six-floor tenement about halfway down the block. Two minutes later, the lights go on and the shades come down on the corner apartment four flights up.

*Gotcha!*

*I've caught the fugitive.*

# Chapter Twenty-Four

## Loco

And give that lucky man a cigar!

I get back to the Big Black Beast, and everything, including my slowly burning Graycliff, is just like I left it. Seeing as we're in Crooklyn, I pop in an old-school Eric B and Rakim CD and head for the Williamsburg Bridge.

At 8:00 p.m. the Manhattan-bound lanes are flowing, and twenty minutes later, as my cigar burns down to the finish, I'm in Chinatown, Jake. *Killing time.*

It's a way different world down here, lots of tiny people scurrying over the packed sidewalks with feverish energy, and it never fails to get me jazzed. Makes me think of *Saigon*, *Apocalypse Now*, and *The Deer Hunter*.

I luck into a parking spot big enough for the Beast, a miracle down here, and wander around for a while until I find a familiar place, where I wash down a couple plates of sweet, soggy dim sum with a couple of sweet, soggy beers.

After dinner for one, I walk around some more, *killing time*, then drive to even darker, quieter Tribeca.

I park on Franklin, climb into the back, and stretch out on my foam mattresses.

With my blacked-out windows cracked for ventilation, sleeping conditions are pretty damn good, and the next time I open my eyes it's 3:30 a.m. and I have that pounding in my chest you get when your alarm rips you out of sleep in the middle of the night. I rub the gunk out of my eyes, and when the street comes back into focus, I see that the shadows fluttering over the cobblestones are rats. Is that what Frank meant about waking up in a city that never sleeps?

Without stopping for coffee, I head back to Bed-Stuy, and half an hour after my alarm went off, I pick the lock in the vestibule of Michael Walker's building. Then I climb the stairs two, three at a time to the fugitive's roof.

It's cool and quiet up here, and at this hour, Bed-Stuy looks peaceful as Bethlehem on a starry night, even beautiful.

When a lone, nocturnal civilian finally turns the corner, I climb down the fire escape to Walker's kitchen.

I need a break here and I get it. The window is half open, and I don't have to break it to slip inside. There's plenty of light to screw the silencer to the end of my Beretta Cougar, which is a beauty by the way.

Like I been saying: *killing time.*

A sleeping person is so unbelievably vulnerable it almost feels wrong to stare at him. Michael Walker looks about twelve years old, and for a second I think back to what I was like when I was young and inno-cent. Wasn't that long ago, either.

I cough gently.

Walker stirs, and then his dark eyes blink open. 'What the—'

'Good morning, Michael,' I say.

But the bullet flying then bulldozing into the back of his brain is more like good night.

And I guarantee, Walker had no idea what just happened, or why.

I don't need to tell you there's nothing but crap on TV at this hour. I settle on a *Saturday Night Live* rerun with Rob Lowe as guest host, and he performs his monologue as I carefully wrap Walker's cool fingers around the handle of my gun. Then I slip it into a sealed plastic bag.

After I find Walker's piece in the corner of his closet, the only thing left to do here is drop off Officer Lindgren's gift – *the red Miami Heat cap* – on the kitchen floor before I step back out onto the fire escape.

Sunrise is still an hour away when I lower my window on the Brooklyn Bridge and toss Walker's one-hundred-dollar pistola into the East River.

I sing that real nice Norah Jones song 'Sunrise' most of the way home. Kind of sad what happened to Walker, but actually I don't feel a thing. Nada.

# Chapter Twenty-Five

## Tom

E ventually, I will think of this downtime with affection, call it the calm before the shitstorm.

At work the next day, in my office, I wad up a sheet of printing paper, lean back in my desk chair ($59), and let fly. The paper ball bounces off the slanting dormer ceiling of my second-floor attic office ($650 a month), glances off the side of a beige metal filing cabinet ($39), bounces on the end of my worktable ($109), and drops softly into the white plastic wastebasket ($6).

The tasteful furnishings are all from IKEA, and the successful shot – nothing but wastebasket – is my eleventh in a row.

To give you a sense of the breakneck pace of my legal career, that's not even close to a personal best. I have reached the high fifties on multiple occasions, and one lively afternoon, when I was really feeling it, I canned eighty-seven triple-bankers in a row, a record I suspect will last as long as man has paper and too much time on his hands.

After two years as the sole owner and employee of Tom Dunleavy, Esquire, Inc., headquartered in a charming wooden house directly above Montauk Books, my paper-tossing skills are definitely world-class. But I know it's a sorry state of affairs for an educated, able-bodied thirty-two-year-old, and after visiting Dante's grandmother Marie, and realizing what she's going through, it feels even lamer than it did twenty-four hours ago.

It could be my imagination, but even Wingo stares at me with disappointment. 'C'mon, Wingoman, cut me a little slack. Be a pal,' I tell him, but to no avail.

Marie is still on my mind when the phone shatters the doldrums. To maintain a little dignity, I let it ring twice.

It is *not* Dante.

No, it's Peter Lampke, an old friend. He's just

accepted an offer on his house in Hither Hills and wants to know if I can handle the closing.

'I'm up to my eyeballs, Peter, but I'll make time for a pal. I'll call the broker right now and get her to send over the contracts. Congratulations.'

It may not be challenging work, but it's at least two or three hours of bona fide billable, legal employment. I immediately call the broker, Phyllis Schessel, another old friend, leave her a message, and with the rent paid for another couple of months, call it a day.

I don't even attempt a twelfth shot, just leave the crumpled-up paper in the basket.

I'm halfway out the door, key in hand, when the phone rings again. I step back inside and answer.

'Tom,' says a deep voice at the other end of the line, 'it's Dante.'

# Chapter Twenty-Six

## Tom

Three hours later, I'm in New York City, and I must admit, the whole thing feels surreal.

Two bolts turn over, a chain scrapes in its track, and Dante Halleyville's frame fills door 3A at 26 Clinton Street. Dante hasn't stepped out of the apartment in more than a week or opened a shade or cracked a window, and what's left of the air inside smells of sweat and fear and greasy Chinese food.

'I'm starving,' are the first words out of his mouth. 'Three days ago a delivery guy looked at me funny, and I've been afraid to order anything since. Plus, I'm down to twelve dollars.'

'Good thing we stopped on the way,' I say, pulling the first of three large pizza boxes out of a bag and placing it in front of him.

He sits down with Clarence on a low, vintage couch, a forty-year-old picture of Mick Jagger looking back at me over their shoulders. I'm not saying I approve of Dante's decision to bolt, but an old immigrant neighborhood filled with young white bohemians, half of whose rent is paid by their parents, is not the first place the police are going to look for a black teenager on the run. The apartment belongs to the older sister of a kid Dante met this summer at the Nike camp.

Dante wolfs down a slice of pie, only stopping long enough to say, 'Me and Michael were there that night. I mean, we were right there,' he says, taking another bite and a long drink from his Coke. 'Ten yards away. Maybe less than that. Hard to talk about it.'

'What are you saying, Dante? You *saw* Feifer, Walco, and Rochie get shot? Are you telling me you're a *witness*?'

Dante stops eating and stares into my eyes. I can't tell whether he's angry or hurt. 'Didn't see it, no. Me and Michael were hiding in the bushes, but I heard it clear as I hear you now. First, a voice saying, "Get on your knees, bitches," then another. Feifer maybe asking,

"What's going on?" Sort of friendly, like maybe this is all a joke. Then, when they realize it's serious, all of them bawling and begging right up to the last gunshot. I'll never forget it. The sound of them begging for their lives.'

'Dante, why'd you go back there that night?' I ask. 'After what happened that afternoon? Makes no sense to me.' *Or to the police*, I don't bother to add.

'Feifer asked us to come. Said it was important.'

This makes even less sense.

'Feifer? Why?'

'Feifer calls us that afternoon. That's why I recognized his voice over at the beach. Said he wants to put all this drama behind us, wants things to be cool. Michael didn't want to go. I figured we should.'

'Michael still have his gun?' asks Clarence, and if he hadn't, I would have.

'Got rid of it. Said he sold it to his cousin in Brooklyn.'

'We *got* to get the gun back,' says Clarence. 'But first, you got to turn yourself in to the police. The longer you stay out, the worse this looks. You *have* to do this, Dante.'

'Clarence is right,' I say, and leave it at that. I know from Clarence that Dante has always looked up to me some. Dante doesn't say anything for a couple of minutes, *long* minutes. I understand completely – he's just been fed, and he's free.

'Let's do it tonight then,' Dante finally says. 'But Tom's coming with us, okay? I don't want nothing outlandish happening when I show up at that police station.'

# Chapter Twenty-Seven

## Tom

On the ride back to Bridgehampton, I make one call, and it's not to the cops to tell them we're on our way. It's to Len Levitt, an AP sports photographer I've known for years, and almost trust.

'Yeah, I know what time it is, Len. Now you want to find out why I woke you up or not?' When he hears me out, Levitt is thanking instead of cursing me.

As soon as we're out of the city and through the Midtown Tunnel, Clarence shows us his big Buick can still move. We get to Marie's place just before 3:00 a.m.

When we pull up, Marie is outside waiting. Her back is as straight as a board, and her game face is on. If people thought she'd been shattered by the events of the past week, they're wrong.

She's wearing her Sunday clothes and beside her is a big plastic bag filled with food she's been cooking all night and stuffing into Tupperware containers just in case Dante has to spend the night in jail. Who knows how long she's been standing there already, but it doesn't matter because you know she'd stay there all night if she had to.

Then again, one look at her face and you know she'd march into hell for her grandson. Grandmothers are something.

But right now, more than anything else in this world, Marie is relieved to finally be able to lay her eyes and hands on Dante, and when she wraps her arms around his waist, the love in her eyes is as naked as it is ferocious. And then another surprise – Dante starts to cry in her arms.

'Don't worry, Grandma, I'm going to be okay,' he says through his tears.

'You most certainly will be, Dante. You're *innocent*.'

# PART TWO

---

# KATE COSTELLO

# Chapter Twenty-Eight

## Tom

It's 4:15 a.m. In the moonlight, East Hampton's deserted Main Street looks almost wholesome. The only car in sight is a banged-up white Subaru parked in front of the quaint fifties-era movie theater marquee.

As Clarence plows slowly through town, the Subaru's lights go on and it tears off down the road. We follow it to the tiny police station, and when we arrive, the Subaru is already parked out front.

Short, solid, and determined, Lenny Levitt stands beside it, one Nikon hanging around his neck, another being screwed into a tripod.

I hop out of Clarence's car and read Levitt the brief

statement I composed during the drive from New York City. 'Dante Halleyville and Michael Walker,' I say slowly enough for him to take it down in his notebook, 'had absolutely nothing to do with the murders of Eric Feifer, Patrick Roche, and Robert Walco. Dante Halleyville is an exceptional young man with no criminal record or reason to commit these crimes.'

'So where's Walker?' asks Levitt.

'Walker will turn himself in tomorrow. There will be no further comment at this point.'

'Why did they run?'

'What did I just say, Len? Now start taking pictures. This is your chance to get out of the Sports section.'

I called Lenny for PR reasons. The tabloids and cops love that shot of the black suspect in shackles paraded through a gauntlet of blue and shoved into a squad car. But that's not what they're getting this morning.

The image Lenny captures is much more peaceful, almost poetic: a frightened teenager and his diminutive grandmother walking arm in arm toward the door of a small-town police station. The American flag flutters in the moonlight. Not a cop is in sight.

As soon as he has the shots, Levitt races off with his film as agreed, and Clarence and I catch up to Dante and Marie as they hesitantly enter the East

Hampton station. Marty Diallo is the sergeant behind the desk. His eyes are shut and his mouth wide open, and when the door closes behind us, he almost falls out of his chair.

'Marty,' I say, and I've been rehearsing this, 'Dante Halleyville is here to turn himself in.'

'There's no one here,' says Diallo, rubbing the cobwebs out of his eyes, and also taking out his gun. 'What the hell am I supposed to do?'

'This is a *good* thing, Marty. We're going to sit down here while you make some calls. Dante just turned himself in. Put down the gun.'

'It's four thirty in the morning, Dunleavy. You couldn't have waited a couple hours?'

'Of course we couldn't. Just pick up the phone.'

Marty looks at me with some strange mixture of confusion and contempt, and gives us our first inkling of why Dante was so insistent that I accompany him.

'I don't even know why you're here with this piece of shit,' Diallo finally says.

Then he cuffs Dante.

# Chapter Twenty-Nine

## Dante

S oon as the desk sergeant wakes all the way up, something pretty scared and angry clicks in his doughy face, and he pulls his gun and jumps out of his chair like he thinks the four of us are going to rough him up or maybe steal his wallet. The gun points straight at me, but everyone puts their hands up in the air, even my grandmoms.

Just like on the court at Smitty Wilson's, Tom's the only one steady enough to say anything.

'This is bullshit, Marty,' he says. 'Dante just turned himself in. Put down the gun.'

But the cop doesn't say a word or take his eyes off

me. Folks being scared of me is something I'm used to. With white strangers, it's so common, I've almost stopped taking it personally. But with Diallo – I can read his name tag – I can almost smell the fear, and the hand with the gun, with the finger on the trigger, is dancing in the air, and the other one, fumbling for the handcuffs on his belt, doesn't work too well either. For everyone's sake, I put out my hands to be cuffed, and even though the cuffs are way too small and hurt, I don't say a word.

Even when the cuffs are on me, Diallo still seems nervous and unsure of himself. He tells me I'm under arrest for suspicion of murder and reads me my rights. It's like he's cursing me out, only with different words, and every time he pauses, I hear *nigger*.

'You have the right to remain silent (*pause*). And everything you say (*pause*) can and will be held against you. Got that (*pause*)?' Then he pulls me toward the door to inside, and he's rough about it.

'Where you taking my grandson?' asks Marie, and I know she's mad, and so does Diallo.

'Marty, let me wait with Dante until the detectives arrive,' says Tom Dunleavy. 'He's just a kid.'

Without another word, Diallo shoves me through a small back office crammed with desks and then down a short, tight hallway, until we're standing in front of three empty jail cells, which are painted blue.

He pushes me into the middle one and slams the door shut, and the noise of that door shutting is about the worst sound I ever heard.

'What about these?' I ask, holding up my cuffed wrists. 'They hurt pretty bad.'

'Get used to it.'

# Chapter Thirty

## Dante

I sit on the cold wooden bench and try to hold my head together. I tell myself that with Grandmoms, Clarence, and most of all Tom Dunleavy outside, nothing bad is going to happen to me. I hope to God that's the truth. But I'm wondering, *How long am I going to have to be here?*

After twenty minutes, a new cop takes me out to be fingerprinted, which is some bad shit. Half an hour later, two detectives arrive in plainclothes. One is young and short and about as excited as the sergeant was scared. The older guy looks more like a real cop, heavyset, with a big square face and thick gray hair. His name is J. T. Knight.

'Dante,' says the younger one. 'All right if we talk to you for a while?'

'The sergeant says I have the right to an attorney,' I say, trying not to sound too much like a wiseguy.

'Yeah, if you're a candy ass with something to hide,' says the older one. 'Of course, the only ones who ask for lawyers are guilty as sin. You guilty, Dante?'

My heart is banging, because once I tell them what happened, I know they'll understand, but I calm down enough to say, 'I want Tom Dunleavy in the room.'

'Is he your lawyer?' asks the younger detective.

'I'm not sure.'

'If you're not even sure he's your lawyer, why do you want him in the room?'

'I just do.'

The younger one leads me down some steps, then another tight hallway, to a room the size of a big closet with a bare bulb hanging from the ceiling. There's nothing in it but a steel desk and four chairs, and we sit there until the older, bigger one returns with Tom.

From the apologetic way Tom looks at me, I can tell that none of this is happening like he imagined it would. Him and me both.

# Chapter Thirty-One

## Tom

'Why don't you start by telling us about the fight,' says Barney Van Buren. He is so amped to have a suspect in the box in his first big case that he's practically shaking. 'The fight that afternoon between you and Eric Feifer.'

Dante waits for my nod, then begins the story he's waited almost two weeks to tell.

'I barely know why we squared off. I don't think he did either. People just started shoving, and a couple punches were thrown. But no one got hurt. It was over in maybe thirty seconds.'

'I hear he tagged you pretty good,' says Detective

J. T. Knight, his right knee bouncing under the metal table.

'He might have got a couple shots in,' says Dante. 'But like I said, it was no big deal.'

'I'm curious,' says Knight. 'How does it feel to get your ass kicked by somebody a foot and fifty pounds smaller than you, what with all your buddies standing on the sidelines watching it happen?'

'It wasn't like that,' says Dante, looking at me as much as Knight.

'If it was such a minor deal,' asks Van Buren, 'why'd your friend run to the car and get his gun? Why did he put the gun to Feifer's head?'

'That was messed up,' says Dante, his forehead already beaded with sweat. 'It wasn't my idea he did that. I didn't even know he had a gun. I had never seen it before.'

I wonder if Dante is telling the truth about that. And if he can tell *small* lies, then what?

'And how about when Walker threatens Feifer again, says this still isn't over?' says Van Buren. 'It sounds like a big deal to me.'

'He was fronting.'

'Fronting?' says Knight, snorting. 'What's that?'

'Acting tough,' says Dante, glancing at me again for

help. 'Trying to save face for letting Tom talk him into putting the gun down.'

'*You two think we're idiots? Is that it?*' says Knight, suddenly leaning across the table to stick his face in Dante's. 'Ten hours after a fight that's "no big deal" and a threat that didn't mean a thing, Fiefer, Roche, and Walco are shot through the head. A triple homicide – over *nothing*?'

'That's what I was trying to tell you about it being no big deal,' says Dante, his eyes begging the two detectives to please understand and see that what he's saying makes perfect sense. 'The only reason we're there that night is because Feifer *called* Michael and asked us to meet him there so we could put this drama behind us. And look, here's the *truth* – Michael was looking to maybe buy some weed on Beach Road. The only reason we ran is because we heard the whole terrible thing happen and thought the killer saw us. The fact that Feifer called and asked us to meet him shows what I say is true.'

'How'd he get Walker's number?' asks Van Buren.

'I really don't know. I saw Feifer talking to my cousin Nikki at Wilson's; maybe he got it from her.'

'And how did you feel about *that*?' asks Detective Knight.

'About what?'

'About Eric Feifer putting the moves on your cousin.'

When Knight says that, he's leaning halfway across the small table again, so when I bring my hand down hard in the middle of the table, he jumps back as if a gun went off.

'You're the one with the problem,' I say, my face in Knight's now, even more than his was in Dante's. I'm bluffing, but Knight doesn't know that. 'Dante had nothing to do with these murders. He was there. That's all. Now he's here to share everything he saw and heard that night. But either the tone of this questioning changes, or this interview is over!'

Knight looks at me as though he's going to throw a punch, and I kind of hope he will. But before he makes up his mind to do it, there's a hard knock on the door.

# Chapter Thirty-Two

## Tom

Van Buren steps outside, and J. T. Knight and I continue to glower at each other until his partner returns with a large brown paper bag. Van Buren places the bag behind his chair and whispers something to Knight.

I can't make out Van Buren's words, but I can't miss his smirk. Or Knight's, either. *What the hell is this about?*

'Let's all calm down here for a second,' says Van Buren, a trill in his voice belying his words. 'Dante, did you stop at the Princess Diner in Southampton on your way out here tonight?'

Dante looks over at me again, then answers. 'Yeah, so Tom could use the bathroom.'

'Tom the only one who used the bathroom?'

'No, I think Clarence went too.'

'You think or you're sure?'

'I'm sure.'

'So that left you alone in the car? Is that right?'

'I didn't need to go.'

'Really?'

'What are you getting at?' I ask Van Buren, who maybe isn't as dumb as he seems.

'An hour ago we got a call from someone who was at the diner at about two thirty this morning. The caller says they saw a very tall black man throw a gun into the Dumpster in the parking lot.'

'That's a lie,' says Dante, shaking his head and looking at me desperately. 'I never got out of the car. Didn't happen.'

'You sure about that?'

'Yes, why don't you send a cop out there and look for yourself?'

'We did,' says Van Buren, a smug smile creasing his lips. Then he reaches behind his back and drops a sealed plastic bag on the table like a poker player triumphantly laying down a full house.

Staring up at us through the plastic and looking almost obscene is a handgun with a black plastic handle and a dull steel barrel.

'I've never seen that gun in my life!' cries Dante. 'And it's not Michael's gun either.'

I cut him off. 'Dante's not saying another word.'

# Chapter Thirty-Three

## Tom

I don't know what feels worse – what just happened, or the thought of facing Marie. I stagger up the stairs into the small waiting area, where Marie and Clarence jump from their chairs and surround me.

Behind them, steep sunlight streams through the glass door to the parking lot. It's 8:00 a.m. Dante and I were in that box for two hours.

'What's happening to my grandson, Mr Dunleavy?'

'I need some air, Marie,' I say, and walk through the door into the cool morning.

Marie follows and stops me in my tracks. 'What's

happening to my grandson? Why won't you look at me, Mr Dunleavy? I'm standing right in front of you.'

'They don't believe him,' I say, finally meeting her eye. 'They don't believe his story.'

'How can that be? The young man has never lied in his life. Did you tell them that?'

Clarence puts his arm around her and looks at me sympathetically. 'Tom's doing his best, Marie.'

'His best? What do you mean, his best? Did he tell them Dante had no reason on earth to commit these crimes? And where's the gun? There's no weapon.'

I look at Clarence, then back at Marie. 'Actually, they have the gun.'

I sit on a bench and look at the early morning traffic rolling by on Route 27. What a mess this is; what a complete disaster. And it's only just starting.

'So, what are you going to do now, Mr Dunleavy?' asks Marie. 'You're his lawyer, aren't you?'

Before I can come up with any kind of response, the door swings open behind us. Dante, in handcuffs again, is being led out by two more cops, this time from the Suffolk County Sheriff's Department.

The cops try to fend off Marie, but they're no match for her, and she runs between them and throws her arms around her grandson's chest. Dante looks ready to cry, and Marie's face looks even more heartbroken. The cops don't want to grab her, so they turn to me.

'Where are you taking him?' I ask.

'Suffolk County Courthouse.'

'We'll follow them in Clarence's cab,' I tell Marie. She whispers something to Dante as Clarence gently pries away her arms. Both of them are crying, and I'm pretty close myself.

'Are you in over your head?' Marie suddenly asks me.

I look at her, and I don't say *absolutely*, but I'm pretty sure she can read my mind.

# Chapter Thirty-Four

## Tom

Thirty years ago, when the county slapped it together at the outskirts of Riverhead, the Arthur M. Cromarty Complex, a sprawling campus of county courtrooms, might have looked almost impressive and modern, with its big white walls and tall glass doors.

Now it looks as plain and shoddy as any out-of-date corporate park. We pull into the complex just as Dante is being led into the main building. Hustling past a flock of off-course seagulls, we follow him in through the glass doors.

The guard behind the metal detector tells us that arraignments are handled by Judge Barreiro on the third floor, and with a beefy, heavily tattooed arm, he points us to the elevator.

Courtroom 301 has the same stench of catastrophe as an inner-city emergency room, which in a way it is. The distraught members of two dozen families have rushed here on short notice, and they're scattered in clusters throughout the forty rows of seats.

Clarence, Marie, and I find an empty section and sit and wait as a parade of men, mostly young and dark-skinned, are processed.

One after another, they're ushered through a side door with a sheriff on each arm and, as devastated moms and girlfriends and court-appointed attorneys look on, are formally charged with burglary, drug sale, domestic battery and assault. For three years I was one of those public defenders, so I know the drill.

'Such a shame,' Marie whispers, talking to herself. 'This is so wrong.'

The system proceeds with brutal efficiency, each arraignment taking less than ten minutes, but it's still more than two hours before a disembodied voice announces, *The people in the county of Suffolk in the state of New York versus Dante Halleyville.*' And now it's Marie and Clarence's turn to gasp.

Like the others before him, Dante wears handcuffs

and a bright-orange county-issued jumpsuit, in his case several inches too short in the legs and arms.

He is marched to a rectangular table in front of the judge. Already sitting there is his court-appointed attorney, a tall, stooped man close to sixty with overly large horn-rimmed glasses. This is mostly Marie's doing. She *knows* Dante is innocent, so she's advised him to use what the court gives him. I don't necessarily agree, but I'm just here to give free advice when I'm asked, *if* I'm asked.

Judge Joseph Barreiro leans into the microphone mounted on his podium and says, 'Dante Halleyville is charged with three counts of first-degree murder.' Murmurs of disbelief instantly sweep through all the rows of the courtroom.

'The defendant pleads not guilty to all three counts, Your Honor,' says Dante's lawyer. 'And in the setting of bail, we ask that the court bear in mind that this is a young man who turned himself in of his own volition, has never previously been charged with a single significant offense, and has strong ties to the community. For these reasons, Dante Halleyville represents a negligible risk of flight, and we strongly urge that any bail that is set be within the reach of his family's modest income.'

Dante's lawyer sits down, and his more energized adversary jumps up. He is around my age, and with his short haircut and inexpensive suit, he reminds me of half the kids I went to law school with.

'The state's position is the opposite, Your Honor. Three young men were bound and executed in cold blood. Because of the nature of the crimes and the severe penalties facing the defendant, as well as the fact that before turning himself in he remained at large for several days, we believe he represents a *substantial* flight risk.'

The black-robed judge weighs the relative merits of both arguments for a full thirty seconds. 'This court sets bail for the defendant at six million dollars. Two million dollars for each victim.'

Plea to bail, the whole process takes about as long as it does to place and pick up your order at the drive-through window of a McDonald's. The echo of Judge Barreiro's gavel has barely receded when the two sheriffs reappear and lead Dante out the side door.

'He's innocent,' Marie whispers at my side. 'Dante never hurt anyone in his entire life.'

# Chapter Thirty-Five

## Tom

It's Monday morning, and the only person feeling semi-okay with the world is AP photographer and friend Lenny Levitt. Since the weekend, Len's moonlight shot of Dante and his grandmother has appeared on the covers of the *Post,* the *Daily News,* and *Newsday.* My minor role in his affair barely rates a mention – in *Newsday* – and I think I have a pretty good chance of crawling back into my old and comfortable, if uninspiring, life.

Even though the only thing I've got to do is that real estate closing for my buddy Pete Lampke, I'm parked outside my office at 8:15 a.m. Like every weekday morning for three years, I leave Wingo on the front seat and step into the Montauk Bakery for my Danish and coffee.

Why I've been so loyal to the bakery is a mystery. It's certainly not the flakiness of the pastry or the richness of the coffee. Must be the comforts of consistency and the dependable early morning cheer of owner Lucy Kalin.

Today, the only thing Lucy's got to say is, 'Two twenty-five.' I guess she had a bad night too.

'I think I know the price by now, Lucy, girl. And top of the morning to you too.'

Breakfast in hand, I grab my pooch and head for the office.

Grossman Realty has the ground floor of the building next to mine, and the eponymous owner is also arriving bright and early. Normally, Jake Grossman is a sinkhole of bonhomie, upbeat, full of chatter even by the outsized standards of his profession.

This morning though, the way he reacts to my greeting, you'd swear he's deaf and blind.

Whatever. I'm still relieved to be back in my office where I can quietly read the papers again before checking in with Clarence.

When I call him, the poor guy's so twisted up about

what's happening to Dante he can barely talk and admits he had to go to the emergency room in Southampton for sedatives to get through the night. I hope I'm imagining it, but he sounds a little *chilly* too. What's up with everybody this morning?

I know Marie has to be feeling worse because she doesn't even pick up her phone.

When Lampke's contracts haven't arrived by noon, I get Phyllis at the broker's on the line.

'I owe you a call,' she says. 'Peter decided to go with a lawyer with a little more real estate experience.'

'Really?'

'Really.'

The bad news makes me hungry, but rather than getting shunned across the street at John's, Wingo and I drive to a little grocery run by a Honduran man and his three daughters at the edge of Amagansett.

As always, the place is packed with the Hispanic carpenters, gardeners, and day workers who keep the Hamptons buff. Despite the stack of newspapers with Dante's picture plastered all over them, no one here could care less about the latest Hampton drama. In this disconnected Spanish-speaking pocket of town, I'm invisible, and it feels pretty good.

I eat the pork-and-assorted-veggies sandwich at my

desk, where despite my best efforts, I think about Dante scared in his cell and about his tired old public-defender lawyer. The only good thing I come up with is that big as Dante is, no one will mess with him.

As of yesterday, Michael Walker still hadn't turned himself in, and I call Lenny at the AP offices to find out what, if anything, he's heard. We're talking the talk when something is thrown through the window in the office. What the hell? Shattered glass covers my desk. Then I see a burning bag on the floor.

'Call you back, Lenny! Somebody just broke my damn window.'

I douse the flames with the extinguisher hanging in the hall, but the room is already full of acrid yellow smoke and a horrendous stench, which Wingo and I soon discover is the smell of a plastic bag of burning shit.

I think I get the point – somebody is mad at me. And guess what? I'm a wee bit angry at them too.

# Chapter Thirty-Six

## Detective Connie P. Raiborne

I give Detective Yates the address for today's first reported homicide – 838 MacDonough – and he swerves out of the traffic and barrels down the middle of Fulton, his screaming siren and flashing lights barely denting the usual cacophony of a lovely Bed-Stuy afternoon.

Our banged-up Crown Vic barely gets a glance from the sleepy-eyed schoolkids hanging out in front of Price Wise. In this neighborhood police sirens are part of the soundtrack, like the strings and horns in a Nelson Riddle chart.

'Joe, take it easy. I got it on good authority our man will sit tight till we get there.'

Joe Yates has three of the more annoying qualities you'll ever find in a colleague or friend – tireless good humor, a full head of hair, and a beautiful girlfriend. Maybe the three are related, but that doesn't make them any less annoying.

Yates doesn't reply to my request, but apparently he listens. The car slows to double the speed limit, and there's less screeching around the corners. When we finally pull up in front of a redbrick six-floor walk-up and park behind the two double-parked squad cars, half my ice coffee is still in my cup.

'Smooth enough for you, Gramps?'

When we reach the fourth floor, everyone is already here – Heekin from Forensics, Nicolo and Hart from Homicide, and the street cop who broke down the door after a neighbor alerted the super to the funky smell inside.

But except for the guys in white gloves dusting the doorknobs, faucets, light switches, and window, everyone's been waiting for me to get here and see the scene as it was found.

No one's touched the teenage brother half lying, half sitting on the bed. Judging by the smell and the pallor and the chunk a rat gnawed off his big toe, I'd say the kid's been dead about a week.

'TV on when you got here?' I ask.

'Yup,' says Hart, the younger of the two Homicide detectives and a bit of a kiss-ass. 'Same volume. Same channel. No one touched a thing, Connie.'

Blaring away on the tube is one of those stand-up comedian shows. Right now some skinny black female comic is riffing about large black women, and Heekin seems to think it's hysterical.

'We catch you at a bad time, Jimmyboy? Because if we did, we can reschedule.'

'That's okay, Chief.'

'You sure? Girlfriend's pretty damn funny. I mean, she's killing our friend over here.'

I get one of the guys from Forensics to dust the TV remote for prints so we can turn the set off and I can ask the question of the hour.

'So who is this poor, unfortunate deceased individual?'

# Chapter Thirty-Seven

## Raiborne

There are three characteristics I find particularly endearing in a friend or coworker – a deep and dependable level of misery, male-pattern baldness, and a sexually stingy wife. Again, maybe all these traits work together, but that doesn't make them any less likable, and my favorite medical examiner, Clifford Krauss, bless his heart, has all three.

Because of all his winning qualities, it doesn't bother me in the least that Krauss, who took over the morgue nine years ago, one year after I made chief of Homicide, is two or three times better at his job than anyone else in the Seventeenth. And he definitely knows it.

By now we all know that the kid stretched out on his back on the metal gurney in the morgue is Michael Walker, seventeen, from Bridgehampton, Long Island, and one of the kids wanted in connection with three East Hampton homicides. Till this morning I didn't even know there were black people in the Hamptons, let alone triple homicides. But hey, I'm just a street cop from Bed-Stuy.

When I walk in, Krauss is at his desk in front of his laptop. He cups one hand over the mouthpiece of the phone and says, 'Suffolk County coroner.'

'They just went through my report,' he says after hanging up, 'and are pretty sure that the same gun that killed Walker was also used in the three Hampton homicides on Labor Day weekend.'

Then Krauss grabs his long yellow pad, comes over to where I'm standing next to Walker, and, wielding a stained Hunan Village chopstick for a pointer, takes me on a dead man's tour.

The crispness and intensity of Krauss's delivery hasn't softened in nine years, and if anything, his enthusiasm for gleaning secrets from a corpse has only increased. He starts with the exact size and location of the entrance and exit wounds, and the angle at which the bullet traveled. Reading from his notes, he describes the caliber, make, and casing of the bullet picked out of the plaster from behind the bed, and says all three are consistent with the weapon and silencer recovered by police in Long Island.

'I put the time of death at early in the morning of September eleventh,' he says, 'very early in the morning, approximately four a.m.'

'Approximately?'

'Yeah,' says Krauss, with a twinkle in his eyes. 'Could have been four thirty. All his blood work and the amount of dilation of his pupils indicate someone who'd been in a deep sleep right up to the moment he was shot.'

'Hell of a way to wake up,' I say.

'I'd prefer a kiss from J-Lo,' says Krauss.

'So Walker wasn't the one watching the tube?'

'Not unless he left it on. Also, we found a basket-ball cap on the floor of the closet, where it looked like someone was searching for something. The hat's barely been worn and is about three sizes too big for this guy here.'

'Isn't that how they wear everything now?'

'Jeans, coats, sweatshirts, but not hats. And none of Mr Walker's prints are on it. Maybe if we're really lucky, it was left by the shooter.'

'That's all you got for me, Cliffy?'

'One last thing. The rat who snacked on Walker's big toe – a black Norwegian, four to six pounds, female, pregnant.'

'Why's it always got to be a black rat, Krauss? Why never a white one?'

One thing, just for the record. That description of Cliffy's wife – pure bullshit. Her name is Emily, and she's a sweetheart.

# Chapter Thirty-Eight

## Marie Scott

L ast week this very same Riverhead courtroom was
filled with a sickening indifference. It is even worse
now. It turns my stomach inside out.

Today the room's *bursting* with reporters, family and
friends of the victims, and, more than anything else,
a lust for blood. The parents of the three dead boys
stare at me with powerful hatred, and Lucinda Walker,
Michael's mom, who I've known since she was a grade-
school student at Saint Vincent's, looks at me as if she
doesn't know what to think. I feel so badly for Lucinda.
I cried for her last night. Deep down she must realize
Dante would no more kill Michael than Michael would

kill Dante, but there's so much hurt in her eyes that I look away and squeeze Clarence's arm and rub the embossed leather cover of my Bible.

The spectators crane their necks and gawk as my grandson Dante, in handcuffs and an orange jump-suit, is led to that bare table with nothing but a water pitcher in the middle of it. They stir with anticipation or whatever as a booming voice intones, '*The State of New York versus Dante Halleyville*,' as if it were the ring announcement before a disgusting boxing match. Dante looks so scared and sad up there it breaks my heart. I need to go and hug him but I can't, and that makes me feel almost as bad.

The electricity builds as the judge leans into his microphone and says, 'The state of New York charges Mr Halleyville with a fourth count of first-degree murder.' Then the judge asks, 'How does the defen-dant plead?'

Dante's court lawyer says, 'Not guilty.' But it's as if he has said nothing at all. No one seems to believe him, or even listen to the man. Until this very moment, I don't think I believed that a trial could ever really happen, but now I know it can.

The crowd's only interest is the district attorney, and now that white man, so young he can't possibly understand what he's saying, so forgive him Lord, addresses the judge.

'Your Honor,' he says, 'in light of the heinous nature of the original crimes and the wanton disregard the defendant displayed in executing his accomplice, just as he did in the first three execution-style murders, the state of New York has no choice but to seek the ultimate penalty available to defend its citizens. In this case, the prosecution takes the extraordinary step of seeking the death penalty.'

I nearly collapse, but I won't let myself fall in front of all these people. The state of New York wants to murder my grandson! *Lord,* it's as simple as that. The state wants to murder my miraculous grandson who is as innocent as your own son, Jesus Christ, and the crowd thrills, THRILLS, to these terrible words. If they could, or if it were fifty years ago, they'd surely drag Dante from his chair and pull him out of this so-called courtroom and hang him from the nearest tree.

*Lord, help me, and please help Dante in his terrible time of need.*

I look at Clarence, and then I look at Mr Dunleavy. 'Please help us,' I say to him. 'Please help Dante. He didn't kill those boys.'

# Chapter Thirty-Nine

## Tom

If you've never seen a live media courtroom circus, consider yourself lucky.

Vans from all the TV networks and the big cable shows have been double-lined outside the courtroom building all day, and everywhere I look a correspondent is summoning the required fake gravitas to describe the ins and outs of such a high-profile death-penalty case.

I can't get away from the courthouse fast enough. Eyes cast downward, I thread my way through the crowded parking lot, trying to avoid an encounter with people I've known my whole life.

I'm so eager to get into my car, I don't notice Clarence

in the front seat until my key is almost in the ignition. He's shattered, sobbing into the back of his hand.

'They want to kill him, Tom. He'll never get a fair trial. You see what it's like in there.'

'Clarence, come back to my place tonight. I could use the company,' I tell him.

'I'm not after your sympathy, Tom. I'm here to ask you to be Dante's lawyer.'

'Clarence, I haven't been in a courtroom in over a year. Even then I was nothing special.'

'That's because you never tried, Tom. Not like you did playing ball. Put your mind to it, I believe you can do anything well. Folks *like* you. They *listen* to you.'

'Just because Dante's lawyer is older doesn't mean he's not doing a good job,' I say. 'Besides, he's Marie's choice.'

Clarence shakes his head. 'Marie wants *you*, Tom. She told me to ask. If you were on trial for murder, would you want that guy representing you? Or if your son was on trial? Be real with me.'

'I'm being real, Clarence. I can't be Dante's lawyer. The answer is no. I'm sorry.'

As soon as the words are out of my mouth, Clarence opens the door and pulls himself out of the seat. 'You're a big disappointment, Tom. Not that I should be surprised. It's been that way for years.'

# Chapter Forty

## Tom

Highly agitated now, I drive to Jeff's house. I need to talk to somebody I trust – because I am thinking about being Dante's lawyer. I need somebody to talk me out of my craziness.

Ten years ago my brother bought just about the last affordable house in Montauk. I loaned him the down payment from my signing bonus, and now the house is worth five times what he paid. That doesn't make us geniuses. Anything you bought then has gone through the roof. It's sweet in this case, however, because Jeff's wife had just left him for, as she put it, 'not being sufficiently ambitious.' Now Jeff and his three kids are living in a house worth more than a million dollars.

When she ran out on my brother, Lizbeth assumed she'd be getting Sean, Leslie, and Mickey. But Jeff dug in and hired one of the best lawyers out here. The lawyer, a friend of mine named Mary Warner, pointed out, among other things, that except in football season, Jeff was home by three thirty every day and had summers off, and to everyone's amazement, the judge awarded him full custody of the three kids.

Sean, the oldest, just turned twenty-five, and when I pull into the driveway, he's in the garage lifting weights. The two of us talk for a couple of minutes; then he starts breaking my chops.

'So, Uncle,' he asks between reps, 'how's it make you feel to be the least popular person in Montauk?'

'The old man around?' I ask.

'He's not back yet. The first game of the year against Patchogue is two weeks away.'

'I guess I'll head over to the high school then. I need to talk to him.'

'You spot me on my bench before you go?'

I've got a soft spot for Sean, maybe because he reminds me a little of myself. Because he's the oldest, the divorce fell hardest on him. And he had that 'son of the coach' crap in school, which is why despite being a natural athlete, he never went out for a high school team.

The last couple years, Sean's been lifting weights. Maybe he wants to look good in his lifeguard chair, or make a point to his old man. Well, now he's making a point with me because he doesn't stop adding black rings until he's got a hundred sixty pounds on each end. Add the weight of the bar, that's over three hundred fifty, and Sean can't weigh more than one seventy.

'You sure you're ready for this?' I ask, looking down at his fiercely determined face.

'One way to find out.'

The son of a gun lifts it twelve times, and a huge grin rushes across his beet-red face.

'Thanks for nothing, Uncle Tommy.'

'My pleasure. Okay if I tell the old man how impressive you are?'

'Nah. It'll only get him talking about all my wasted potential.'

'Don't feel bad, Sean. For us Dunleavys, squandered talent is a family tradition.'

# Chapter Forty-One

## Tom

I've been back in town three years, and this is my first visit to the old high school. Truth is, I'd rather have a root canal than go to a reunion, but as I step onto the freshly waxed gym floor, the memories rush back all the same. Nothing's changed too much. Same fiberglass backboards. Same wooden-plank bleachers. Same smell of Lysol. I kind of love it, actually.

Jeff's office is just above the locker room, and a very small step up in terms of accommodations and aroma. He sits in the corner, Celtic-green sneakers up on his metal desk, staring at a game film projected on the white cinder-block wall. The black-and-white images and the purr of the projector and the dust motes caught in the air make me feel as if I've fallen into a time warp.

'Got a game plan, Parcells?' Jeff has always worshipped Parcells and even looks like him a little.

'I was about to ask you the same thing, baby brother. What I hear, you need a plan more than me. An *escape* plan.'

'You could be right.'

There's a punt on the screen, and the pigskin seems to hang forever in the fall air.

'All I did was help a scared kid turn himself in,' I say to Jeff. I don't tell him that I've been asked to represent that kid. Or that I'm actually considering it.

'What about Walco, Rochie, and Feifer? You don't think they were scared? I don't get what you're up to, Tom.'

'I'm not sure I do either. I think it has something to do with meeting Dante's grandmother. Seeing where they lived, how they lived. Oh, and one other small detail – the kid didn't do it.'

Jeff doesn't seem to hear me, but maybe he does because he flicks off the projector.

'Between you and me,' he says, 'season hasn't started

and I'm already sick to death of football. Let's grab a beer, bro.'

'See, there's a plan,' I say, and grin, but Jeff doesn't smile back.

# Chapter Forty-Two

## Tom

Fifteen minutes later, Jeff stops in Amagansett and parks in the lot behind McKendrick's, the one bar most likely to be full of townies on a Wednesday night. But I guess that's the point. Or the plan. Make peace with the locals?

We enter through the back door and grab a booth by the pool table, so it takes a minute or so for the place to fall silent.

When Jeff is sure that everyone knows we're here, he sends me to the bar for our beer. He wants me to see exactly what I could be getting myself into, wants me to feel the hate up close and personal.

Chucky Watkins, a crazy Irish laborer who used to work for Walco now and then, is sitting at a table as I shoulder my way to the bar. 'Guess you're afraid to come here without your football-coach chaperon?'

'Kev,' I say, ignoring Watkins, 'a pitcher of Bass when you get a chance.'

'*When you get a chance, Kev,*' says Pete Zacannino, mocking me from the corner. By the way, a week ago, every face in this room was a pretty good friend of mine.

Kevin, who's a particularly good guy, hands me the beer and two mugs, and I'm ferrying back to the table when Martell, another former pal, sticks out his foot, causing half my pitcher to spill onto the floor. Snorts of laughter erupt from one end of the bar to the other.

'You all right, Tom?' asks Jeff from the back booth. A week ago, with Jeff or alone, I'd have cracked the pitcher over Martell's skull if only to see what would happen next.

'No problem, Jeff,' I shout back at the room. 'I just seem to have spilled a little of our beer, and I'm going to go back to the bar now and ask Kev if he would be so kind as to refill it.'

When I finally get back to our booth, Jeff takes an enormous gulp of beer and says, 'Welcome to your new life, buddy.'

I know what he's trying to do, and I love him for it. But for some reason, knee-jerk contrariness or just blind stupidity, it must not sink in. Because three beers later, I stand up and unplug the jukebox in the middle of a Stones song. Then, with a full mug in my left hand, I address the multitudes.

'I'm glad all you rednecks are here tonight because I have an announcement. As you all apparently know, I helped Dante Halleyville turn himself in. In the process, I've gotten to know him and his grandmother, Marie. And guess what? I like and admire them both a hell of a lot. Because of that and other reasons, I've decided to represent him. You heard correct. I'm going to be Dante Halleyville's lawyer, and as his lawyer, I'll do everything I can to get him off. Thanks very much for coming. Good night. And get home safely.'

A couple of seconds later, Chucky Watkins and Martell come at me. Something goes off inside me, and this is a side of Tom Dunleavy most of these guys know. I hit Watkins full in the face with the beer mug, and he goes down like a shot and stays down. I think his nose is broken. It could be worse.

'*C'mon!*' I yell at Martell, but he just backs away from me. I may not be Dante Halleyville's size, but I'm six three and over two hundred, and I know how to scrap.

'C'mon! Anybody!' I yell at the other cowards in the room. 'Take your best shot! Somebody?'

But only Jeff comes forward. He tucks me under his beefy arm and pushes me toward the back door.

'Same old Tommy,' he says, once we're in his truck. 'Same hothead.'

I stare out the windshield, still steaming as Jeff steps on the gas and we roar out of the parking lot.

'Not at all,' I say. 'I've mellowed.'

# Chapter Forty-Three

## Tom

The next day, at the Riverhead Correctional Facility, I place my wallet, watch, and keys in a small locker, then step through a series of heavy barred doors, one clanging shut behind me as another slides open in front.

The difference between the life of a visitor and those locked inside is so vast it chills me to the bone. It's like crossing from the land of the living into the land of the dead. Or having a day pass to hell.

To the right, a long, hopeless corridor leads to the various wings of the overflowing fifteen-hundred-bed jail.

I'm led to the left into a warren of airless little rooms set aside for inmates and their lawyers.

I wait patiently in one of them until Dante is led into the room. He's been inside a little less than a week but already seems harder and more distant. There's no trace of a smile.

But then he clasps my hand and bumps my chest, and says, 'Good to see you, Tom. It means a lot.'

'It means a lot to me too, Dante,' I say, surprisingly touched by his greeting. 'I need the work.'

'That's what Clarence says.' And his two-hundred-watt smile finally cracks through the shell. *This kid is no murderer. Anyone should be able to see that, even the local police.*

I really do need the work too. It feels like the first day of high school as I take out a new pack of legal pads and a box of pens.

'Other than the fact that I will believe everything you tell me,' I say, 'today's going to be like being in that box with the detectives, because we're going through that day and that night again and again. And we're doing it until every detail you can remember is on these pads.'

I have him start by telling me everything he knows about Kevin Sledge, Gary McCauley, and Dave Bond, his three other teammates that day. He tells me where they live, work, and hang out. He gives me their cell phone numbers and tells me how to track them down if they try to avoid me.

'All have been in some scrapes,' says Dante, 'but that doesn't mean much where I'm from. McCauley's on probation for drugs, and Bond served ten months right in here for armed robbery. But the real gangster is Kevin, who has never spent a day in jail.'

'How did they react to Michael pulling the gun?'

'They thought it was wack. Even Kevin.'

We talk about what happened the night of the murder. Unfortunately, his grandmother was visiting relatives in Brooklyn, so she hadn't seen him before or after the shootings. Dante swears to me that he didn't know where Michael Walker was hiding.

I'd forgotten how tedious this kind of work can be. Hartstein, my professor at St John's, used to call it 'ass in the chair' work, because that's what it comes down to, the willingness to keep asking questions and the persistence to go through events again and again even if it only yields a few crumbs of new, probably useless, information.

And it's twice as hard in here because Dante and I have to do it without caffeine or sugar.

Nevertheless, we keep on slogging, turning our attention to what he and Michael Walker saw and heard when they arrived to meet Feifer that night. These few minutes are the key to everything, and I keep pressing Dante for more details. But it's not until our third time through that Dante recalls smelling a cigar. *Okay, that could be something.*

And in the midst of his fourth pass, he sits up straight in his chair and says, 'There was a guy on the bench.'

My posture suddenly improves too. 'Someone was there?'

'You know that bench at the far side of the court? A guy was sleeping on it when we arrived. And five minutes later, when we ran past it, he was gone.'

'You sure about that, Dante? This is important.'

'Positive. Hispanic-looking dude, Mexican, or maybe Colombian. About thirty, long black hair in a pony-tail.'

# Chapter Forty-Four

## Tom

*A* cigar. Maybe belonging to one of the killers.

*The news that somebody else may have been at the murder scene who could confirm or add to Dante's story, who maybe saw the three kids killed.*

Both are significant leads that need to be tracked down, but there's something else I need to do first. So the next morning, when the doors of the shuttle slide open in Times Square, I'm one of the five hundred or so suckers ready to go to war for four hundred spaces.

The same quick first step that got me to the NBA gets me onto the car, and as the subway lurches the quarter mile to Grand Central, I feel as full of purpose and anxiety as any other working stiff in New York. I'm a workingman now. Why shouldn't I be a commuter too? Jeez, I'm even wearing a suit. And it's neatly pressed.

At the other end of the line, the urgent scramble resumes, this time upward toward Forty-second Street. I drop a dollar in the purple lining of an open trumpet case and head east until I'm standing in front of the marble facade of 461 Third Avenue, the suitably impressive home of one of New York's most venerable white-glove law firms – Walmark, Reid and Blundell.

Before I have a chance to lose my nerve, I push through the gleaming brass doors and catch an elevator to the thirty-seventh floor.

But that just gets me to the wrong side of another barrier, as daunting in its way as the walls that ring the Riverhead jail. Instead of barbed wire and concrete, it's a giant piece of polished mahogany so immense it must have arrived from the rain forest in the hold of a tanker and been hoisted to its new, unlikely home by a cloud-scraping crane.

Instead of an armed sentry, there's a stunning blond receptionist wearing a headset and looking like a cyborg.

'Good morning. I'm here to see Kate Costello,' I say.

'Do you have an appointment?'

'No.'

'Is she expecting you?'

'I'm a friend.'

To the receptionist, that's the same as a no. Maybe worse. She directs me toward a leather purgatory, where for the next twenty minutes I sweat into a thirty-thousand-dollar couch. Last night, coming here un-announced seemed a stroke of genius, and during the three-and-a-half-hour train ride from Montauk, my confidence never flagged. Well, not too much anyway.

But witty conversations with yourself and mock rehearsals can never duplicate the tension of the actual moment – and now Kate strides toward me, low heels clicking like little hammers on the marble floor.

I wonder if she knows how little her austere navy suit does to conceal her beauty. And does she care?

'What are you doing here?' she asks, and before I say a word, I'm back at the bottom of the hole I dug with Kate ten years ago.

'I need your help to defend Dante Halleyville.'

This is the point where I figured Kate would invite me back to her office, but all she does is stare through me. So I make my pitch right there in the lobby, laying it out as succinctly as I can. What I say makes perfect sense to me, but I have no idea how it's being received. I stare into Kate's bright blue eyes but can't read them, and when I stop to catch my breath, she cuts me off.

'Tom,' she says, 'don't ever come here again.'

Then she spins and walks down the hall, the clicking of her heels sounding even chillier than when she arrived. She never looks back.

# Chapter Forty-Five

## Kate

I retreat from Tom Dunleavy's totally unexpected ambush to the sanctuary of my office. I know that sounds superficial. It's just a room. But I've only had it a month, and the elegant furniture and dazzling East River view haven't lost the power to make me feel better the instant I step inside.

Thirty-one e-mails have come in since nine last night. Eight are related to the cease-and-desist letter I messengered to the lead attorney for Pixmen Entertainment last night. Our client, Watermark, Inc., considers Pixmen's new logo too close to one used by one of their divisions, and my letter accused them of trademark infringement and raised the prospect of aggressive legal action, including a possible freeze on all Pixmen income for the last fourteen months.

In an e-mail sent at 3:43 a.m., Pixmen's attorney reports that the logo has been deleted from all outgoing products, and e-mails from Watermark's attorneys express their satisfaction and gratitude. Persuasively threatening cataclysmic doom is one of the cheap thrills of my job.

A dozen other e-mails are the fallout of an embarrassing feature in *American Lawyer* about rising female legal stars. Many are from headhunters, but the most interesting is from the president of Columbia University, who asks if I have time to serve on the committee to find the new dean of the law school. *Yes, I will find the time.*

At exactly 9:00 a.m., Mitchell Susser arrives to brief me on the upcoming insider-trading trial of former Credit Mercantile managing partner Franklin Wolfe. An earlier trial, handled by one of our senior partners, ended in a hung jury, and I've been assigned the retrial.

'Relax, Mitch,' I say, not that it does much good. Susser, a brand-new hire who was Law Review at Harvard, has been reviewing the trial transcripts. 'Wolfe,' he says, 'spends way too much time implausibly denying activity that isn't clearly illegal. It costs him his credibility and gains him almost nothing. I think a second trial is a great opportunity.'

We're considering which of our defendant-preppers would make the best pretrial coach, when Tony Reid, the 'Reid' of Walmark, Reid and Blundell, sticks his eminent gray head into the room. Beside him is Randall Kane, arguably the firm's most valuable client.

'Got a minute, Kate?' Reid asks rhetorically.

Susser sweeps up his papers and bolts, and Tony Reid and Kane take his place in the seating area at the far end of my office. 'Of course, you know Randy, Kate.'

I don't need to have met Kane to know him. In the process of making Bancroft Subsidiaries one of the fastest-growing corporations in the world, Kane has become an iconic business leader, the embodiment of the hard-charging CEO. With a proposal jotted down on a napkin, a colleague in another division just got him a six-million-dollar advance for a business book.

But as Reid explains with exactly the right degree of urgency, all that could be jeopardized by a just-filed class-action lawsuit. It charges Bancroft with tolerating a work environment hostile to women and allowing a pattern of widespread sexual harassment. The suit names Kane directly.

'I know I don't need to tell you,' says Reid, 'that this opportunistic litigation is nothing but thinly veiled extortion.' Based on my own experience with class-action lawyers, that's probably true. Sophisticated ambulance-chasers, these lawyers come up with a target, prepare a suit, and then trawl for victims.

'I'm not rolling over on this one, Kate,' says Kane. 'It's total crap! Three of Bancroft's eight senior vice presidents are women, and the company was co-founded by my wife. They've got the wrong guy. If I have to, I'll take it all the way to trial.'

'I can't believe that will be necessary,' I say, 'but I assure you our response will be aggressive.'

'You bet it will!' says Randall Kane.

The rest of the day is wall-to-wall briefings, meetings, and conference calls. The company dining room delivers a chef's salad for lunch and sushi for dinner, and when I turn off the light at 11:00 p.m., I'm not the last person to leave.

The lovely fall night reminds me of the lovely fall day I've missed, and I decide to walk awhile before catching a cab.

I'm taking my first steps toward mostly deserted Park Avenue – when a tall figure rises from the shadows of the small stone plaza beside our office building.

# Chapter Forty-Six

## Kate

Walking stiffly, the man hurries toward me, then stops before he reaches the brightly lit sidewalk.

'Half-day?' he asks.

*It's Tom!*

'How long you been here?' I ask.

'I don't know. I've always sucked at math.'

I'm shocked to see him again but, much as I hate to admit it, kind of impressed. Tom's always been too charming by half but has never seemed the kind of guy capable of sitting on a stone bench for fifteen hours. Hell, one of our problems was that I never knew what he was capable of.

'Kate, you have got to hear me out. Can I please buy you a drink?' In the streetlight now, he looks exhausted, and his eyes plead. 'This is a matter of life and death. That may sound lame to you, but not to Dante Halleyville.'

'A cup of coffee,' I say.

'Really? That's the best news I've had in ten years.'

'I'm sorry to hear that,' I say, hoping I caught my smile in time.

The least intimate place I can think of is a Starbucks around the corner, where Tom wolfs a muffin in three or four bites and gulps down a bottle of water.

'Here's my spiel, Kate, the one I didn't get a chance to give you this morning. Dante Halleyville has never had one good thing happen in his entire life. When he was twelve, his father was stabbed in front of him, and he watched him bleed to death because in his neighborhood ambulances get there a lot slower than on Beach Road. His mother – a crack addict, prostitute, and thief – wasn't much better than no mother at all. She'd been in and out of jail even before his father died. So how does Dante deal with all this? He sees he has a talent that can take him out of this world and help everyone in his family. He can play ball.'

'Sounds familiar.'

'I mean *really* play, Kate. A whole different level than me. The Michael Jordan–Magic Johnson level. He makes himself the best schoolboy player in the country. He's easily good enough to go hardship and enter the League out of high school, but out of respect for his grandmother, Marie, he agrees to go to college. Three weeks ago, he's framed for four murders he had nothing to do with, Kate. Now the state of New York is seeking the death penalty. The least he deserves is a great lawyer.'

'What are you?'

'I don't know what I am, Kate, but we both know it's not a great lawyer. On a good day, I'm an okay lawyer trying his ass off. He needs a brilliant lawyer trying her ass off.'

'Excuse me?'

'Kate, it's a figure of speech.'

It's a good pitch. Tom didn't waste those fifteen hours – but I don't even think about it. The bastard could charm the birds out of the trees, but I'm not falling for it. Not TWICE. It's a big world. He can find another sucker.

'Sorry, Tom. I can't do it. But keep trying your ass off – you might surprise yourself.'

'Excuse me?'

'Tom, it's a figure of speech. And thanks for the coffee.'

# Chapter Forty-Seven

## Tom

Come what may, I am definitely on the case now, and in the spotlight again.

Since Lucy and the Montauk Bakery don't want my business anymore, me and Wingnut, who by the way was named after the great Knicks reserve player Harthorne Nathaniel Wingo but answers to anything with a *wing* in it, have been forced to refine our morning routine. Now we start our workday at that Honduran-owned grocery where no one knows our names. There I can sit alone at the outdoor table ten feet from Route 27 and try to figure out how to keep New York from executing an innocent eighteen-year-old kid.

Since I've taken on Dante Halleyville's case, my days pass in a blur and end wherever I fall asleep over my notebooks. I am nothing if not dedicated, and a little crazy.

As I sit in the steep October-morning light, pickups roll in and out and traffic streams west on 27, ten feet from my nose, but I'm too preoccupied to be distracted. When Dante dredged that 'witness' on the bench from his memory, he gave me a tantalizing lead. But I'm having a hard time following up on it.

If there's a person out there who can corroborate Dante's version of events or saw the real killers, the state has no case. But I barely have a description, let alone a name.

Maybe Artis LaFontaine, dealer, pimp, whatever he is, stayed at the basketball court long enough to see the guy arrive, but I have no idea how to get in touch with him. If I went to the police, they might have him on their radar, but I hate to do that unless I absolutely have to.

As I take a pull of coffee, a yellow VW bug rolls by. Yellow is the color du jour, I guess, and that makes me think of Artis's canary-yellow convertible.

*There can't be that many places where a person can buy a four-hundred-thousand-dollar Ferrari, right?*

I flip open my cell and start using up my minutes.

The dealership in Hempstead refers me to an exotic-car dealership on Eleventh Avenue in Manhattan. They refer me to a dealership in Greenwich, Connecticut.

Two hours later, still at my outdoor office on the side of the road, I'm talking to Bree Elizabeth Pedi. Bree Elizabeth is the top salesperson at the Miami Auto Emporium in South Beach. 'Of course I know Artis. He's putting my kids through college.'

I persuade Pedi to give Artis a call, and a couple minutes later he is on the line, but he's chillier than I expect. 'If you're calling about that night at the basketball court, I wasn't there.'

'Artis, if I have to, I'll subpoena you.'

'First, you got to find me.'

'Dante's facing the death penalty. You know something, and you're going to keep it to yourself?'

'You don't know Loco. I'll do time rather than testify against him. But as long as you understand that I was NOT THERE, I might be able to help.'

I describe the man lying on the bench, and Artis knows who I'm talking about right away.

'You're looking for Manny Rodriguez,' he says. 'Like everyone else, he's an aspiring rapper. He told me he works for a tiny label called Cold Ground, Inc. I bet they're in the phone book.'

# Chapter Forty-Eight

## Tom

Okay, so now I'm an amateur detective. And I'm back in Manhattan because Cold Ground, Inc., turns out to be in a funky postwar building right below Union Square.

A mirrored elevator drops me on seven, where a thumping baseline pulls me down a maroon-and-yellow hallway, and the scent of reefer takes me the rest of the way.

Inside the last door on the left, a little hip-hop factory is chugging industriously. What had been the living room of a one-bedroom apartment is now a recording studio.

Behind a glass wall a baby-faced rapper, his

immaculate Yankee cap precisely askew, rhythmically spits rhymes into a brass microphone.

> I ice him and vanish
> No trace of what I done
> Finding me is harder
> Than finding a smoking gun.

The artist looks no more than seventeen and neither does his girl, who sits on the leather couch on the other side of the glass with an infant on her lap dressed just like his dad, right down to the cockeyed cap and retro Nikes. A dozen other people are scattered around, and whether dazzlingly elongated or powerfully compact, they all seem like the fullest expression of who they are.

*Who is in charge?* No one that I can tell, and there's no desk or receptionist in front.

'Manny's making dupes,' says a tall woman named Erica, and she nods helpfully when a cable-thin guy with a jet-black ponytail steps out of a back room.

In Manny's arms is a stack of what look like pizza boxes. 'Got to deliver these to another studio,' he says, heading out the door. 'Come and we'll talk on the way.'

In a cross town cab, Manny lays down the plotlines of his frenetic life. 'I was born in Havana,' he says. 'My father was a doctor. A good one, which meant he made a hundred dollars a month. One morning, after a great big breakfast, I got on an eight-foot sailboat, pushed off from the beach, and just kept going. Twenty hours later, I almost drowned swimming to shore fifty miles south of Miami. I was wearing this watch. If I died, I died, but I had to come to America.'

Three years later, Manny says he's a break away from becoming the Cuban-American Eminem. 'I'm dope, and I'm not the only one who knows it.'

I suspect he's confused about why I'm here, but I'll set him straight in a minute. We get off on West Twenty-first Street in front of a Chelsea townhouse, and he drops his tapes at another apartment-turned-recording-studio.

'I'm not going to be doing this much longer,' he tells me.

I offer to buy him lunch around the corner at the Empire Diner, and we take a seat at a black-lacquered table overlooking Tenth Avenue.

'So what label you with?' Manny asks once our orders are in.

'I'm not with a label, Manny. I'm a lawyer, and I'm representing Dante Halleyville. He's falsely charged with killing three people at Smitty Wilson's court in

East Hampton. I know you were there that night. I'm hoping you saw something that can save his life.'

If Manny is disappointed that I'm not a talent scout looking to sign him to a huge deal, he keeps it to himself. He looks at me hard, as if he's running through his loop of images from that night.

'You're the ballplayer,' he says. 'I seen you there. You were a pro.'

'That's right. For about ten minutes.'

'You got a tape recorder?' he asks.

'No, but I've got a pad. I'll take careful notes for now.'

'Good. Let me hit the bathroom. Then maybe I got a story that could save that tall black boy.'

I wrestle my legal pad out of my case and hurriedly scribble a list of key questions in my barely legible shorthand. *Stay calm,* I tell myself, *and listen.*

I've been lost in my notes, and Manny still isn't back when the waiter drops the food on the table. I twist around, and see that the bathroom door is wide open.

I jump out of my chair and run like a maniac to the street.

I'm just in time to see Manny Rodriguez hop into a cab and roar away up Tenth Avenue. He finger-waves out the back window at me.

# Chapter Forty-Nine

## Loco

There's a gray, pebbly beach on the bay side of East Hampton where on Sunday afternoons the Dominicans, Ecuadorians, and Costa Ricans play volleyball. During the week, they put in seventy hours mowing lawns, clipping hedges, and skimming pools. At night, they cram into ranch houses that look normal from the street but have been partitioned into thirty cubes. By Sunday afternoon, they're ready to explode.

These games are wild. You got drinking, gambling, salsa, and all kinds of over-the-top Latin drama. Every three minutes or so two brown bantamweights are being pulled apart. Five minutes later they're patting each other on the back. Another five minutes, they're swinging again.

I'm taking in this Latin soap opera from a peeling green bench fifty yards above the fray.

It's six fifteen, and as always, I'm early.

It's no accident. This is part of the gig, the required display of fealty and respect. Which is fine with me. It gives me time to light my cigar and watch the sail-boats tack for home at the Devon Yacht Club.

I should cut back. The Davidoff torpedo is my third this week. But what's life without a vice? What's life *with* a vice? Did you know Freud smoked half a dozen cigars a day? He also died of mouth cancer, which I like to think was poetic payback for telling the world that all every guy wants to do is kill his father and boff his mom. I don't know about you, but I didn't need to know that.

Speaking of authority figures, a drumroll please, because here comes mine – *BW* – and he's right on time, eleven minutes late.

With his three-hundred-dollar Helmut Lang jeans, torn and faded just right, and his God-knows-how-expensive light-blue cashmere hoodie and week-old growth, he's looking more like a goddamn weekender every day. But who's got the stones to tell him? Not me, bro, and they call me Loco for a reason.

'What's up?' asks BW, but not in the convivial way most people use it. Out of BW's mouth, it sounds more like 'What's your problem?' or 'So what's your problem now?' But this time it's not just *my* problem, it's *our* problem, which pisses him off ten times more.

'Apparently, we had company,' I say. 'Out behind Wilson's house.'

'Oh, yeah? Who told you that?'

'Lindgren.'

'That sucks.' For all his peccadilloes, BW has an impressive ability to cut to the chase.

Down in the sand, a drunk volleyballer is pointing at a ball mark and screaming bloody murder in either Spanish or Portuguese.

'What should I do now, boss?'

'Whatever you think is best.'

'Whatever *I* think is best, BW?'

'And let me know when you've done it.'

Then, like a puff of smoke from an overpriced cigar, BW's gone, and it's just me, the night, and the salsa.

# Chapter Fifty

## Loco

*W*hatever I think is best, huh? I think I get BW's point, which means another trip to Brooklyn and another *shitty, shitty, bang, bang.*

Like his compadres out in the Hamptons, Manny Rodriguez works way too hard. It's three in the morning, and I've been parked across the street from Manny's apartment since eleven, and everyone in Bed-Stuy is asleep but him. Is it that immigrant work ethic or is something boiling in their blood? *Quien sabe, ay?*

Wait just a second – here comes Manny. Just in time, because my stomach couldn't take any more bad coffee tonight.

Even now, our boy is still hopped up, bouncing to the music pumping through his headphones.

If you ask me, nothing's ruined the city more than headphones and iPods and computers. It used to be New York offered the kind of random interaction you couldn't get anywhere else. You never knew when you might have a moment with the beautiful girl waiting next to you for the light to change.

Or maybe you'd say something to a guy, not a gay thing, just two people traveling through this world acknowledging each other's existence. Now everyone walks around obliviously, listening to their own little music downloaded from their own little computer. It's lonely, brother.

Plus, it's dangerous. You step off the curb and don't hear the crosstown bus till you're under it, and you certainly don't hear the Chinese guy pedaling around the corner on his greasy bike.

Well, now you can add the sad cautionary tale of Manny Rodriguez. He's so caught up in his own tunes he doesn't hear me walk up behind him and pull out my gun. He doesn't sense anything's the slightest bit amiss until a bullet is crashing through the back of his skull and boring into his brain. The poor guy doesn't know he's been murdered until he's dead.

# Chapter Fifty-One

## Kate

The blueback laying out the formal complaint against Randall Kane hits my desk at Walmark, Reid and Blundell around 2:30 p.m. I shut my door and clear my calendar for the rest of the day.

I'm well aware that this choice assignment is not based entirely on my skill as a litigator. For the high-powered CEO charged with crossing the line, walking into court with a female lawyer is pretty much textbook. And I don't have a problem with that. There are still so many more disadvantages than advantages to being a woman, career-wise, that in those rare instances where it plays in your favor, I believe in going with the flow.

Once I read the language at the top of the complaint, I'm confident this is something we can win not only in court but in the media. It's sprinkled with phrases like 'hostile work environment,' which usually refers to off-color jokes and pages of the *Sports Illustrated* swimsuit issues pinned to cubicle walls.

Then I read the affidavit from the first of Randall Kane's alleged victims. She's a thirty-seven-year-old mother of three who spent nine years as Kane's executive secretary. In her written statement, sworn under oath and the penalty of perjury, she describes how on more than thirty occasions, she repelled Kane's physical and verbal sexual advances, and how when she finally quit and filed a complaint, he used all the corporate resources at his disposal to destroy her life.

By the time I finish reading the complaint, I realize that *Randy* Kane's problems aren't going away with a scary letter or pretrial motion. And there are eleven other women whose sworn testimonies are essentially identical, right down to the phone call they receive from Kane's corporate lackey telling them they'll never work again if they keep this up. Three of the women recorded the calls.

I close the file on my desk and ponder the East River. Kane apparently isn't just an unfaithful husband.

He's a scumbag and possibly a serial rapist who just happens to be worth a billion dollars. He deserves to pay a high price for his actions, and if I help him avoid it, I'm no different from that in-house lackey of his making obscenely threatening phone calls.

For a decade I've punched all the right tickets, from Law Review at Columbia to two years prosecuting white-collar crime for the DA's southern circuit, and after three and a half years at Walmark, Reid and Blundell, I've got senior partner in my sights.

You know how many female senior partners there are or have been at Walmark, Reid and Blundell? None.

So why am I walking down the corridor to Tony Reid's corner office?

Is it possible that Tom's midnight pitch hit the mark? *God help me if it did.* Tom has made me feel like crap in a hundred ways, but I never dreamed he'd make me feel professionally jealous, or worse, that he'd pass me on the ethical ladder.

But now I'm a very well-paid consigliere, and he's defending someone he believes is innocent – for free.

Reid waves me into his office, and I drop the stack of affidavits on his antique desk.

'You better read this,' I say. 'We go to trial, Randall Kane will be exposed as a ruthless sexual predator.'

'Then it can't go to trial,' says Reid.

'I can't represent this man, Tony.'

Reid calmly gets up and closes the door. It barely makes a sound.

'I wouldn't think I'd have to remind you, of all people, how important Randy Kane is to this firm. In every department, from corporate to real estate to labor management, he bills hundreds of hours a year. A dozen unfortunate women have been manipulated by a shameless lawyer, an ambulance-chaser out for his own gain. You know the game. And if by some chance they're telling the truth? Guess what, ladies? It's a tough world.'

'Get someone else then, Tony. Please. I'm serious about this.'

Tony Reid thinks about what I've said before he responds. Then he speaks in the same persuasive tone that has made him one of the most successful trial lawyers in New York.

'For an ambitious attorney, Kate – and everything I know about you indicates you are as ambitious and talented as any young lawyer I know – cases like this one are a rite of passage. So unless you come back to this office at eight tomorrow morning and tell me otherwise, I'm going to do you and this firm the favor of pretending this conversation never happened.'

# Chapter Fifty-Two

## Kate

That night, I get back to my apartment at the unheard-of hour of 7:00 p.m. Three years ago, I bought this ridiculously expensive one-bedroom apartment in the eighties on the Upper West Side because it had a garden. Now, having poured myself a glass of pricey Pinot Noir, I'm actually sitting in my garden and listening to the sounds of the city as the lights blink on in the surrounding apartments.

I watch the sky go black on this late October night, then go back inside for a refill and a blanket. *The scene is almost but not quite right.* So I drag out my ottoman and put my feet up. Now that's more like it

– comfortable, warm, and miserable, my life in a nutshell.

That arrogant prick Reid is right about one thing: I should hardly have been shocked to discover Randy Kane is a scumbag. Wealthy scumbags pretty much fill the coffers at Walmark, Reid and Blundell. If the firm is ever in need of a catchy motto to chisel into the marble lobby, I'd suggest Scumbags Are Us.

But I don't want to be the person defending those clients anymore. How did this happen? When I went to law school, aiding and abetting white-collar crime couldn't have been further from my career goal. But then I did well at Columbia, got on the fast track, and wanted to prove I could stay on it, earn just as much money, make partner just as fast, etc., etc., etc.

Sitting in the cold dark of my lovely garden with my third glass of Pinot, I realize there have been other consequences of my fab career. You may have noticed that I'm sharing my depressing thoughts with myself tonight rather than bouncing them off a succession of dear old friends. That's because I really don't have any. Forget a boyfriend. I don't even have a really close girl-friend I'd be comfortable pouring my heart out to right now.

I think it's that competitiveness and pride thing again.

In law school I had two wonderful, very close friends – Jane Anne and Rachel. The three of us were tight as thieves and swore we'd be soul mates to the end and bring the bastards to their knees.

But then Jane Anne gets happy and pregnant, and Rachel stays on a fast track for a couple of years before dropping out to work for Amnesty International. Both resent my 'success' a little, and I'm miffed by their resentment. Then one time a week goes by without one of us returning a call, and then it's a couple of weeks, and eventually no one wants to give in and pick up the phone. So I finally break down and make the call but feel the chilliness on the other end, or think I do, and wonder, who needs that?

It turns out I do, because the next thing you know I'm alone in the dark with only a blanket and a glass of wine for company.

Now it's 2:00 a.m., and the empty bottle of Etude lies next to the half-empty box of Marlboros, which was full when it was delivered from the bodega three hours ago. Let the record show that I never once represented a cigarette manufacturer. Of course, no one asked me to, but it should still count for something.

An hour and a couple more cigarettes later, I'm dialing the number of the one person on this planet

I'm reasonably confident will be delighted to hear from me at three in the morning.

'Of course I'm not sleeping,' says Macklin as if he's just been told he hit the Lotto. 'At my age you never sleep, unless that is you're trying to stay awake. Kate, it's so lovely to hear your voice.'

Mack, why did you have to say that? Because now I'm crying and can't stop. It's five minutes before I can blurt, 'Macklin, I'm sorry.'

'Sorry? What are you talking about, darling girl? That's what unlimited minutes are for.'

That sets off more sobbing. 'Macklin, you still there?'

'Yup. Always.'

'So, Mack, I'm thinking of coming out to Montauk for a while and was wondering if that offer about your extra bedroom is still on the table?'

'What do you think, Kate?'

And then I lose it again.

And in the morning, I call Jane Anne and Rachel too.

# Chapter Fifty-Three

## Tom

B ack in the days when an East Hampton billionaire turned fifty he'd buy his way out of his second marriage, get a Harley and a tattoo, and find a nice twenty-something girl (or boy) who admired him for what he truly was – a very, very rich person.

Now instead of a scooter he can barely ride, maybe he buys a surfboard he can't ride at all. And instead of a leather jacket, he squeezes into a full-body polyurethane girdle, otherwise known as a wet suit.

I have nothing but respect for real surfers. Feif, for example, was a wicked athlete and a bona fide badass on the water. It's the middle-aged nouveau surfers I have trouble with, the guys who wander into what used to be perfectly decent dive bars and try to get the ball rolling with that pretentiously simple two-word question: 'You surf?'

Still, the surfing craze has been good to my pals. Sometimes, Feif made five hundred dollars a day giving lessons, and it's been manna from heaven for Griffin Stenger, who owns the Amagansett Surf and Bike Shop. Grif tells me that on Saturday mornings the Beach Road crew tries to catch the baby waves that come off the breaker at the end of Georgica Beach. Since the spot is no more than two hundred yards from where Feif, Walco, and Rochie were murdered, and because there's no point going back to Cold Ground, Inc., till Monday, I'm here to see if one of these ocean gods saw anything the night of the murder.

Saturday morning, I'm out of the house at dawn and waiting at the breaker when the surfer lads start to waddle in.

In the first group, flanked by a burly duo, is Mort Semel, who sold his company to eBay last year for $3 billion.

When I approach him to introduce myself, the two younger, muscular guys drop their boards and get in my face. 'Can we help you, sir?'

'I was hoping to talk to Mort for a minute.'

'About what, sir?'

'I'm a lawyer representing a young man accused of committing a murder near here a couple months ago. I know Mr Semel is a close neighbor of Mr Wilson's and often surfs here. I need to find out if he saw or heard anything that night, or knows anyone who did.'

One bodyguard stays with me, the other walks over to Semel, then trots back as if he can't wait to tell me the good news. 'Nope. Mort didn't see or hear a thing.'

'Oh, yeah. Well, since I came all the way out here, I'd kind of like to ask him myself.'

'Not a good idea.'

'This is not his home,' I say, and my temperature is starting to rise a little. 'This is a public beach, asshole. I'm talking to Mort.' I start to walk his way.

Apparently not a good idea either, because now I'm flat on my back in the sand, and the bigger of the two has his foot on my throat.

'Stay *down*,' he says. 'Stay *still*.'

# Chapter Fifty-Four

## Tom

'I get the picture,' I say. 'I get it, all right?'

But I'm thinking, *A surfer with two bodyguards. How rad is that?* It's almost funny, except as I tried to point out, this is a public beach. Also, my face was just in the public sand.

So I grab the foot in my face and twist it around like little Linda Blair's head in *The Exorcist*. The ankle makes a satisfyingly unnatural sound; then the cartilage around the bully bodyguard's knee cracks, and a scream comes out of his mouth. I don't see him fall because I've already turned my attention to his colleague, and the two of us pretty much break even until some of the other surfers pull us apart.

*Break even* might have been a slight exaggeration on my part. When I get back to my car one eye is closed already. And back at my house, a half-hour later, there's some blood in it. But I'd be feeling worse if I let those jerks scare me off my own beach.

Besides, one eye still works fine, so I go back to the notes from my last interview with Dante.

In addition to the aching ribs and the eye, I must have taken a blow to the head, because I swear a woman who looks exactly like Kate Costello just walked into my backyard. The woman in question wears blue jeans, a white Penguin shirt, and black Converse sneakers, and she comes over to where I'm sitting at a wooden table and takes the chair next to mine.

'What happened to you?' she asks.

'A couple of bodyguards.'

'Belonging to whom?'

'Oh, some guy on Beach Road I tried to talk to about the murders this morning.'

She wrinkles her nose and sighs. 'You haven't changed, have you?'

'Actually, I have.'

Then this woman, who I'm pretty sure actually is Kate Costello, says, 'I've changed my mind. I want to help you defend Dante Halleyville.'

And as I sit there too stunned to reply, she continues, 'The thing is, you've got to say yes because I quit my job yesterday and moved out here.'

'You know there's no pay, right? No perks. No medical insurance. Nothing.'

'I'm feeling healthy.'

'So did I when I woke up.'

'Sorry about that.'

'And you're okay working as an equal with someone who couldn't even get hired by Walmark, Reid and Blundell?'

And then Kate nearly smiles. 'I consider your unworthiness of Walmark, Reid and Blundell an important point in your favor.'

# Chapter Fifty-Five

## Kate

*H*e's just a kid.
*A very tall kid who looks frightened.*

Those are my first unformed thoughts when Dante Halleyville, bending at the waist so as not to bang his head, steps into the tiny attorney's room where Tom and I are waiting. Now I'm thinking that it's one thing for an eighteen-year-old to hold his own with men on a basketball court but another to do it at a fifteen-hundred-man maximum-security jail. And Dante's eyes definitely reveal he's as terrified as my kid, or your kid, or any kid would be who suddenly found himself locked up in this terrible place.

'I've got good news,' says Tom. 'This is Kate Costello. Kate is a top New York lawyer. She's just taken temporary leave from her job at a major firm to help with your case.'

Dante, who has already gotten way too much bad news, only grimaces. 'You're not backing out on me, are you, Tom?'

'No way,' says Tom, straining to make himself understood better. 'Defending you is all I'm doing and all I will be doing until you're out of here. But now you've got yourself a legal team – a shaky ex-jock and an A-list attorney. And Kate is from Montauk, so she's local too,' he says, reaching out for Dante's hand. 'It's all good, Dante.'

Dante grabs for Tom's hand and they embrace, and then Dante very shyly makes eye contact with me for the first time.

'Thanks, Kate. I appreciate it.'

'It's good to meet you, Dante,' I say, and already feel more invested in this case than any I've handled in the last few years. Very strange, but true.

The first thing Tom and I do is talk with Dante about the murder of Michael Walker. He's close to tears when he tells us about his friend, and it's difficult to believe he had anything to do with the killing. Still, I've met some very convincing liars and con artists in my day, and Dante Halleyville has everything to lose.

'I got another piece of good news,' says Tom. 'I tracked down the guy who was at the basketball court that night – a Cuban named Manny Rodriguez. We couldn't talk for long, but he told me he saw something that night, something heavy. And now that I know where he works, it won't be hard to find him again.'

As Dante's young face brightens slightly, I can see all the courage that's been required to keep it together in this place, and my heart goes out to him. I think, *I like this kid. So will the right jury.*

'How are you holding up?' I ask.

'It's kind of rough,' says Dante slowly, 'and some people can't take it. Last night, about three in the morning, these bells go off and a shout comes over the intercom: "*Hang-up in cell eight!*" That's what they say when an inmate tries to hang himself, and it happens so often the guards carry a special tool on their belts to cut them down.

'I'm in block nine, across the way, so I see the guard race into a cell and cut some guy down from where he's hanging. I don't know if they got him in time. I don't think so.'

I haven't read through the materials yet, but Tom and I stay with Dante all afternoon to keep him company and give him a chance to get to know me a little. I tell him about cases I've worked on and why I got sick of it, and Tom recounts some NBA lowlights – like the night Michael Jordan dunked the ball off his head. 'I wanted to ask the ref to stop the game and give me the ball,' says Tom, 'but I didn't think it would go over too well with my coach.'

Dante cracks up, and for a second I catch a glimpse of his smile, which is so pure it's heartbreaking. But at six, when our time is up, his face clouds over again. It feels awful to leave him here.

It's after eight when we get back to Montauk, but Tom wants to show me the office. Our office. He grabs the newspapers lying on the first step and leads me up a steep, creaking staircase. His attic space – with dormer walls slanting down on both sides so he can only stand up straight in half of it – is a far cry from Walmark, Reid and Blundell, but I kind of like it. It feels like rooms I had in college. Hopeful and genuine, like starting over.

'As I'm sure you've noticed,' says Tom, 'every piece in the room is original IKEA.'

Tom leafs through the *Times* while I look around.

'Remember,' he says, 'when I used to just read the Sports? Now all I read is the Metro section. It's the only part that seems connected to anything I under—'

He stops midsentence – and looks as though he's been kicked in the stomach.

'What? What's the matter?' I say, and walk around to look for myself.

Near the top of the page is a picture of a sidewalk in Bedford-Stuyvesant. Candles have been set out and lit in front of a makeshift shrine, an attempt to mark and protest one more pointless street killing in the neighborhood.

Beneath the picture is a story with the headline, HIP-HOP FEUD CLAIMS ANOTHER VICTIM.

The name of the vic is right there in the first paragraph, staring up at both of us – *Manny Rodriguez.*

# Chapter Fifty-Six

## Tom

I am quickly learning that misery *does* like company. And let's hope two lawyers without a chance in hell are better than one.

When Kate and I pull into the lot behind East Hampton High School, all that's left of the sudden November dusk is a violet smudge in a desolate sky. We park behind the gym and wait, doing our best to ignore the awkward reunion feeling of sitting next to each other in pretty much the exact spot where we met almost twenty years before.

'It's like déjà vu all over again,' I finally say, and regret it immediately.

'Still quoting Yogi,' says Kate.

'Only when it's absolutely appropriate.'

A parade of students, all looking ridiculously young, pushes through the rear doors of the gym, and each drives off in one of the cars or SUVs parked or idling in the lot.

'Where's our girl?' Kate asks.

'Don't know. Our luck, she has the flu.'

'Our luck, she was run over by a semi this morning.'

At six thirty, when only a couple of cars are left, Lisa Feifer – Eric's kid sister – steps through the door into the chilly air. Like her brother, Lisa is thin and graceful, the star on the girl's state-championship lacrosse team. She moves across the empty lot with the relaxed shuffle of a spent athlete.

As she drops her gym bag on the roof of her old Jeep and unlocks the door, Kate and I get out of our car.

'We can't waste time feeling sorry for ourselves about Rodriguez,' Kate had told me first thing in the morning when she walked into the office. By then she had already read through my interviews with Dante and thought there were several areas worth pursuing. 'It's not our job to find out who actually killed Feifer, Walco, Rochie, and Walker. But it would sure help if we could steer the jury *somewhere else.* We've definitely got to find out more about the deceased.'

'You mean, dig up dirt on the dead?'

'If that's how you want to put it,' Kate said, 'that's fine with me. Feifer, Walco, and Rochie were my friends too. But now our only loyalty is to Dante. So we have to dig, unmercifully, and see where it leads. And if it pisses certain people off, so be it.'

'Certain people are already pissed off.'

'So be it.'

I know Kate's right, and I like the concept of *unmerciful* action on our part, but when Lisa Feifer turns around and sees us coming toward her, she looks at us as if we're muggers, or worse.

'Hi there, Lisa,' says Kate, in a voice that manages to sound natural. 'Can we talk to you for a minute?'

'About what?'

'*Eric,*' says Kate. 'You know that we're representing Dante Halleyville.'

'How messed up is that? You were his babysitter. Now you're defending the guy who put a bullet between his eyes.'

'If we thought there was any chance Dante killed your brother, or Rochie, or Walco, we wouldn't be doing this.'

'Bullshit.'

'And if you know anything dangerous that Eric might have been involved in you've got to tell us. If you don't, Lisa, you're just helping his real murderer get away with it.'

'No, that's what you're doing,' says Lisa, pushing past us and getting into her car. If we hadn't jumped back, she probably would have run us over as she tore out of the lot.

'So be it,' I say.

'Very good.' Kate nods. 'You're a fast learner.'

# Chapter Fifty-Seven

## Tom

D igging for dirt on your old pals in a town like Montauk is a lot easier said than done though.

Walco's father slams the door in our face. Rochie's brother grabs a shotgun and gives us thirty seconds to get off his property. And Feifer's mom, a sweet woman who volunteers three days a week at the Montauk Public Library, unlooses a stream of curses foul and vicious enough to earn the approval of Dante's most hardened fellow inmates over at Riverhead.

We get the same obscene kiss-off from Feifer, Walco, and Rochie's old friends and coworkers. Even ex-girlfriends, whose hearts have been stomped on by the victims, become ferociously protective of their memory at the sight of us.

Dante thinks being represented by locals is helping him, but right now it's a hindrance, because to townies our decision has made the whole thing personal. Just acknowledging Kate or me on the street is viewed as giving aid and comfort to the enemy.

Being treated like a pariah is harder on me than it is on Kate. She hasn't lived here for years, and working at Walmark, Reid and Blundell has thickened her skin.

But the lack of progress frays her nerves, and after a week and little to show for our efforts, my cramped dormer office has lost its charm. Same goes for the absurdly loud-creaking stairs leading to the chiropractor next door. I, on the other hand, kind of like having Kate around. It gives me confidence. Makes the whole thing feel real.

Another visitor to the chiropractor and Kate yells out, 'This is like working in a theme-park haunted house.'

'I'll get you coffee,' I say.

It's a half-hour round trip to the nearest deli whose owners are unlikely to poison us, so I've brought my antique Mr Coffee from home. But even the time-honored combination of caffeine and desperation doesn't seem to be working anymore.

'We need to find an outsider,' Kate finally says. 'Somebody who grew up here but never fit in.'

'You mean, other than the two of us?'

'Somebody has to be willing to talk to us, Tom. C'mon, think. Who's our Deep Throat?'

I think about her question for a bit. 'How about Sean?' I finally say.

'He was a friend of all three of those guys. Plus, he's a *lifeguard*, for God's sake. I was thinking of a little more of an outcast.'

'He's not a social pariah, Kate. But he's got the guts to go against the flow. People talk to Sean. He could have heard something.'

'You think you'd have better luck talking to him alone?'

I shake my head. 'Actually, I think you'd have a better chance, me being his uncle and everything. Plus, he probably has a crush on you.'

Kate screws up her face. 'What makes you think that?'

'I don't know. Why wouldn't he?'

# Chapter Fifty-Eight

## Kate

L.I. Sounds, where Tom's nephew Sean has been working since the lifeguard chairs came down, is one of the few stores still open in East Hampton, and it's not clear why to me.

At nine that night, there are exactly two people in the brightly lit, narrow space. Sean is up front by the register, as his one potential customer browses the aisles. Sean's a good-looking kid with long blond hair. Actually, he looks more like Tom than Jeff.

I glance around the store. Sounds will always have a special place in my heart. Until they built the mall in Bridgehampton, it was the only record store for thirty miles. With posters of Hendrix, Dylan, and Lennon up on the walls and a staff of zealots preaching about the eternal difference between Good and Awful music, it felt as serious as stepping into a church.

Sean smiles in welcome as I step into the light. He puts on a spacey CD I don't recognize.

The other customer, a tall, skinny guy with wire-rimmed glasses, glances at me then looks away. Nothing changes. He's pushing fifty but has the self-conscious slouch of an eighteen-year-old. The guy is working the back of the alphabet, so I start on the other end and move happily from AC/DC to the Clash to Fleetwood Mac.

When he leaves, I take a reissue of *Rumors* up to the register.

'Classic,' says Sean.

'You approve? I was sure you'd think it was too girly and lame.'

'What are you talking about, Kate? I was playing it an hour ago. Me and the cross-eyed cat couldn't get enough of it.'

'Also, the title seemed kind of appropriate,' I say.

'You lost me.'

'You know, have you heard any?'

Sean seems a little disappointed, but I'm not sure if it's the subject matter or my attempt at humor.

'Is that really why you're here?'

'It is, Sean.'

'You mean information about Feifer, Walco, and Rochie?' asks Sean.

'Or anything that might help explain why someone would want to kill them.'

'Even if I did – I'm not sure I'd tell you.'

'Because people told you not to.'

Sean looks at me as if I just insulted him in the worst possible way. 'I could care less about that bullshit. But these dudes were my pals, and they're not here to defend themselves.'

'We're just trying to figure out who killed them, Sean. If you're a friend, I'd think you'd want to know too.'

'Spare me the lecture, Kate,' says Sean. But then he flashes one of those gracious Dunleavy smiles. 'So you going to buy this CD, or you loitering?'

'I'm buying.'

I take my CD out to a dark bench a couple doors down and claw at the cellophane as I take in the elegant street and cool, fragrant air. East Hampton is one of the prettiest towns you'll ever see. It's the people who can be ugly sometimes.

Beside the bench is a mailbox. Looking closely, I see I'm not the only Sounds customer to make this their first stop. The blue surface is covered with hundreds of tiny little peeled-off CD titles, and now *Rumors* is part of the graffiti montage.

*Rumors* is even better than I remembered, and when I get to Mack's place, I sit in the car in the driveway until I've heard the whole thing.

When I finally go inside, Mack is snoring on the living-room couch, and my beeping cell doesn't faze him at all.

It's *Sean*, and he's *whispering*. 'I have heard something, Kate, and from people I trust – which is that in the last few weeks, Feif, Walco, and Rochie were all hitting the pipe. This summer, crack was all the rage out here, particularly on Beach Road. Supposedly, all three of them got into it. Once you hit the pipe, you can go from zero to a hundred in a weekend. That's what I know. So how'd you like the CD?'

'Great. Thanks. For *everything*, Sean.'

I hang up and look over at my sleeping host. Grateful that Mack still hasn't stirred, I pull the blanket up to his chin and head upstairs. *So they say the dead boys were hitting the pipe. I wonder if it's true.*

# Chapter Fifty-Nine

## Tom

The call from my nephew Sean seems to break the frustrating logjam on the case, because the very next afternoon, eighteen-year-old Jarvis Maloney climbs the creaking stairs to our office. He is the first visitor we've had in a week, and Wingo is beside himself, not to mention all over Jarvis.

'I've got something that might not mean anything,' he says. 'But Coach told me I should tell you about it right away.'

Every summer, the village of East Hampton shows its appreciation for the influx of free-spending visitors by siccing a teenage army of meter maids on them.

Dressed in brown pants and white shirts, they hump up and down Main Street chalking tires, reading dates on registration and inspection stickers, writing tickets, and basically printing money for the town. Jarvis, a jug-headed high school senior, who also happens to play noseguard for the East Hampton High School football team, was a member of last summer's infantry, and once we get Wingo off him, he shares what's on his mind.

'About nine o'clock on the Saturday night that Feifer, Walco, and Rochie were murdered, I ticketed a car at Georgica Beach. Actually, I wrote two tickets – one for not having a valid 2003 beach sticker and another for the missing emissions sticker. Only reason it stuck in my mind was the car – a maroon nine-eleven with seven hundred miles on the odometer.

'The next day, I'm shooting the breeze with my buddy who works the early shift. We had a little competition about who ticketed the sweetest car, and I throw out the Porsche. He says *he ticketed it too,* at the same spot, early the next morning. That means it was sitting there all night, right next to where the bodies were found. Like I said, it probably doesn't mean a thing, but Coach says I should tell you.'

Soon as Jarvis leaves, I drive over to Village police

headquarters. What little crime there is out here is divvied up two ways. The Hampton police patrol the roads from Southampton to Montauk, but the Village police are in charge of everything falling inside the village itself, and as you might expect, the two departments pretty much hate each other's guts.

Mickey Porter, the chief of the Village police, is a friend. Unlike the Hampton police, who tend to take themselves very seriously, Porter, a tall guy with a big red mustache, doesn't pretend he's a character on some cop show. Plus, he's got no issue with Kate and me representing Dante.

After 9/11, the Village Police Department, like others all over the country, received a powerful fifty-thousand-dollar computer from the Bureau of Homeland Security. In thirty seconds, Mickey has the registration of the ticketed Porsche on his screen – a New York plate, IZD235, registered to my beach buddy Mort Semel at his Manhattan address, 850 Park Avenue.

*Bingo.*

*Well, not quite.*

'Even though it's registered to Semel,' says Porter, 'I'm pretty sure the only one who drove it was his daughter Teresa.' He scrolls down on the screen and says, 'See, Teresa Semel, eighteen. One week in August she got three tickets, two of them for speeding.'

'What do you expect, you give a hundred-thousand-dollar car to an eighteen-year-old?'

'On Beach Road, a nine-eleven is a Honda Civic,' says Porter. 'An act of parental restraint. Besides, Tess is no ordinary teenager.'

'She's a fashion model, right? Dated some guy in Guns N' Roses?'

'Stone Temple Pilots, but close enough. Beautiful girl. Was on the cover of *Vogue* at fourteen and played the hottie in a couple teen flicks. Since then, she's been in and out of rehab.'

'It sucks being rich and beautiful.'

'I wouldn't know. I'm just beautiful.'

'Trust me then. So, Mickey, I gotta see this girl. For whatever reason, she was at the murder scene.'

# Chapter Sixty

## Tom

I reinforce with Mickey that I need to talk to Teresa soon. *Before* she does something bad to herself or someone decides to do something bad to her. Still, I don't expect him to report in before I'm halfway back to Montauk.

'Tom, you're in luck. Teresa Semel just got back in town after a stint at Betty Ford. Hurry, maybe you can catch her while she's still clean. What I hear, she's replaced her heroin addiction with exercise. Spends all day at the Wellness Center.'

'The proper word's *dependency*.'

'I mean it, Tom. The girl's got a thousand-dollar-a-day Pilates habit.'

Fifteen minutes later, I'm at the Wellness Center myself, watching Teresa's class through a green-tinted oval window.

Spaced evenly on the floor are five female acolytes. All exhibit near-perfect form as far as I can tell – but no one can match Teresa Semel's desperate concentration.

Seeing her effort, I regret mocking her. Instead of sitting at home and feeling sorry for herself, she's literally taking her demons to the mat and fighting them off one after another.

Informing the client that time is up is always a delicate moment in the service industry, and the instructor shuts down her hundred-dollar session with a cleansing breath and a round of congratulations.

The women collect themselves and their belongings and serenely slide out of the room.

Everyone except Teresa, who lingers on her mat as if terrified at the prospect of being left on her own with time on her hands. She actually seems relieved when I introduce myself.

'I'm sure you've heard about the murders on the beach last summer,' I say. 'I represent the young man charged with the killings.'

'Dante Halleyville,' Teresa says. 'He didn't do it.'

'How do you know that?'

'Just do,' she says as if the answer floated into her beautiful head like the message in a plastic eight ball.

'I'm here because your car was parked at the beach nearby that night.'

'I almost died that night too,' says Teresa. 'Or maybe that was the night I got saved. I'd been so good, but that night I went out and copped. I met my connection in the parking lot. Shot up on a blanket on the beach. Slept there the whole night.'

'See anything? Hear anything?'

'No. That's the point, isn't it? The next morning I told Daddy, and twelve hours later, I was back in rehab.'

'Who'd you buy from?'

'As if there's a choice,' says Teresa.

I don't want to seem too eager, even though I am. 'What do you mean?'

'There's only one person you can cop from on Beach Road. It's been that way as long as I can remember.'

'Does he have a name?'

'A nickname, anyway. Loco. As in *crazy*.'

# Chapter Sixty-One

## Kate

Five minutes after we lift off from the East Hampton heliport, the guy seated next to me glances down at the traffic crawling west on 27 and flashes a high-watt smile. 'I love catching the heli back to town,' he says. 'An hour after going for a run on the beach I'm back in my apartment on Fifth Avenue sipping a martini. It makes the whole weekend.'

'And it's even lovelier when it's bumper to bumper for the poor slobs down below, right?'

'Caught me peeking,' he says with a chuckle. He's in his late forties, tan and trim and dressed in the traveling uniform of the überclass – overly creased jeans, dress shirt, a cashmere blazer. On his wrist is a plat-inum Patek Philippe; on his sockless feet, Italian loafers.

'Fifteen seconds and you've seen right through me. It takes most people at least an hour.' He extends a hand and says, 'Roberto Nuñez, a pleasure.'

'Katie. Lovely to meet you too, Roberto.'

In fact, I already knew his name and that he owns a South American investment boutique and is Mort Semel's neighbor in the Hamptons. After Tom's run-in with Semel's bodyguards taught us how hard it would be to talk to Beach Road types, I called Ed Yourkewicz, the brother of a law school roommate. A helicopter pilot, Ed has recently gone from transporting emergency supplies between Baghdad and Fallujah to shuttling billionaires between Manhattan and the Hamptons.

Last week, I e-mailed him a list of Beach Road residents and asked if on a less-than-full flight he could put me beside one of them for the forty-minute, thirty-five-hundred-dollar trip. He called this after-noon and told me to be at the southern tip of the airport at 6:55 p.m. 'And don't come a minute earlier unless you want to blow your cover.'

For the next ten minutes Roberto struggles in vain to capture and convey the miracle that is Roberto. There are the half-dozen homes, the Lamborghini and Maybach, the ceaseless stress of presiding over a 'modest little empire,' and the desire, growing stronger by the day, to chuck it all for a 'simpler, more real' life.

It's a well-oiled monologue, and when he's done he smiles shyly as if relieved it's finally over and says, 'Your turn, Katie. What do you do?'

'God, I dread that question. It's so embarrassing. Try to enjoy my life, I guess. Try to help others enjoy it a little more too. I run a couple foundations – one helps inner-city kids land prep-school scholarships. The other involves a summer camp for the same kind of at-risk kids.'

'A do-gooder. How impressive.'

'At least by day.'

'And when the sun goes down? By the way, I love what you're wearing.'

After getting Ed's call, I had just enough time to race to the Bridgehampton mall and buy a black Lacoste shirt dress three sizes too small.

'The usual vices, I'm afraid. Can't they invent some new ones?'

'Altruistic and naughty. You sound perfect.'

'Speaking of perfection, you know where an over-bred philanthropist can score some ecstasy?'

Roberto purses his lips a second, and I think I've lost him. *But, hey, he wants to be my friend, right?*

'I imagine from the same person who supplies anything you might need along those lines, the outlandishly expensive Loco. I'm surprised you aren't a client already. From what I hear he has a tidy monopoly of the high-end drug trade and is quite committed to maintaining it. Thus, the nickname. On the plus side, he is utterly discreet and reliable and has paid off the local constabulary so there's no need to fret about it.'

'Sounds like quite the impressive dude. You ever meet him?'

'No, and I intend to keep it that way. But give me your number and I'll have something for you next weekend.'

Below us, the Long Island Expressway disappears into the Midtown Tunnel, and a second later all of Lower Manhattan springs up behind it.

'Why don't you give me yours?' I say. 'I'll call Saturday afternoon.'

The width of Manhattan is traversed in a New York minute, and the helicopter drops onto a tiny strip of cement between the West Side Highway and the Hudson.

'I look forward to it,' says Roberto, handing me his card. It says, *Roberto Nuñez – human being.* Good God almighty.

'In the meantime, is there any chance I can persuade you to join me for a martini? My butler makes a very good one,' he continues.

'Not tonight.'

'Don't like martinis?'

'I adore them.'

'Then what?'

'I'm a decadent do-gooder, Roberto, but I'm not easy.'

He laughs. I'm such a funny girl – when I want to be.

# Chapter Sixty-Two

## Tom

About the same time that Kate catches her whirly-bird to Manhattan, I squeeze into a tiny seat in a fourth-grade Amagansett homeroom smelling of chalk and sour milk.

Like her, I have a role to play, and to be honest, I'm not sure it's much of a stretch.

As I take in the scene, more adults enter the classroom and wedge themselves into small chairs, and despite how rich most of them are, there's none of the usual posturing. The leader closes the door and signals me, and I walk to the front of the room and clear my throat.

'My name is John Smith,' I say, 'and I'm an alcoholic.'

The crowd murmurs with self-recognition and support as I lay out a familiar story.

'My father gave me my first glass of beer when I was eleven,' I say, which happens to be true. 'The next night, I went out with my pals and got gloriously drunk.' Also true, but from here on, I'm winging it.

'It felt so perfect I spent the next twenty years trying to re-create that feeling. Never happened, but as you know, it didn't keep me from trying.'

There are more murmurs and empathetic nods, and maybe I actually belong here – I'm hardly a model of sobriety. But I try not to think about that and keep my performance marching along.

'Six years ago, my wife walked out and I ended up in the hospital. That's when I went to my first meeting, and thank God, I've been sober since. But lately my life and work have gotten much more stressful.' I assume some of the people in the room know me or the work I'm referring to, but Amagansett is a different world from Montauk, and I don't recognize anyone personally.

'In the last couple of weeks, I've felt myself inching closer to the precipice, so I came here tonight,' I say,

which is also true in a way. 'It's hard for me to admit
– but I need a little help.'

When the meeting comes to a close, I have a set of
new friends, and a handful of them linger in the parking
lot. They don't want to leave here and be alone just
yet. So they lean on their Beamers and Benzes, and
trade war stories. And guys being guys, it gets competi-
tive.

When one describes being escorted by two cops
from the delivery room the morning his son was born,
another tops him – or bottoms him – by passing out
at his old man's funeral. I'm starting to feel kind of
sane, actually.

'What was your poison?' asks a gray-bearded
Hollywood producer who owns one of the homes on
Beach Road. He catches me off guard.

'Specifically?' I ask, buying time as I frantically
canvass my brain.

'Yeah, *specifically*,' he says, snorting, provoking a
round of laughs.

'White Russians,' I spit out. 'I know it sounds funny,
but it wasn't. I'd go through two bottles of vodka a
night. How about you?'

'I was shooting three thousand dollars a week, and
one of my problems was *I could afford it.*'

'You cop from Loco?' I ask, and as soon as I do, I know I've crossed some kind of line.

Suddenly the lot goes quiet, and the producer fixes me with a stare. Scrambling, I say, 'I ask because that's the crazy fuck I used to cop from.'

'Oh, yeah?' says the producer, leaning toward me from the hood of his black Range Rover. 'Then get your stories straight. You an alkie or a junkie?'

'Junkie,' I say, looking down at the cement. 'I don't know you guys, so I made that shit up about the drinking.'

'Come over here,' he says.

If he looks at my arms for tracks, I'm busted, but I have no choice.

I step closer to his car, and for what seems like a full minute, he stares into my eyes. Then he pushes off his car, grabs my shoulders, and digs his gray beard into my neck.

'Kid,' he says, 'if I can beat it, you can too. And don't go anywhere near that fucker Loco. What I hear, he was the one who offed those kids on the beach last summer.'

# Chapter Sixty-Three

## Tom

At the office the next morning, Kate and I lay out our notes like fishermen dumping their catch on a Montauk wharf. In a month of digging, some straightforward and a lot of it shamelessly underhanded, we have managed to complicate the case against Dante in half a dozen ways. According to Kate, every new wrinkle should make it easier to cast doubt about what really happened that night.

'For the prosecution, this is going to be about the fear of young black males,' she says. 'Well, now we can flip the stereotype. If what we have is accurate, then in the weeks before their death, the white kids were messing up. And they weren't doing coke or ecstasy or pills, but *crack,* the blackest and most ghetto drug of all. Then there's this mysterious dealer, Loco.'

'What do we do now?' I ask.

'Try to confirm what we have. Look for more. Look for *Loco.* But in the meantime, we're also going to *share* what we have.'

'Share?'

Kate pulls a white shoe box out of her gym bag and places it on the table. With the same sense of ceremony as a samurai unsheathing a sword, she takes out an old-fashioned Rolodex. 'In here are the numbers of every top reporter and editor in New York,' she says. 'It's the most valuable thing I took with me from Walmark, Reid and Blundell.'

For the rest of the day, Kate works the phone, pitching Dante's story to one top editor after another, from the murders and his arrest to his background and the upcoming trial.

'This case has everything,' she tells *Vanity Fair*'s Betsy Hall, then editor Graydon Carter. 'Celebrities, gangsters, billionaires. There's race, class, and an eighteen-year-old future NBA star who's facing the death penalty. And it's all happening *in the Hamptons.*'

In fact, it *is* a huge story, and before the afternoon

is over, we're negotiating with half a dozen major magazines clamoring for special access to both Dante and us.

'The cat is out of the bag,' says Kate when the last call has been made and her Rolodex is tucked away. 'Now, God help us.'

# PART THREE

---

# DOWN AND OUT IN THE HAMPTONS

# Chapter Sixty-Four

## Raiborne

When I need to work something out, I don't go to a shrink like Tony Soprano. I wander into Fort Greene Park and sit down across from an impenetrable Methuselah of a chess hustler named Ezekiel Whitaker. That way I can think instead of talk, and sit outside instead of being cooped up in a shade-drawn room.

It suits me better, particularly on an Indian summer Sunday afternoon with the last brown leaves rustling sweetly in this Brooklyn park.

'Your move,' says Zeke impatiently as soon as my butt hits the stone bench. For Zeke, time is money, just like a shrink. He has a face that looks as if it were carved out of hard wood and the long, graceful fingers of a former migrant fruit picker, and me and him, we've been going at it alfresco for years. So I know I got my work cut out for me.

But when I snatch his rook right out from under his haughty nose ten minutes into the game, I have to crow about it.

'You sure you're feeling all right, brother man?' I ask. 'Cold? Flu? Alzheimer's?'

I should have kept my mouth shut, because of course, that's when my mind leaves the board and circles back to work and the name chalked on the dirty blackboard of the precinct house. Instead of concentrating on how I might solidify my position on this chessboard and teach this old goat some much-needed humility, I think about *Manny Rodriguez.* Rodriguez's unsolved murder has been eating at me for weeks. Every time I walk into the precinct, his name admonishes me from the board.

I never for a second bought that story the papers put out about a feud between Glock, Inc., and Cold Ground, Inc. Thing is, rappers are too hotheaded to make good assassins, and this killer didn't leave a trace. Not only that, but Rodriguez, who picked up lunch and ran out in the rain to put quarters in the meter, was too low on the food chain to make any sense as a target.

Rodriguez was a gofer, or as we chess masters like to say, a pawn, and as I ponder that, Zeke reaches across the board with the precision of a pickpocket and plucks my queen off her square.

'Take her, Zeke. I never liked the bitch anyway.'

Now a win is out of the question, a draw unlikely, and the board looks like a big rusty steel trap waiting to clamp shut on my ass. If I had any dignity I'd resign, but I came here to think about Rodriguez anyway, so I'll let Zeke earn his money while I try to earn mine. As I do that, Zeke sweeps through my ranks like Sherman went through Georgia. He picks off my last bishop and knight, and when my castle drops among all my other casualties, he says, 'I guess you don't have to worry yourself about my deteriorating mind no more, Connie.'

'That's a relief.'

The end is swift but not particularly merciful, and like always, it reminds me of some Latin rumba – check, check, check, checkmate.

I pry open my wallet and hand Zeke a twenty and still feel better than I have in weeks – because I finally got an idea about who might have killed Manny Rodriguez.

# Chapter Sixty-Five

## Raiborne

I hate calling 'Corpseman' Krauss on a weekend, but not so much that I don't do it. He agrees to drive in from Queens, and when I pull into the fenced-in lot behind the morgue, he's already there, sitting cross-legged on the hood of his Volvo. Except for the burning ciggie hanging from his mouth, Krauss looks like a little Buddha.

'Thanks for coming in,' I tell him

'Keep your thanks, Connie. The in-laws have been over since Friday night. I was praying you'd call.'

We trade the sun-filled parking lot for beige linoleum corridors, which are even quieter than usual. We head to

Krauss's office, where he reads me the ballistics report on Rodriguez.

When he's finished, I say, 'Now do me a favor, Kraussie, and call up Michael Walker's report.'

Walker is the teenager we found murdered in his bed three blocks away, about a month before. I'm thinking that maybe the two are connected. I know there are superficial similarities between them, but I'm after something more specific and telling than the fact that both were essentially executed at close range at night in the same neighborhood.

But as Kraussie reads off the two lists of bullet calibers, bore size, etc., nothing matches up. Even the style and make of the silencers are different.

'The logic is different too,' says Krauss. 'I mean, it's not that hard to understand why Walker, prime suspect in a triple homicide, might get his ticket punched. But a messenger who had never been in any kind of trouble? That's some domestic thing, or who knows what.'

'Or maybe they're so different they have to be connected.'

We each grab a report and read through them again in the deep, depressing silence you'd be hard-pressed to find anywhere other than a morgue on a Sunday afternoon.

Neither of us can find a damn thing worth discussing, and finally it's the ocean-floor silence, so deep it's deafening, that drives us back out into the sunshine and our so-called lives.

# Chapter Sixty-Six

## Tom

On Monday evening, Kate and I go to Barnes Pharmacy to check out the new January mags. Like any media-savvy couple, we grab copies of *Vanity Fair*, *New York*, and *The New Yorker* and hustle them back to my car.

At Sam's we get a table in the back room and spread out our glossy booty, the luxe, shiny covers sparkling like showroom sheet metal. Kate grabs *New York* and slides *Vanity Fair* to me. On page 188, Dante looks up at me through prison bars. It's a devastating photograph, capturing Dante's youth and fear, and also the false bravado that attempts to conceal it.

In all of the magazines, his face has been lit to make his skin appear darker. Race and the Hamptons are a winning newsstand combination, and they're milking it for all it's worth.

On top of everything else, it's kind of nice to be here with Kate. Almost like a date. For the next hour, we read our mags and slide them back and forth, stopping only for a bite of artichoke-and-bacon pie or a gulp of cold beer. The *New Yorker* piece, accompanied by a stark black-and-white photograph that makes Dante look like a dancer or a pop star, is quite short, but Dominick Dunne's, in *Vanity Fair*, and Pete Hamill's, in *New York*, are ten thousand words easy, and both are fair, even sympathetic, to Dante. Every major theme Kate planted on the phone, from racism to an overzealous prosecution team to the rumored drug use of the victims, has bloomed into stylish, glossy print. To see it all spread out on the table, particularly since so much of it is little more than rumor, is a bit overwhelming.

Even more so is the amount of space given to the 'courageous pair of young Montauk-born-and-raised attorneys' who have made the brave decision to represent the accused killer of their old friends.

I had no idea Kate and I were going to be such a big part of the story.

Dunne describes us as 'a red-haired Jackie and a burlier JFK' and writes that 'even Dunleavy's Boston terrier, Wingo, is ridiculously photogenic.' According to Hamill, 'their chemistry is not imagined. In their teens and early twenties, the two were a couple for more than five years.' Both *Vanity Fair* and *New York* run the same snapshot of us taken after a St John's victory in 1992.

'It's a good thing everyone in town hates us already,' I say. 'Because this is beyond embarrassing.'

We pay up and untie Wingo from the bench out front. Wingo seems to be adjusting quite well to sudden fame but is bothered by a foul burning smell in the air. As we walk to the lot behind the restaurant, a pumper truck from the East Hampton Fire Department races by.

The smell gets stronger, and when we round the corner of the white stone building, we see that what the local firemen have just put out was *my car*. Or what's left of it.

All the windows have been smashed, the roof ripped off, and on the passenger seat is a soggy, charred stack of glossy magazines.

# Chapter Sixty-Seven

## Tom

Whether in downtown Baghdad or downtown East Hampton, a burned out shell of a car is a riveting sight, even if the smoking remains are yours. For a while, Kate, Wingo, and I stare at it, transfixed. When it gets chilly, we retreat to Sam's again, where we have a pair of Maker's Marks on the rocks, and I give Clarence a call.

'A bunch of rednecks out here,' says Clarence when we return to the scene and he sees what's left of my once-trendy convertible.

Then we all pile into his big yellow wagon, and he gives us a lift to Mack's place in Montauk.

'Tom loved that old car,' says Kate, 'but he hardly seems fazed at all. I've got to admit, I'm almost impressed.'

'Hey, it's just a car. *A thing,*' I say, pandering for a little more of Kate's respect.

The truth is, even I'm surprised by how little I care about the car. More than that, seeing it smoking in the lot made me feel kind of righteous.

Once we're on the road, Clarence is somber, and his face and posture still bear the terrible effect of Dante's arrest and the upcoming trial.

'Clarence, it may not look like it,' I say, 'but things are turning our way.'

'How you figure that?'

'Those magazines burning on my front seat are filled with stories that are going to help us win this case. Even my car is going to make a great picture and will open people's eyes to what's happening out here.'

But nothing I say registers on Clarence's face. It's as if whatever optimism he has been able to muster and cling to over the course of a hard lifetime has been exposed as bunk.

On this Monday night in January, the Ditch Plains neighborhood is quiet and dark. Not Mack's place, though! It's lit up like a Christmas tree, and when we pull up, Mack stands in the doorway in his raggy plaid bathrobe. Two police cars are just leaving.

'Oh, no!' cries Kate, and jumps out of the car. But Mack, who's got his walking stick in one hand and a Scotch in the other, won't hear of it.

'It's nothing at all, darling girl,' he says. 'Just a pebble through the window. At my age, I'm grateful for whatever attention I can get.'

Despite Mack's protests, I insist on leaving Wingo with the two of them. A sweet-natured pooch who hasn't met a face he didn't want to lick isn't much of a watchdog, but at least he'll make some noise.

Then I get back into the car with Clarence. 'You hear that shite Mack was saying to Kate on the porch?' I put on my best Irish brogue; '"No big deal, darlin' girl. Just a pebble." It's the same shameless tripe I was saying about my car ten minutes ago. That son of a bitch is after my girl, Clarence, and we've got the same strategy.'

'You better keep an eye on the old goat,' says Clarence, almost smiling. 'I hear he's been stockpiling Viagra. Buys it over the Internet in bulk.'

'That's not even close to being funny.'

# Chapter Sixty-Eight

## Tom

I don't like leaving Kate at Mack's, but she insisted she'll be okay, that *they'll* be okay. The thing is, I wish that Kate would stay with me tonight. I've felt that way for a while, and it's driving me a little crazy, but especially after what's just happened.

It feels strange to enter my house and not hear Wingo scamper on down the long, dark hallway, to not hear the jangle of his collar against his metal bowl or his tongue slurping up water.

Along with the dogless quiet is a faint metallic odor I can't quite identify. Unpleasant, like dried sweat. Maybe it's me. It's been a long day.

I follow the hallway into the kitchen, grab a beer, and stare through the sliding glass doors at my backyard. I still don't care that much about my car, but the intensity of the town's hatred toward Kate and me is getting me down, particularly because I realize it's never going away.

I've got two choices: the couch and some cathode rays, or the vertical pleasures of a hot shower. I opt for the shower, and as I walk back to my bedroom, that same metallic scent stops me in the hall.

This time it's even stronger, so I guess it can't be me.

Then I realize what it is. It's the smell of fear, and then a floorboard creaks, there's an urgent rustle of fabric and a rush of movement, and a large fist hits me square in the face.

Blood pours out of my nose, and the force of the punch throws me into whoever is standing behind me. He hits me too. My elbow digs a grunt out of the bastard, and the next half-minute is the red-hot chaos of flying fists, elbows, and knees. This is my house, my hall, and even outnumbered, I like my chances, right up till the moment I start to go down.

I'm on the ground taking kicks to the head and ribs

when a voice cuts through the pain. *'That's enough, I said! That's enough.'*

But I can't say for sure if I'm hearing it, or thinking it, or praying it.

# Chapter Sixty-Nine

## Kate

With the ruckus Wingo is raising in my car, it's hardly necessary, but I grab the wrought-iron ring and deliver three hard raps to Tom's front door.

It's eight in the morning, so Tom has to be in the house, but neither Wingo's barking nor my steady banging gets a response. I'm guessing he's in the shower.

A towing service has dropped off what's left of Tom's car in the driveway, and Wingo and I walk around the burned-out shell to the backyard.

The sliding doors off the patio are locked, but I can see inside the house well enough. A living-room chair has been knocked over. So has a bookcase.

I dial Tom's cell and get his voice mail, and I'm starting to panic, when on the far side of the house, Wingo barks as if he's treed a fox.

I race over and find him howling at a small shed off the kitchen.

The door has been left open. Inside are two tattered folding chairs and a musty beach umbrella. I call Tom's cell again, with no more luck than the first time.

I hadn't told Tom I was going to pick him up, so instead of breaking in, or calling the police just yet, I cling to the hope that he arranged a ride with Clarence. I shove Wingo back in the car and race toward our office in Montauk.

With everything going on in my head, and the steep early morning sun in my eyes, I very nearly hit a cyclist pedaling furiously along the shoulder of the road.

Only when Wingo yelps deliriously and tugs at my sleeve do I see in the rearview mirror that the man on the bike is Tom. I brake to a stop, then back up in a hurry.

My relief is enormous, but it only lasts as long as it takes me to see his face. One eye is completely shut, the other raw purple. There are welts and cuts on his neck and ear, and a jagged gash over one eyebrow.

'Two guys were waiting for me when I got home,' says Tom. 'I mean, *four* guys.'

'You call the police?'

'Didn't see the point. Like Mack said, it was more symbolic than anything.'

'It's not a good idea to get hit in the head like this every couple of months. Concussions can be dangerous, Tom.'

'Tom? Is that my name?'

'That's not funny.'

'No, it's pretty funny.'

'It is pretty funny actually.'

'I'm getting better with age, Kate, admit it.'

'You left yourself a lot of room for improvement.'

I stop at Barnes Pharmacy for disinfectants and sterile pads, tape and bandages. Back at the office, we clean the cuts. I do my best to remind myself that this is a slippery slope and that I didn't take this case to hook up with Tom Dunleavy one more time. But beneath it all, I guess I'm just a sap, because I'm also wondering how smart it is to hold a grudge against someone based on how they acted when they were twenty-two, and if there isn't a statute of limitations on bad behavior.

# Chapter Seventy

## Tom

At the office the next day, Kate writes up some interviews we did around the apartment where Dante was hiding out in New York City. Meanwhile, I pull the file on the .45 caliber semiautomatic pistol found behind the diner the night Dante turned himself in. In some ways, it's the prosecution's most persuasive piece of evidence.

*So how can we use it?*

The file includes five black-and-white eight-by-ten photographs of the weapon, and I lay them on the table. According to Suffolk County Forensics, there was one set of prints on the handle, and they're a perfect match for Michael Walker; ballistics tests prove the weapon was used to kill all four victims. But Dante swears he's never seen the gun before.

'It's not even close,'Dante told me in that first long, grueling session in Riverhead. 'Michael's gun was small, cheap, a Saturday-night special. This is a real gun. Twice the size and a different color. You were there, bro.'

It's true. I was standing right next to Walker as he held the gun to Feif's head, and if anyone could accurately describe the revolver, it should be me. But I never looked at it, made a point of not looking at it actually, and that's why I was able to get him to put the thing down. I pretended the gun didn't exist, that we were just two reasonable guys having a conversation on a Saturday morning.

But it's the *circumstances* by which the gun was found that are particularly suspect. 'If Dante kills Michael in Brooklyn when they say he does,' I say, half to Kate, half to myself, 'he had plenty of time to get rid of the murder weapon. He can dump it in Bed-Stuy somewhere, or toss it in the East River. Instead he hangs on to it so he can throw it away at the last minute behind a diner in Southampton?'

'What's the name on the police report?' asks Kate.

'I don't recognize it,' I say, trying to read the signature on the bottom. 'Looks like *Lincoln*. The first name begins with an *h*. Harry, maybe.'

# Chapter Seventy-One

## Tom

The desk sergeant tells me the officer's name is Lindgren, not Lincoln, first name Hugo, and he's working nights this week.

After locking up our office, Kate and I head to the barracklike station house and loiter by the back door, hoping to catch Lindgren as he arrives for his shift.

After being up for the last twenty hours, there's not much left in me. Actually, I'm burned to a crisp, but I'm still not sharing that info with my partner.

'After we're through here,' I say, stretching my legs and glancing at my Casio, 'I think old Wingo and I are going to take ourselves a little run. Help us fall asleep.'

'Tom, you're so full of shit it's frightening.'

'Nothing ambitious, an easy fifteen, sixteen miles in the sand with boots on.'

An old Jeep rolls in, and a former friend of mine named John Poulis hops out. Then Mike Caruso, another former friend, shows up on his Honda. At this point 'former' describes most of my friends, and both cops stare through us as if we're made of glass.

The next car into the lot is a shiny silver Datsun Z.

'Pretty sporty for thirty-four grand a year,' I say.

'How do you know how much he makes?' asks Kate.

'Let's just say that if the admissions director of St John's Law School hadn't been a hoops fan, I might be arriving for work myself right now.'

'Officer Lindgren?' I call out, and the stocky brown-haired man stops in his tracks. 'Could we talk to you a couple minutes?'

'That's all I got. I'm late already.'

I do the introductions, and then Kate takes over.

'That anonymous call that came in about the gun,' asks Kate, 'did it go directly to you or the main switch-board?'

'Directly to me,' says Lindgren.

'Is that normal? For an anonymous tip to be directed at a specific officer?'

'How should I know what's normal? What are you getting at?'

'I'm trying to prepare a case for my client, Officer Lindgren. It's pretty standard stuff. Why are you getting all defensive? What's the problem here? Am I missing something?'

Watching Kate effortlessly rattle Lindgren's cage will definitely go on our highlight film for today.

'What I mean is,' she continues, 'isn't it odd that a caller who knows who he's talking to would be so anxious to conceal his identity?'

Lindgren adjusts his tone from combative to condescending. 'Not at all. The caller is doing something frightening – getting involved in a murder case and potentially making dangerous enemies. That's why every police department in America has an anonymous hotline.'

'But the caller didn't use the anonymous hotline. He called you directly.'

'Maybe he'd seen me around. Maybe he felt more comfortable calling me. Who the hell knows? Anyway, kids, that's all I got time for. Some people have to work for a living.'

'So the caller was a man,' says Kate. 'You said *he*.'

'Did I?' says Lindgren, and practically walks through us into the back of the police station.

Five minutes later – when Kate drops me off at my place – a silver Mini Cooper is parked behind what's left of my XKE. As I hop out of Kate's car, the driver gets out of the Mini. *Now what?*

He's about twenty-five, Indian or maybe Pakistani, and, if it's the kind of detail that interests you, ridiculously attractive.

'I sincerely apologize for any inconvenience,' says the visitor, who introduces himself as Amin. 'I've been sent by my employer to deliver an invitation to each of you, and lucky day for me, I've found both of you at once.'

'How'd you know who we are?'

'Everyone knows you two, Mr Dunleavy.'

Amin presents us with two envelopes made out of the paper equivalent of, I don't know, maybe cashmere. Our names are scrawled across them in dark-green script.

'Can I ask the name of your employer?'

'Of course,' says Amin with a practiced deadpan. 'Steven Spielberg.'

# Chapter Seventy-Two

## Loco

If the BW is going to keep me waiting every time we get together to talk business, I've got to do the same to the folks working under me. How else will they know where they stand in the pecking order?

So even though I see Officer Lindgren on the bench behind the East Deck Motel, I circle the block and let the cop cool his heels. That's what the BW does to me, right?

This makes Lindgren crankier than usual, and when I finally sit beside him in the shade, he doesn't bother to look up from his *Guns & Ammo*.

'I pegged you more for *House and Garden* or *O.*'

'You're late.'

'Unavoidable,' I say. 'What's got your panties in a twist?'

'Halleyville's lawyers, for one thing. They cornered me last night at the station. That snotty Ivy League bitch was all over me.'

'About what?'

'Why the call about the gun came directly to me and not through the main switchboard.'

I laugh, but it's not that funny. 'She's just fishing in the dark.'

'I don't think so. They're onto something, and what I'd like to know is what are we going to do about it?'

'Not a thing. You expect me to kill somebody every time you get a heart palpitation? If you were the worrying type you should have stuck to the police manual and stayed away from drug-dealing slime like me. Give me your hand.'

'You a fag or something?' Lindgren says, and snorts out a laugh.

'Not that I'm aware of. Open your hand.'

You shouldn't be a drug dealer if you don't believe in the healing power of modern pharmacology, and when Hugo unclenches his fingers, I fill his palm with a dozen lovely white Vicodins.

'These little fellas will chill your ass out.'

'I think we got a real problem,' says Lindgren. 'And I thought you'd want to be the first to know. But I'll keep an open mind.'

And with that, Lindgren lays two Vicodin on his tongue, slips the rest into his shirt pocket, and marches off to fight crime in the Hamptons.

# Chapter Seventy-Three

## Tom

I guess this is what you would call a high point, and actually, it is. At the very least, it's a much-needed break for Kate and me.

Amin greets us as if we're old pals and leads us through a succession of huge, airy rooms adorned with Picassos and Pollocks even I can recognize. Then it's back outside to a flagstone terrace with endless views of Georgica Pond. I've thumbed through the mags with mansions shot like centerfolds, but maybe the real stuff never gets photographed, because this is way beyond that.

On the terrace a small cocktail party is in full swing,

and the moment we step into it, Steven Spielberg, looking far more accessible without his baseball cap, disentangles himself from a nearby conversation.

'Tom! Kate! So wonderful to finally meet you,' he says as if only the most unlikely of circumstances could have delayed it this long, and waves over waiters bearing champagne and oysters.

'We feel the same way, Steven.' Kate grins so that I'm not really sure about her point of view here.

'To new friends then,' he says, 'and, of course, to Dante Halleyville's successful defense.' His bright, merry eyes light up as we take our first sip of his champagne. When I say 'his,' I mean that literally, since it comes from his own Northern California vineyard.

Ten feet away, in front of a three-piece combo, a gorgeous black woman in a floor-length dress sings, 'Just in time, I found you just in time,' and the air is full of silvery murmurings. Yet it's obvious as the whiskers on Spielberg's chin that Kate and I are the center of attention.

Then Steven – we're on a first-name basis now – raises one hand as if he's just remembered his hostly obligations and says, 'Come! Let me introduce you.' We follow him from the periphery to the white-hot center, where the evening quickly slides from over the top to *Twilight Zone*.

'George and Julianne,' says Steven, 'I'd like you to meet Kate and Tom.' And now we have no choice but to shoot the breeze with George Clooney and Julianne Moore, both of whom are as electrically *on* as if they are sitting on the hot seat next to Letterman, Leno, or Jon Stewart. Just as we're getting slightly comfortable, it's time to meet Clive Owen and Kate Winslet, Julia Roberts, Matt Damon, and Ashley Judd. The only unrecognizable face we're introduced to belongs to Alan Shales, whose Oscars are for screenwriting.

There are fewer than a dozen guests on the terrace, but they're a sizable chunk of A-list Hollywood. They can't all just happen to be in the Hamptons this weekend, particularly at this time of year. When I can't resist asking about it, Steven says, 'I flew them in this afternoon.'

A half-hour later, we're shepherded to a second terrace where a table has been set, and for the next two hours Kate and I take turns answering questions about ourselves, our backgrounds, and the case. I guess we're entertainment, the flavor of the month that Spielberg, on a whim, has decided to share with a dozen pals.

But that doesn't make sense either. These actors and actresses are professional acquaintances of his, colleagues not buddies. And why are they all staring at Kate and me so intently and hanging on our every word as if there's going to be a test on us the next morning? I swear I'm not making this up, but as I'm saying something about the case, I notice that Clooney and Damon are holding their hands like I do and sinking into their chairs with the same slouch.

Is that something actors do unconsciously, or am I being *mocked*? Or both? And then it comes to me. The movie about this case is already moving toward production. Steven has signed on, but everything else is up for grabs. What George and Julianne, Julia and Kate and Clive are doing at this glam gathering is auditioning.

To play us.

# Chapter Seventy-Four

## Kate

All visitors to the Riverhead Correctional Facility are welcomed with a hospitable placard:

> GIVING MONEY, FOOD, OR ANY OTHER CONTRA-
> BAND TO AN INMATE IS A FELONY PUNISHABLE
> BY UP TO A YEAR IN JAIL. IF YOU ARE CAUGHT
> BRINGING CONTRABAND INTO THIS FACILITY YOU
> WILL STAY HERE.

Tom and I have walked past it umpteen times, but this morning, Tom nudges me and clears his throat.

'Whatever,' I say.

Five minutes later, after stashing our money and keys and passing through metal detectors and locked-off checkpoints, we are back in the tiny attorney's room that has become our second office.

But this isn't going to be a normal workday, and when Dante steps into the room, I point him to the chair in front of the Mac PowerBook on what's normally my side of the table. Then I close the door behind me.

'Dante,' I say softly, 'we know it's your birthday Sunday, so we're giving you a little party.'

As Dante flashes a smile of surprise and affection I won't forget if I live to be a hundred, Tom slips a pair of headphones over his head. He hits a key on the computer, and I turn off the lights.

'*Happy birthday, Dante!!!*' marches across the screen to a hip-hop beat, and Dante taps his feet with delight. It's pretty amateurish. As auteurs, Tom and I have a ways to go, but after we stumbled out of Spielberg's backyard a couple weeks ago, we figured Dante could use a break from reality too.

Following the birthday greeting, the brand-new, not-yet-released Jamie Foxx movie, which we procured with considerable help from our new best buddy, fills the computer screen, and Dante, eighteen or not, smiles like the kid he still is. As the opening credits roll, I open my briefcase and hand Dante an important legal document. That's not strictly true. What I hand him is a small tub of popcorn. I read the sign. I know it's a felony, but it just isn't a movie without popcorn.

Two hours later, when our feature presentation comes to a close, Tom hits the Return key one last time. Among the countless things Dante has been unfairly denied over seven months is the dunk contest at the NBA All-Star Game. No more. Last night we downloaded it into my laptop, and for the next fifteen minutes, I watch Dante and Tom shake their heads and whisper astute commentary like 'Nasty!' and 'Sick!' and 'Ridiculous!'

I can't remember the last time I had so much fun, and I realize that my whole world is inside this little room.

# Chapter Seventy-Five

## Dante

I didn't think it was possible. Not in this hellhole. Not walking down a long, nasty tunnel, wrists and ankles in chains, locked up for something I didn't do.

But I actually feel good. Instead of thinking about how messed up everything is, about my broken-hearted grandmoms back in her trailer, I'm thinking about what Kate and Tom did this morning. It makes me feel warm inside.

I guess you live in your head more than anyplace else. If your head is in a good place it doesn't matter quite as much if the rest of you isn't. For the first time since I got here, time doesn't feel like a stone I got to drag from one end of the day to the other. It feels like it can pass by on its own.

The tunnel taking me back to my cell runs some two hundred yards before reaching the stairwell up to my block, and because of how unusual the morning's been, it takes me half of that to notice that the guard, whose name is Louis, is kind of quiet today. What's up with that? Most of the time Louis is a chatterbox, always wanting to talk hoops and tell me about all his old-school favorites from the eighties and nineties, but this morning, when I actually feel like talking, he's not saying a word. I realize it must be tough, being a prison turnkey.

'I got to use the bathroom,' says Louis. 'I'm going to leave you for a minute.'

'Whatever. I'm in no hurry.'

Louis bolts the chain running from my ankle to a pipe along the wall, and when I see his expression as he steps into the bathroom, everything comes together in a rush. I know what's happening.

Then I hear heavy footsteps coming fast from the far end of the corridor.

I try to reach for the fire alarm five feet away on the wall, but the way Louis has me attached to the pipe I can't reach it. Then I try to rip the pipe off the wall, but I can't move it, hard as I yank.

A voice from inside a nearby cell cries, 'Run, young-blood! Run!' *But how can I run with my hands and feet in chains?* Too late for that. I can't even grab the fire extinguisher from the wall. The answer has got to be somewhere in my head. The answer has got to be *somewhere,* and it better come fast.

The pounding footsteps are louder now, and when I look down the corridor again, I see they've sent a brother to do the job. A *big* brother. He fills the corridor like a subway coming through a tunnel.

And now I can see his face – it's no one I've seen before – and something shiny is in his right hand.

I can only take three steps, but it's enough to reach the bathroom door, the one behind which Louis is hiding right now, waiting for this to be over so he can jump out and pull the alarm.

I don't bang on the door like a desperate man who is about to die. I tap on it real soft with my knuckles, like the one who has just done the killing, and I whisper in a strange voice – *'Louis, it's done.'*

Then I step to the other side of the door real quick. I also start to pray.

My killer is less than ten feet away, close enough for me to see that he's looking scared too. And I need for him to see that I'm every bit as big as him, and my fists out front let him know I'm not going down without a fight. That makes him pause for a second, but just a second.

Then he takes one more step, with his knife held out in front of him like a spear. He lunges at me with the shiv just as the bathroom door opens, and as I duck down, Louis steps out.

The killer is so startled it gives me time to spring up from my crouch, and holding my fists together, I hit him right under his chin. I catch him solid with all I got. It knocks him out cold and sends the home-made knife clattering to the ground at his feet.

Even with both hands and feet manacled I could reach the knife and kill the thug they sent to kill me, but despite what some people think, I haven't killed anyone yet and don't plan to start now.

# Chapter Seventy-Six

## Raiborne

The fact that there's nothing in the forensic reports linking the murders of Michael Walker and Manny Rodriguez helps me keep my mind off the two dead men for a while. Then I start to get nuts again. I call Vince Meehan. Vince, who runs the evidence room, gives me the number of the individual who picked up Rodriguez's silver crucifix, empty wallet, and packed iPod.

It belongs to a twenty-three-year-old waitress named Moreal Entonces, and a few hours later I'm at the counter of a trendy Cuban diner in Nolita listening to Moreal tell me her and Manny's life story.

This one's sadder than most. Not just because Moreal and Manny had a cute eighteen-month-old daughter, but because she really believed in the guy. And the guy actually may have been worth believing in.

'Manny had talent,'says Moreal, whose caramel skin is the same color as the flan she puts down beside my coffee.'But he couldn't catch a break.

'That's why he was at Cold Ground,'she continues. 'Manny was an artist, but he was working as a gofer for free. Not even that. He bought sandwiches and coffee with his *own* money sometimes, all on a chance that a big-shot producer would give him four minutes of his precious time.

'And what happens when a producer finally *does* agree to hear his song? Manny gets shot in the back of his head the night before, caught in the middle of some nonsense he had nothing to do with.'

'What was the song? The last one?' I ask her.

'"Arroz con Frijoles": "Rice and Beans". And that track was something. For real.'

'Is that what your name means, Moreal? *More real?*'

'That's good. I might even borrow it. But no. In Colombia, where I'm from, Moreal is like Mary or Martha.'

I nurse my café con leche and scan the pictures of Cuba on the wall – beautiful, ornate streets filled with big-finned American cars from the fifties. I let Moreal decide when her story is over, and it's another ten minutes before I ask the one question I came here to ask.

'Moreal, I know this may sound ridiculous, but had Manny been spending time in the Hamptons?'

# Chapter Seventy-Seven

## Raiborne

N ow I feel as if maybe I'm pushing the envelope too far, even for me.

The next morning, instead of driving to the precinct house in Brooklyn, I take the Grand Central Parkway to the Northern State and follow the signs for Eastern Long Island. Two hours later, I'm rolling through the shade of the biggest, oldest elms I've ever seen into downtown East Hampton.

Since it's my first time out here, I squeeze my Taurus between a starter Porsche and a bright-red Ferrari and have a look around.

It's Main Street USA. I'm two hours from Bed-Stuy,

but I feel as though I'm on some kind of National Geographic expedition, like Darwin in the Galapagos. I'd buy a notebook and jot down my impressions, except there's no place to buy one.

The only things for sale seem to be cashmere, coffee, and real estate. Shit, there are more real estate agencies here than bodegas in Brooklyn. In two blocks I count seven, all in white clapboard houses with cute, preppy names: Devlin McNiff and Brown Harris Stevens.

But there's nothing cute about the prices under the black-and-white photographs, eight-by-tens, like the ones Krauss takes in the morgue. Twenty million for something grand, four million for something nice, and $950,000 for a shack on an eighth of an acre. Is that possible?

When I tire of walking, I check out a 'bodega' called the Golden Pear Café, where oddly enough everyone behind the counter *is* Hispanic, like in a real bodega. I pick one of the six kinds of coffee and a four-dollar slice of angel cake, and take them to a bench out front.

The coffee's way better than I'm used to, the pastry beats the hell out of a Hostess Twinkie, and there's something about the light out here. But there's so much money dripping off of everything I can't tell where the town ends and the money begins. Instead of wasting any more time figuring it out, I cut myself a break and spend the next ten minutes warming up in the sun and smiling at the girls walking by, suddenly remembering life's too short to do much else.

# Chapter Seventy-Eight

## Raiborne

The East Hampton Police Station isn't quite as idyllic as the sidewalk outside the Golden Pear. To my disappointment, it looks like a police station – squat and grim and overcrowded and sweaty. Three beefy, Irish-looking detectives are stuffed into one room. The chief detective, the youngest of the four, has got his own little office, the size of a small closet.

'Make yourself at home,' says Detective Van Buren. He dumps the contents of one chair onto the floor. 'We've been about to move to new headquarters for two years now.'

I wasn't expecting much civility, and I don't get any.

Just typical cop shit. Who wants a visit from a big-city cop who's going to look at him like he's some kind of pretend cop? But Van Buren seems like any other young, ambitious detective, and there's nothing pretend about the bodies piled up in his backyard.

'I'm here,' I say, 'because about a month after Michael Walker got shot, I investigated the murder of Manny Rodriguez, a rapper who was also shot. Yesterday I found out he also had been hanging out at Wilson's place. That makes five dead bodies connected to Wilson's court.'

'A starting squad,' cracks Van Buren, and I have to smile because I think it might help me get somewhere with him.

'An all-dead team,' I say.

'You probably should be talking to Suffolk County Homicide. After the first couple weeks, they've been running the show out of Southold. But since you came all the way out, I'll be glad to drive you over to Wilson's place.'

I leave my black banged-up Taurus in the lot and get into Van Buren's black banged-up Crown Vic, and we drive to the good part of town. Soon we're in a neighborhood that makes Main Street look like the projects.

'Through those hedges,' says Van Buren, 'is Seinfeld's place. Stole it from Billy Joel for fifty-six mil. Just up that road to the left is where Martha Stewart used to live.'

'This is all very interesting, but where the black folks live at?'

'We're almost at Wilson's place right now,' says Van Buren, turning onto a particularly wide country lane called Beach Road.

Van Buren unlocks the police chain on the rustic wooden gate, and we take the long driveway toward the ocean. The basketball court is also locked, but Van Buren has the key for that too.

'Were you the one who talked to Wilson originally?' I ask.

'No.'

'One of the other detectives?'

'No one talked to Wilson.'

'Three local kids are piled up on his lawn. Another deceased individual shows up afterward, and no one feels it's necessary to talk to Wilson?'

'Ahh, no. That's not the way we do things out here.'

I look around the estate, but other than the spectacular ocean views, there's not much to see, or make notes on.

Eventually, Van Buren and I are standing on the veranda of the massive house, which, he says, is for sale.

'I'm a little pressed for cash right now,' I tell him.

Van Buren laughs, and actually, we're getting along fairly well under the circumstances.

'There's one name that's come up,' he finally says. 'Local dealer who calls himself Loco.'

I nod, scratch my head some. 'You talk to this Loco?'

'Nobody's been able to find him.'

'Mind if I try?'

# Chapter Seventy-Nine

## Raiborne

W hat's wrong with *this* messed-up picture? Three days ago I was kicking back in the Hamptons. Now I'm in NYC, on my hands and knees on the floor of a beat-up surveillance van eyeing the entrance of a take-out joint in Williamsburg, Brooklyn.

Soon as I got back to the city, we leaned on a network of junkie snitches to see what could be learned about a drug dealer named Loco.

The name didn't mean a thing to several lowlife informants, but we found out that on the last Monday of the month, a major dealer drives in from the Hamptons and replenishes his supply from the

Colombians operating out of a take-out place in South Williamsburg.

It's called Susie's Wok, and for the last two hours, I've had a pretty good view of its side door as a parade of tattooed hipsters in skinny black pants and old-school sneakers comes and goes. Remember when arty white kids like Hemingway went to Paris to write a novel? Well, now junkies from Paris come to Williamsburg to start a rock band.

The DA's office has been doing surveillance on the Colombians for months, running wiretaps, working up to a major sting. So we can't touch Susie's. All they've cleared us to do is watch out for Loco. If there *is* a Loco.

If we spot him, we can follow him back to the Long Island Expressway and pull him over for a traffic violation or something.

That's if Loco shows at all.

I haven't seen a single nonjunkie come up to Susie's door in hours, and my knees are killing me. When I see a lumbering Hasidic Jew sneak in for an illicit fix of outlawed swine – I guess we all got something we're afraid of getting busted for – I call it a wasted day and follow him in.

After staring at Susie's Wok all day, I'm starving for some fried pork myself.

# Chapter Eighty

## Loco

On Mondays, when I make my pickup in Brooklyn, I leave the Tahoe at home and get a loaner.

'Weekenders' not due back till Friday are generous enough to leave a fleet of cars for me to choose from at the railroad station. Today, I select a ten-year-old off-white Accord so generic it's practically invisible. After thirty seconds to pick the lock and hot-wire the ignition, I'm off to Crooklyn.

The cops have their network of snitches, and I got my network too. Actually, it's the same network. I just pay a little better and play a lot rougher.

They tell me Susie's Wok has been getting a lot of

attention lately. Something about too many cops spoiling the Wok, so when I get there, I circle the block a couple times to scope things out.

The first time I drive around, everything looks copacetic to me.

The second time, I notice this white van parked a little too conveniently across the street. The third time by, I can see that the van's blacked-out windows are a lot newer than the banged-up body.

If I had the IQ of a piss clam, or an iota of criminal discipline, I'd turn around and keep going, but I spent three hours getting into makeup and wardrobe, and in my gray-flecked beard and side locks, I barely recognize myself. So I park a quarter of a mile away, put on my wide-brimmed black hat and baggy black jacket, and head back to Susie's Wok on foot.

I know my disguise is kosher because on the four blocks back to Susie's two guys dressed just like me wish me 'Good Yontif,' and a cute little Hasidic mommy gives me the eye.

Inside Susie's, my man Diego is pacing impatiently outside his little back office.

'Shalom,' I say.

'Shalom to you too, my friend,' says Diego, nervously looking at his watch.

'When I say shalom, I truly mean *shalom*. It's not something I'm just saying.'

That gets Diego's attention, and he stares at me warily before a faint smile sneaks across his lips.

'Loco?' he whispers.

'This would be true, my friend.'

Behind closed doors, our transaction is handled with brisk efficiency. Twenty grand for Diego and his people, a hundred thousand dollars' worth of goodies for me. The drugs are packed up in little cardboard boxes and metal takeout tins, with a handful of menus scattered on top.

It's a good thing too, because as I step out the door I almost bump into a large black guy whose carriage and black leather jacket shout NYPD.

'Good chow?' he asks.

'The best,' I say, and keep on stepping. I don't even let myself look in the rearview mirror until my takeout and I are out of Williamsburg and back on the expressway.

'Lo-co!' I shout at the windshield of the stolen Accord. *'You da man!'*

# Chapter Eighty-One

## Tom

It's Friday, just days before the start of Dante Halleyville's trial, and the first buses filled with protesters arrive in East Hampton just after dawn. The people out here are about to understand the scale of this case, its national implications.

The buses aren't Jitneys, the tall, sleek air-conditioned models that drop queerly dressed Manhattanites at quaint bus stops up and down 27. They're a rolling armada of rusted-out school buses, long-retired Greyhounds, and dented-up vans. There are hundreds of them, and they come from as far north as New Hampshire, as far south as the Florida Panhandle.

Like a medieval army laying siege, they stop just outside of East Hampton. Early arrivals fill the field across from the Getty Station, and when it can't hold any more, the protesters fan out onto the tiny south-of-the-highway streets that lead to the water.

At noon, a mile-long column, twelve people across, marches into town, and East Hampton's two perpendicular blocks, where you could go a week without seeing an African American, are overwhelmed with thirty thousand mostly black protesters – men, women, and children.

They are waving home-made signs that read FREE DANTE HALLEYVILLE! and STOP LYNCHING OUR TEENAGERS! They're everything East Hamptonites are not – loud, unselfconscious, and angry.

The crowd marches past the hastily boarded-up windows of Cashmere Hampton, Coach, and Ralph Lauren. They turn left on Newtown Lane and file past Calypso and Scoop and Om Yoga until they reach the middle school.

There, frantic police and just-arrived National Guardsmen steer them across the street into the park.

A low stage has been set up in the infield of the softball diamond in the far corner of the twenty-acre field, and Reverend Marvin Shields, in a dazzling white three-piece suit, grabs the mike.

'No justice!' bellows Shields.

'No peace!' reply thousands of voices in unison.

'I can't hear you,' shouts the reverend, one cupped hand to his ear.

'No peace!'

'What was that?'

'No peace!'

'We've got a very special guest here this morning,' Shields says. 'A man who has proved himself to be a friend time and again, a man who now works out of an office in my neighborhood in Harlem, the former president of the United States, Mr Bill Clinton!'

President Clinton saunters onto the stage to a deafening roar, and for a full minute he waves and smiles, as comfortable in front of this enormous, mostly black crowd as if he was in his backyard. Then he puts one arm around Reverend Shields and grabs the microphone with the other.

'Welcome to the Hamptons, y'all,' he says. 'Nice out here, ain't it?'

# Chapter Eighty-Two

## Tom

Bill Clinton is still talking when Kate takes my hand and pulls me away. East Hampton can burn for all she cares right now. We have a capital murder defense to prepare, and we're still way behind.

The road back to Montauk is so empty it's as if the eastern tip of Long Island has been evacuated. The ride with Kate brings back memories of our days together when we were younger. We used to hold hands all the time, and I want to reach out for Kate's hand now. But of course, I don't, which makes it even worse. When we get to Montauk, there's not a single car in the parking lot outside our office.

Aided by the unlikely quiet, Kate prepares a folder on every witness we might call to the stand, and I attempt a first draft of our opening statement. At one point, she gives me a little hug. I don't make a big deal out of it, even though I don't want it to end.

The historic sense of the day is inspiring, and the sentences and paragraphs begin to flow for me. But Kate is underwhelmed. When she slides back the draft, half of it is crossed out, the rest festooned with notes. 'It's going to be great, Tom,' she offers as encouragement.

Grateful for standards higher than my own, I churn out draft after draft, and until a car pulls into the empty lot outside, I have no sense of the time. I suddenly notice that the afternoon is long gone, and our one window has turned black. In fact, it's close to 10:00 p.m.

Car doors open and slam shut, and then heavy footsteps clomp up the steep stairs. It sounds as if there are three or four people coming, and based on the creaking, they're all large and probably males.

I reach for the baseball bat I've been keeping beside the desk and look over at Kate. She returns my nervous smile and shrugs, but the glint in her eyes says, 'Bring it on.'

# Chapter Eighty-Three

## Tom

The head that pokes through the door doesn't belong to a drunken local lout. It's Calvin Coles, the minister at Riverhead Baptist. Calvin has been over a couple times in the last few months and apologizes for the lateness of the visit as two other formidable black men, both wearing dark suits, follow him into the room. The heads of all three nearly scrape the low ceiling.

Coles smiles awkwardly and introduces his companions, as if it's necessary. One is Reverend Marvin Shields, the other Ronnie Montgomery, the dapper black attorney who became a celeb after winning the acquittal of former Major League Baseball star Lorenzo Lewis for the murder of his wife.

'I've got some very exciting news,' says Reverend Shields, stepping forward and clasping my hands in both of his. 'After some serious cajoling and arm twisting, Mr Montgomery has generously volunteered to take over Dante Halleyville's defense.'

'The trial starts in a few days,' says Kate, her voice calm, her eyes red hot.

Ronnie Montgomery responds with a condescending smile. 'Obviously, I'm going to ask for an extension,' he says. 'And I have no reason to believe I won't get it.'

'Have you spoken to Dante?' I finally say.

'I wanted to come here first,' says Montgomery, 'as a professional courtesy.'

Montgomery takes in our modest office, conveying with a shrug what it suggests about our inappropriateness for this huge case and about our chances in the upcoming trial.

'I know you mean well, and I'm sure you've worked terribly hard. And both of you are welcome to stay on to help with the transition. But you're way out of your depth here, and Dante Halleyville deserves more.'

When Montgomery serves up another condescending smile, I'm kind of sorry I put down that baseball bat.

# Chapter Eighty-Four

## Tom

The next morning as Kate's Jetta pulls into the lot behind the Riverhead Correctional Facility, Ronnie Montgomery's black Mercedes limo pulls out. This is the end of the line for us. It's like arriving for your last day of work to find your replacement already sitting in your chair, cleaning out your desk.

But Kate and I adhere to our routine. We park in our spot, exchange pleasant greetings with Mike and Billy at the front desk, and stash our watches and keys in locker number 1924.

For presumably the last time, Sheila, the only female guard at the maximum-security jail, who has somehow worked here twenty-three years, escorts us through the sliding steel gates into the purgatory of the attorney rooms. Dante, having just met with Montgomery, is already there.

He looks at his feet and says, 'We've got to talk.'

Kate and I sink into our seats at the small metal table. I bite my tongue and wait for the ax. I haven't felt this awful in a long time.

'I just had a visit from Ronnie Montgomery,' says Dante. 'The brother that got off the baseball player Lorenzo Lewis.'

'He stopped by our office last night,' says Kate.

'Then I guess you already know he's offered to take the case. He said he hasn't lost a trial in fifteen years.'

'Might be true,' says Kate.

'He said that this is the most important decision I'll ever make. That I need to take some time with it.'

'What'd you say?'

'Time's up, Mr Montgomery. I already lost ten months in here. I know what I got to do.'

'Which is what?' I ask.

'You got to understand this ain't personal. Lorenzo Lewis's clothes were smeared with his wife's blood. When the cops arrived he locked himself in his bathroom, took thirty sleeping pills, and called his mama. Montgomery still got him off.'

'That was a unique case,' says Kate, 'but we won't take it personally.'

'You sure?'

'For Christ's sake, Dante, what did you tell him?'

'I told him, no thanks, bro'. I like the lawyers I got.

'You think I'm crazy?' says Dante, pointing a long finger at Kate and smiling as though she's just been Punk'd. 'I hire Montgomery, and everyone, including the jury, is going to assume I'm as guilty as Lorenzo Lewis. Plus, I figure Montgomery used up his luck for three lifetimes on that other case. Kate, you crying on me, girl?'

# Chapter Eighty-Five

## Kate

Dante's grandmom, Marie, bows her head and reaches for my hand, which I gratefully give her.

'Thank you, Lord, for the abundance we are about to receive,' she says. 'Thank you for the strength to endure this terrible, terrible ordeal and most of all for delivering such dedicated attorneys as Tom and Kate. Bless this meal, oh Lord, and please find it in your heart to keep an eye out for my grandson Dante. My *innocent* grandson. Amen.'

Saturday evening, two days before the trial, and every friend Tom and I have left sits around Macklin's dining-room table. With only Mack and Marie; Tom's brother, Jeff, and nephew, Sean; Clarence and his wife, Vernell, there's plenty of leg and elbow room.

'To this time next year,' says Mack, raising a glass and trying as always to lighten the mood. 'When Dante sits next to us, stuffs his face, and tells barely believable tales of Shaq and Kobe, Amare and LeBron.'

The guest list for the meal is short, but the table groans under a rarely seen combination of Caribbean and Irish standards. After almost a year in near isolation, the company means more than the food to me. But the food is wonderful too. We're in the process of eating way too much of it when the ringing of Tom's cell pierces the room. 'I better answer it,' he says.

He pulls it from his pocket and raises one hand in apology as the blood drains from his face.

'We've got to turn on Fox News,' he tells everybody.

Half of us are already in the living room with our desserts, and the rest shuffle over and twist a chair to face Mack's antique Zenith. Sean finds channel 16 just as the anchor turns it over to a field reporter.

'I'm live in Queens,' says a perky blonde, 'directly across from St John's Law School, alma mater of Tom Dunleavy, cocounsel in the capital murder trial of Dante Halleyville. According to documents just obtained by Fox, Dunleavy, a star basketball player at St John's, was accepted into the law school despite grades a full point below the admission minimum.'

'Quite a scoop,' says Macklin, snorting.

'Despite graduating in the bottom fifth of his class,' continues the reporter, 'Dunleavy was hired by the Brooklyn Public Defender's Office, where he received mediocre evaluations.

'The most troubling allegation, however, is that in 1997, Dunleavy had someone take the Law Boards for him.

'According to copies of the test obtained by Fox and examined by independent handwriting experts, Dunleavy's LSATs, on which he scored surprisingly well for a student with his grades, were taken by someone who is *right-handed*. Dunleavy, a two-time All-American, is *left-handed*.

'If this is true, Dante Halleyville, who faces capital punishment and whose trial begins in forty-eight hours, has put his life in the hands of someone who is not even a lawyer.'

# Chapter Eighty-Six

## Tom

At 9:00 p.m. the following night, the somber-faced clerk for Suffolk County Supreme Court judge Richard Rothstein waves me, Kate, and District Attorney Dominic Ioli into his well-appointed chambers, where we take our seats at a long mahogany table.

Ioli, a loquacious career pol with a full head of gray hair, makes a couple stabs at idle chatter, but when he sees we're in no mood, he abandons the effort and thumbs through his *Times*. I know this much about Dominic Ioli – he's a whole lot smarter than he looks, and he rarely loses.

When Judge Rothstein strides in, wearing khakis and a button-down white shirt, his penetrating black eyes and long sharp nose tell me I'm exactly the kind of dumb Irish jock he's got no time or use for.

Bypassing pleasantries, he turns to Ioli and asks, 'What's your office's position on this, Dominic?'

'We haven't had time to fully assess the charges,' he says, 'but I don't think it matters. Whatever decision this court makes should be beyond reproach. If defense stays on, we leave the door wide open for appeal. Assigning new counsel will require a delay, but it's better to spend that time now than to have to come back and do this all over again.'

'Sounds reasonable,' says Rothstein, and turns his eyes on me. 'Dunleavy?'

I'm prepared to argue forcefully, but I have no intention of getting down on my knees for anyone. 'Your Honor, the grades and evaluations are what they are,' I say in an offhanded tone. 'But I'm sure in your career you've come across at least a couple of excellent attorneys who weren't brilliant law students. For all I know, the district attorney is one of them.'

Encouraged by the hint of a smile in Rothstein's eyes, I barge ahead.

'So the only charge that matters is that I had someone

take the Law Boards for me, and that's absolutely false. Here's a copy of X-rays of my left wrist, taken the night before I took the boards, and here's a record of my visit to Saint Vincent's emergency room on April 5, 1997.'

'I was playing a pickup game at the Cage in the Village that night and took a hard fall. I could have gotten a medical extension, but I'd spent months preparing and, frankly, at that point, wasn't sure I wanted to be a lawyer. I decided to take them right-handed and let the scores decide for me.'

'You telling me you passed the bar writing with your wrong hand, Dunleavy?'

'I don't have a wrong hand. I'm ambidextrous.'

'The multiple choice maybe, but the essay?'

'It's the truth,' I say, looking straight into his eyes. 'Take it or leave it.'

'We'll see,' says Rothstein, and slides a legal pad across the table. Then he reaches behind him and blindly grabs a book off the shelf.

'You're in luck, Dunleavy – Joyce's *Ulysses*. I'll dictate the first line, you jot it down right-handed as fast as you can. Ready?'

'It's been seven years since I've had to do this.'

'What do you care? You don't have a wrong hand. Ready?'

'Yup.'

'"Stately, plump Buck Mulligan,"' reads Rothstein with pleasure, '"came from the stairhead, bearing a bowl of lather on which a mirror and a razor lay crossed."'

I scribble furiously and slide the pad back.

'Now I know why you went to your right so well, Dunleavy,' says Rothstein, the smile in his eyes moving down to his thin lips. 'Your handwriting's better than mine. By the way, I made a couple phone calls this afternoon, and it turns out this rumor came out of the offices of Ronnie Montgomery. I'll see you in court tomorrow morning.'

'But, Your Honor,' says Ioli.

'I'll see you too, Dominic.'

# Chapter Eighty-Seven

## Kate

Trained by the test in Rothstein's chambers, Tom slowly drives my car through Riverhead toward the Sunrise Highway. Neither of us says a word.

The full moon lights up the road, and some of that light spills onto the front seat where Tom's right hand lays on the armrest between us.

To be honest, I've always loved Tom's strong hands, with their thick, raised veins running from his battered knuckles to his wrists. In two decades of basketball, every finger has been dislocated so many times that not one of them is straight. They've become a kind of relief map of his life revealing everything he's been through.

Without really thinking about it, I lay my hand on his.

Tom's hand jumps, and he looks at me, stunned. Then, just as quickly, he turns away. *Why'd I do it?* I'm not really sure. It could have been for the balls and charm he showed winning over Rothstein and pulling victory out of his hat one more time, or maybe it's everything the two of us have been through in the last year. Or, I've just wanted to do it for months.

But I don't regret it – and to let Tom know it was no accident but an intentional piece of insanity, I wrap my fingers around his.

For the next half-hour, the car is filled with a very different kind of quiet. 'I'll pick you up at seven thirty,' is the only thing Tom says the whole way, but by the time he pulls up in front of Mack's house, I feel as if we've been talking for hours.

'Get a good night's sleep,' I say, and hop out of the car. 'You did good, Tom. I'm proud of you.'

And that makes Tom smile in a way that I haven't seen since we were both kids.

# PART FOUR

# COLD PLAY

# Chapter Eighty-Eight

## Kate

At 8:15 a.m., the sprawling parking lot in front of the Arthur M. Cromarty Court Complex is overrun with media. TV news trucks occupy the half-dozen rows closest to the courthouse; thick black cable stretches over the cement in every possible direction.

Network and cable reporters, comfortably rumpled from the waist down and impeccably dressed and groomed above it, their faces caked with makeup, stand inside circles of white-hot light and file their first remotes.

Tom and I weave our way through the chaos and park. Then we walk briskly toward the entrance of the complex, hurrying to get safely inside before getting grabbed by the journalistic mob.

Our timing is good, because at that moment every TV camera in the lot is aimed at an elegant black man standing dramatically on the courthouse steps. As we hustle past, I see that it's none other than T. Smitty Wilson. I guess he's finally come to pay his respects.

Inside, three hundred or more spectators pack forty rows, and they are split straight down the middle of the courtroom. Dante's supporters, who have arrived from as far away as California, fill the left half of the room. On the right are those who have traveled a much shorter distance to support the families of the victims. I've known most of them my entire life.

Surrounding the divided crowd are at least fifty cops, and in this instance, it doesn't seem unwarranted. Officers from the Sheriff's Department stand shoulder to shoulder along the front and back walls, behind the jury box, and on both sides of the judge's podium.

Except for the journalists in the front two rows, there are few exceptions to the racial seating pattern. One is Macklin, the octogenarian exception to most rules. He sits defiantly between Marie and Clarence, and woe to the man who tries to move him. Hanging just as tough one row back are Jeff and Sean.

Tom, riffling through a stack of file cards, barely looks up when the twelve jurors and two alternates solemnly take their positions.

But neither of us can ignore the loud gasp when Dante, escorted by a pair of county sheriffs, enters the courtroom. He wears an inexpensive blue blazer and dress pants, both a size too small – he's grown an inch in prison. He stares at the ground until he is seated between us.

'You guys good?' Dante asks in the quietest voice I can imagine coming out of his large body.

'Not just good,' I tell him. 'We're the best. And we're ready.'

Dante's slight smile, when it comes, is priceless.

Twenty minutes behind schedule, the sharp nasal voice of the bailiff finally rings through the courtroom. 'Hear yea! Hear yea! All persons having business before the Suffolk County Supreme Court and Honorable Judge Richard Rothstein will now rise!'

# Chapter Eighty-Nine

## Tom

Suffolk County DA Dominic Ioli pushes his chair back from the prosecution table and then carefully folds his reading glasses into a leather case. Only after they're safely tucked away in the jacket pocket of his new gray suit coat does he stand and face the two rows of jurors.

'Ladies and gentlemen, over the next several weeks you're going to hear about the cold-blooded murder of four young men last summer. Before this trial is over, the state will have proven beyond any reasonable doubt that the defendant seated on my left, Dante Halleyville, carefully and deliberately planned and carried out all four heinous crimes.

'We will prove that in the first three murders, Mr Halleyville acted with Michael Walker, and that eleven days later, he turned the same weapon on his best friend and accomplice.'

Ioli has logged his share of court time, and you can hear it in his measured delivery. As he refers to 'a gun and a hat and a body of evidence that places the defendant at both crime scenes,' I glance back at the divided sea of faces staring from opposite sides of the courtroom. I scan the expressions of Jeff, Sean, Clarence, and Mack, and linger on Marie.

'*Murder* is too gentle a word,' bellows Ioli, bringing me back to his speech. 'The more accurate word, the *only* word that captures the horror of these crimes, is *execution.*'

As Ioli winds down, I look around for one last piece of incentive, this time in the row of journalists and brand-name lawyers the networks have flown in as talking heads.

Sitting beside Alan Dershowitz, in a rumpled suit, and Gerry Spence, in a fringed leather jacket, is Ronnie Montgomery. For a second, we lock eyes.

The moment makes me think of Cecil Felderson, a fellow benchwarmer in my short time playing with the

Timberwolves. According to Cecil, who hoarded his resentments like gold, 'The worst thing of all, the thing that sticks in your craw more than anything, is having to listen to some guy say, "I told you so."'

With one haughty look at us and our tiny office, Montgomery wrote me off as an amateur and a loser, hopelessly out of my depth. Now I can either prove him right and hear about it, one way or another, for the rest of my life, or I can prove him wrong and shut him, and everybody else, the fuck up.

I rise from my seat.

# Chapter Ninety

## Kate

I don't know who's more nervous right now, Tom or me, but somehow I think it might be me. This is it, a bigger, more important trial than either of us has any right to be involved in probably ever in our careers, but certainly right now.

'Ladies and gentlemen,' says Tom, turning to face the jury, 'I have only one request of each one of you this morning, and it's harder than it sounds. I ask you *to listen*.

'For as long as it takes for justice to be delivered to the nineteen-year-old sitting behind me, I need you to listen with a sharp, open, and critical mind.'

Tom looked green on the drive over, and he hasn't said a dozen words all morning, but suddenly his game face is screwed on tight. 'Because if you do, if you just listen, the prosecution's case will collapse like a house of cards.

'The district attorney of Suffolk County has just told you that this is an open-and-shut case and that he has a mountain of evidence against Dante Halleyville. Ladies and gentlemen, *nothing could be further from the truth.* Not only did Dante Halleyville have no motive to commit these murders, he had enormous incentive *not* to commit them.

'For the past half a dozen years, Dante Halleyville has concentrated all his considerable energy, talent, and determination on becoming the top schoolboy basketball player in the country. Lofty as that goal was, he accomplished it. Dante Halleyville succeeded so well that pro scouts guaranteed him that whenever he chose to enter the NBA draft he would be among the very top selections, maybe even number one. Growing up under extremely difficult circumstances and surrounded by family members who made one disastrous choice after another, Dante never took his eye off his goal. Not once, until these false charges, has Dante been in any kind of trouble, either

at Bridgehampton High School or in his neighborhood, with the law.

'So why now, when he is so close to achieving his
dream, would he commit such self-destructive crimes?
The answer – *he wouldn't*. It's as simple as that. He
wouldn't do it.

'Ladies and gentlemen, your selection as jurors was
random, but the next few weeks could be the most
important in your lives. The future of a fellow human
being is in your hands. Not just the life of an innocent nineteen-year-old, but of a truly remarkable young
man. And both Dante and you will have to live with
your decision for the rest of your lives.

'*Someone* did kill those young men on Beach Road.
And in that Brooklyn apartment. Murdered them in
cold blood. Whoever committed these horrible crimes
will eventually be apprehended and brought to justice,
but that person was not and *could not* have been Dante
Halleyville.

'So I ask you to listen carefully and dispassionately
and critically to everything presented to you in this
courtroom. Don't let anyone but yourself decide how
strong or weak the prosecution's case is. I have faith
that you can and will do that. Thanks.'

When Tom turns away from the jury, three hundred

bodies readjust themselves in their seats. In addition to the rustling, you can almost feel the surprise, and it runs from Judge Rothstein in his pulpit to the last beer-bellied cop leaning against the far wall. This inexperienced lawyer, with mediocre credentials and crap grades, can handle himself in a courtroom.

# Chapter Ninety-One

## Kate

**T**om sits, and Melvin Howard, Ioli's assistant DA, stands. Howard is a tall, thin man in his late thirties with a trimmed salt-and-pepper beard and antique wire-rimmed spectacles. He's also African American, and none of these things is coincidental.

For the same transparently cynical reasons that my old firm chose me to help Randall Kane fend off sexual harassment charges brought by his female employees, the prosecution has selected a black man, with the mild-mannered appearance of a college professor, to prosecute Dante Halleyville. The selection is an attempt to tell the jury that this case is not about race, but about crime, a vicious murder that should outrage blacks as much as whites.

And just because this strategy is obvious and self-serving doesn't mean it won't work.

'In addition to *listening,*' Melvin Howard begins, as he tapes a twelve-by-fourteen-inch color photograph to a large easel set up directly in front of the jury, 'I'm afraid you're going to have to *look* too.'

He slowly attaches three more photographs to the easel – and when he steps out of the way, the jurors push back in their chairs, trying to get as far away from the lurid images as possible.

'These are crime-scene photographs of each of the four victims, and it's your sworn duty *not* to look away.'

Caught in the white light of the flash, the skin of the victims is a ghostly white; the lips blue-gray; the raw, burned edges where the bullets entered the foreheads orange; the ample blood that poured down into eyes and cheeks, over chins and down the necks of shirts a deep maroon, a red so deep it looks almost black.

'This man here, with the bullethole between his eyes, is Eric Feifer. He was twenty-three years of age, and before the defendant executed him on August thirtieth, he was a professional-level surfer.

'This young man is Robert Walco, also twenty-three. While other kids were going to college and business school, he put in ten-hour days with a shovel. The result of his sweat and labor was a successful landscaping business he owned with his dad, Richard Walco.

'And this is Patrick Roche, twenty-five, a painter who paid the bills by moonlighting as a bartender, and whose good nature earned him the affection of just about everyone who knew him.

'Finally, this is Michael Walker, and no matter what else you might say about him, he was seventeen years old, a high school senior.

'*Don't look away.* The victims couldn't. The killer and his accomplice wouldn't let them. In fact, the killer took sadistic pleasure in making sure that each of these four victims saw exactly what was happening to them as they were shot at such close range that the barrel of the gun singed the skin of their foreheads.

'And the killer got exactly what he wanted, because you can still read the shock and the fear and the pain in their eyes.

'In ten years, I've prosecuted eleven murder cases, but I've never seen crime-scene photographs like these. I've never seen head-on executions like these. And I've never seen eyes like these either. Ladies and gentlemen, don't assume this is run-of-the-mill horror. This is very different. This is what evil looks like up close.'

Then Melvin Howard turns away from the jury and stares directly at Dante.

# Chapter Ninety-Two

## Tom

On this stifling early June morning, with the temperature on its way to the mid-nineties, the state initiates its pursuit of justice by calling drug dealer Artis LaFontaine's former girlfriend, Mammy Richardson, to the stand. Mammy was at the basketball court when Feif and Dante came to blows. She saw it all.

A large, pretty woman in her early thirties, Mammy cut a striking figure at Wilson's estate last summer, and as strong rays slant in through the courtroom's only window, she steps into the booth in a cream-colored pantsuit that she fills to bursting.

'Directing your attention to last August thirtieth, Ms

Richardson, do you recall where you were that afternoon?'

'Watching a basketball game at Smitty Wilson's estate,' says Richardson, clearly enjoying her cameo, a trill of excitement in her voice.

'Could you tell us who was playing in this game?'

'Young fellas from Bridgehampton taking on an older squad from Montauk.'

'Was it a friendly game?'

'I wouldn't say that. Way both squads were going at it, you'd think it was game seven of the NBA finals.'

'Ms Richardson, do you have any idea why a weekend pickup game would be so intense?'

'Objection!' snaps Kate. 'The witness isn't a mind-reader.'

'Sustained.'

'Ms Richardson, were the players on the Bridge-hampton squad all African American?'

'Yeah,' says Richardson.

'And the Montauk team?'

'White.'

'Which team won the game, Ms Richardson?'

'The white fellas.'

'And then what happened, Ms Richardson?'

'That's when the trouble happened. Some of the

Montauk guys started showboating. One of the Bridgehampton fellas didn't appreciate it. He shoved somebody. They shoved back. Before anyone could calm things down, one of the victims and the defendant were throwing down.'

'Throwing down?' asks Howard, feigning ignorance.

Richardson flashes him a look. 'You know, scrapping.'

'How far away were you sitting from the court, Ms Richardson?'

'Closer than I am to the jury right now.'

'About how big was Eric Feifer?'

'Six feet, and skinny. One hundred seventy pounds, tops.'

'You've got a pretty good eye, Ms Richardson. According to the coroner's report, Eric Feifer was five eleven and weighed one hundred sixty-three pounds. And the defendant?'

'Anyone can see, he's got some size on him.'

'Six foot nine inches and two hundred fifty-five pounds to be exact. How did Eric Feifer do in the fight?'

'That skinny white boy could fight. He put a whooping on Dante.'

'What happened next?'

'Michael Walker, one of Dante's teammates, ran to

his car and came back with a gun. Which he put upside Eric Feifer's head.'

'How far away did he hold the gun from Eric Feifer's head?'

'He pressed it right up against it. Just like those pictures showed.'

'Objection,' shouts Kate like a fan screaming at the refs about a bad call. 'Your Honor, the witness has clearly been coached and has no right or authority to equate what she saw to the pictures taken of the crime scene. This is grounds for a mistrial.'

'The jury will disregard Ms Richardson's last remark, and the stenographer will expunge it from the record.'

Howard moves on. 'Then what happened, Ms Richardson?'

'Walker put the gun down.'

'Did Michael Walker say anything?'

'Objection, Your Honor,' says Kate, increasingly exasperated. 'This is nothing but hearsay.'

'Overruled,' says Rothstein.

'What did Michael Walker say, Ms Richardson?'

'This shit ain't over, white boy. Not by a long shot.'

'No further questions, Your Honor,' says Howard, and Kate is already up out of her chair.

# Chapter Ninety-Three

## Tom

I lean in close to Dante, figuring he needs some re-assurance. 'This isn't going to be as much fun as Mammy thought,' I say.

'Ms Richardson, what do you do for a living?' Kate begins.

'I'm unemployed at the moment.'

'How about last summer? What were you doing then?'

'I was unemployed then too.'

'So you've been unemployed for a bit more than a moment, Ms Richardson. How long exactly?'

'Three and a half years.'

'You seem bright and personable, not handicapped in any way. Is there a reason you haven't been able to find a job?'

'Objection, Your Honor.'

'Sustained.'

'Did you come to Mr Wilson's estate alone that afternoon?'

'I came with Artis LaFontaine.'

'What was your relationship with Mr LaFontaine?'

'Girlfriend.'

'Were you aware at the time that Mr LaFontaine had spent a dozen years in jail for two separate drug convictions?'

'I knew he'd been incarcerated, but I didn't know for what.'

'Really? Did you know that according to police your former boyfriend was and remains a major drug dealer?'

'I never asked him what he did for a living.'

'You weren't curious how a man with no apparent job could drive a four-hundred-thousand-dollar Ferrari?'

'Not really,' says Richardson, the trill in her voice long gone.

'Are you in a relationship right now, Ms Richardson?'

'Not really.'

'You aren't involved with Roscoe Hughes?'

'We date some.'

'Are you aware that he has also served time for a drug conviction?'

'I don't ask about the specifics.'

'But I do, Ms Richardson, so could you tell me, do you date drug dealers exclusively or just most of the time?'

'Objection,' shouts Howard.

'Sustained,' says Rothstein.

Mammy Richardson has been skillfully discredited as a witness, but she can defend herself a little too.

'Why?' she asks, squaring her shoulders at Kate and putting her hands on her ample hips. 'You want me to fix you up?'

# Chapter Ninety-Four

## Tom

Next up, Detective Van Buren. He takes the stand and, among other things, says that a call had come to the station establishing that someone matching Dante's description tossed a .45 caliber Beretta in a Dumpster behind the Princess Diner. After Barney's testimony, Rothstein offers an hour recess for lunch, but the stone plaza outside is so hot and shadeless that despite the anemic air-conditioning in the courtroom, the crowd is relieved to get back to their seats.

Once they're settled, Melvin Howard pops right up from his table and approaches the bench with a large plastic bag in each hand.

'The state,' says Howard, 'submits to this court as evidence the forty-five-caliber Beretta recovered behind the Princess Diner in Southampton early on the morning of September twelfth. Henceforth referred to as Exhibit A. And a red Miami Heat basketball cap recovered at eight thirty-eight MacDonough Street in Brooklyn four days later, from here on referred to as Exhibit B.'

Howard then calls a second member of East Hampton's finest, Officer Hugo Lindgren.

'Officer Lindgren, were you on duty the morning the defendant turned himself in?'

'I wasn't assigned to work that day, but I got a call to come in. I arrived at the police station just after Van Buren and Geddes.'

'Were you privy to anything that the defendant told the detectives that morning?'

'Yes, the discussion about the gun. I retrieved it from the Princess Diner.'

'Tell us about it, please.'

'At about five thirty in the morning, five thirty-three to be exact, an anonymous call came into the station and was routed to my desk. The caller reported that a few hours before, he'd seen a man discard a weapon in the Dumpster behind the Princess Diner.'

'Did the caller describe the man?'

'Yes. He said the man was extremely tall and African American.'

'What did you do then?'

'I drove to the diner with Officer Richard Hume. We found the weapon in the garbage.'

'Is this the weapon that you found that morning?'

'Yes, it is.'

When Howard informs Rothstein he has no further questions, Kate stands to face off with our old buddy Lindgren one more time.

'According to the defendant and receipts, what time was Dante Halleyville at the diner that morning?' she asks.

'Between two thirty and two thirty-seven a.m.'

'And what time did you get to the police station?'

'A little after five.'

'So the caller, whoever it was, sat on the information for three hours.'

Lindgren shrugs and frowns. 'People are resistant to get involved.'

'Or maybe the caller just waited for *you* to get to the station, Officer Lindgren. Now why in the world would that be? Hmmmm?'

And Dante whispers to me, 'She's *damn* good.'

Yes, she is.

# Chapter Ninety-Five

## Kate

The next morning, Melvin Howard, who is patiently and pretty skillfully building the state's case block by block, puts Dr Ewald Olson on the stand.

Olson, an itinerant forensic scientist, travels the land from courtroom to courtroom offering his expert testimony to whoever is willing to pick up the tab. He arrives with his own video setup and an assistant, who controls it from a laptop. Only after Olson has spent nearly an hour going through every last published article and citation does the assistant DA turn his attention to the images on the monitor.

'Dr Olson, could you tell us about the photograph on the left?'

'It's an enlargement of the recovered forty-five-caliber shell that entered and exited the skull of Patrick Roche,' says Olson, a tall, stooped man with a crawling monotone.

When he says all there is to say about the bullet, he talks about the Beretta and all the tests performed on the inside of its barrel.

'The photographs on the right,' he says, wielding a red laser light, 'are impressions taken from the Beretta's barrel. As you can see, the markings on the barrel conform exactly to the markings on the bullet.'

'And what does that indicate?'

'That the bullet that killed Patrick Roche was fired from the recovered weapon.'

'Based on twenty-eight years as a forensic scientist, Dr Olson, how certain are you that this is the murder weapon?'

'Entirely certain,' says Olson. 'Barrel and bullets are a perfect match.'

At noon, Rothstein mercifully recesses for lunch, but an hour later, Olson picks up where he left off, this time going through a similarly exhaustive drill with the *fingerprints* found on the handgun.

'As you can see,' says Olson, 'the set of prints taken from the handle is an exact match to the prints later taken from Walker's right hand.'

'Dr Olson, is there any doubt that the prints on the recovered weapon belong to Michael Walker?'

'Every print is unique, Mr Howard. These could belong to *no one other than Michael Walker*.'

Then Howard holds up Exhibit B, the red Miami Heat cap found in the Brooklyn apartment where Walker was killed. He asks Olson to compare two more sets of fingerprints displayed on the monitor.

'The prints on the left, Dr Olson,' asks Howard, 'whom do they belong to?'

'They were taken from the defendant, Dante Halleyville.'

'And the prints on the right?'

'An identical set of prints lifted from the bill of the basketball cap found in the apartment where Michael Walker was murdered.'

'Again, Dr Olson, could you give us the odds of these prints belonging to anyone but the defendant?'

'These prints could belong to no one other than Dante Halleyville.'

When the prosecution is through, Olson has been plodding along like the tortoise that always catches the hare – for six hours.

So long that there are groans of disappointment when Tom pushes out of his chair.

My own feelings are even stronger. We hadn't planned on cross-examining Olson. Tom is recklessly winging it.

'Dr Olson, no one questions that the handgun recovered behind the Princess Diner was the murder weapon. The question is, who fired it? Is there *any physical evidence,* anything at all, linking the defendant to that weapon?'

'No. The only fingerprints left on that gun belong to Michael Walker.'

'As for the prints found on the gun, the ones belonging to Michael Walker, what kind of quality are we talking about?'

'*Very* good. The highest quality.'

'On a scale of one to ten?'

'Nine, maybe even a ten,' Olson says with pride in his voice. Maybe he's been watching a little too much *CSI.*

'Doesn't it strike you as suspicious, Dr Olson, that on a gun that has been *carefully cleaned* there would be one complete set of prints and every fingertip would be perfect?'

Now, for the first time in hours, the crowd is actually awake and paying attention.

'Not in this case,' says Olson.

'But you have, in the past, on at least two occasions that I'm aware of, concluded that prints found on murder weapons were, in your words, "too good to be credible." That was your conclusion in the *State of Rhode Island versus John Paul Newport*. Is that not true?'

'Yes, but that's not my conclusion about these prints.'

'Defense has no further questions.'

The crowd is still buzzing when Judge Rothstein calls an adjournment for the day, but whether or not Tom's high-risk two-minute gambit succeeded in undermining six hours of testimony, we don't have long to dwell on it.

After Dante gives us both hugs and the sheriffs escort him back to his holding cell, the paralegal for the prosecution delivers a note.

They've just added Dante's eighteen-year-old cousin, Nikki Robinson, to their list of witnesses.

Nikki was among the group of spectators who saw Walker pull the gun on Feifer, but the prosecution has already established what happened after the game. *So the decision to put Nikki on the stand now doesn't make sense.*

And when the prosecution makes a move I don't understand, I get scared.

# Chapter Ninety-Six

## Tom

When Nikki Robinson, eyes averted, walks past our table and takes the witness stand, the morning crowd ripples with anticipation. To be honest, Kate and I are a lot more on edge than the spectators. Nikki works as a maid for a local house-cleaning service. She hung around at Smitty Wilson's – *but what else? Why is she being called now?*

'Ms Robinson,' says Melvin Howard, 'could you please tell us your relationship with the defendant?'

'Dante is my cousin,' says Robinson, her girlish voice faint.

'And were you at the game at Smitty Wilson's that afternoon?'

'I got there just before the fight broke out, and Michael Walker got that gun.'

'Did you leave right after?'

'No, sir.'

'What were you doing?'

'Talking to Eric Feifer,' says Robinson, her voice getting even fainter.

'Was that the first time you met?'

'I had seen him around.'

'Did you talk long that afternoon?'

'No. I clean for Maidstone Interiors and had to go do a house. Eric asked if he could go with me. Swim in the pool while I worked. I said okay.'

'So the two of you left together?'

'He put his bicycle in my trunk.'

'What happened when you got to the house you had to clean?'

'Eric hung by the pool. I got to work. House wasn't much of a mess. The owner's gay, and gay people are usually neat.'

'Then what happened?'

'I was vacuuming the master bedroom,' says Nikki, her voice reduced to a whisper, 'and something made me turn around. Eric was standing right behind me. Naked. At first, I was so shocked, I didn't notice the knife in his hand.'

The entire courtroom stares at Robinson now, and Rothstein gently taps his gavel. I resist looking over at Kate, or especially Dante. What is *this* all about?

'What did you do then, Nikki?'

'I screamed,' she says, fighting through tears. 'I ran and tried to lock myself in the bathroom. But Eric, he grabbed the handle. He was strong for his size.'

'I know this is painful,' says Howard, handing her a tissue. 'What happened next?'

'He *raped* me,' says Nikki Robinson in a tiny, anguished squeak.

Then Robinson's head falls onto her chest, and for the first time since the trial began, both sides of the courtroom are equally distressed. Within seconds of each other, one woman cries out, 'Liar!' and another yells, 'Lying bitch.' Each has different reasons for their anger.

'One more outburst,' shouts Judge Rothstein, trying to control his courtroom, 'and I'll clear the room.'

Still, it's another minute or so before Howard asks, 'What happened after you were raped?'

'I pulled myself off the floor. Finished my work. I don't know why. Shock, I guess. Then I left the house.'

'Where'd you go, Ms Robinson?'

'I was going to go home. But I got more and more upset. I went to the courts behind the high school. Dante and Michael were there. I told them what happened. That Feifer raped me.'

'How did Dante react?'

'He went crazy. He was screaming, stomping around. He and Michael.'

'Quiet!' shouts Rothstein again, calming the room some.

'What did you think when you heard about the killings, Ms Robinson?'

'It was my fault,' says Robinson, staring at her lap. 'I never should have let Feifer come to the house. Most of all, I never should have told Dante and Michael Walker.'

Dante leans in to me. 'She's lying, Tom. She made that whole thing up. Every word.'

# Chapter Ninety-Seven

## Kate

As Rothstein bangs his gavel like a jockey flogging a fading horse on the home stretch, Tom writes *Lindgren* on a piece of paper. He slides it to me before I get out of my chair. I'm already there.

'Ms Robinson, we're all hearing this for the first time. To say the least, we're a bit overwhelmed. And confused. Could you tell us again why you decided to come forward now?'

'*Jesus*,' says Nikki, then pauses as if to let this sink in. 'He came to me in a dream and told me it was my duty to tell what happened.'

'Does Jesus often come to you in dreams, Nikki?' I

ask, provoking enough derisive laughter to have Rothstein pound his desk some more.

'That was the first time.'

'Ahh. But why wait this long to come forward? And why do it now?'

'I was afraid. I didn't want to hurt my cousin. But Jesus said I should say what I knew.'

'After the rape, did you go to the hospital?'

'No.'

'Really? Did you see a doctor anywhere?'

'No.'

'You weren't examined by anyone?'

Robinson shakes her head, and I say, 'I didn't hear your response, Ms Robinson.'

'No, I was not examined by a doctor.'

'Weren't you worried about contracting a sexually transmitted disease or getting pregnant?' I ask.

'I was on the Patch.'

'But you weren't worried about an STD?'

'Not really.'

'So you didn't tell anyone at all about the incident at the time. No one. There is no police record, no medical record, and you finished cleaning the house after the rape. So there's not a single bit of evidence, even circumstantial evidence, to support or confirm your story.'

'Objection,' cries Howard.

'What's your question, Counselor?' asks Judge Rothstein.

'When you decided to come forward two days ago – after your visit from Jesus – *who'd you talk to first*?'

'I called the East Hampton Police Department.'

'And who exactly did you talk to?'

'Officer Lindgren.'

I am thinking on my feet now, trying to anyway. 'Ms Robinson, have you been arrested lately? Say, in the last few months?'

'Yes, ma'am. For possession.'

'Possession of drugs?'

'Yes.'

'And who arrested you?'

Nikki Robinson looks left and right, anywhere but at me, but there's no getting around this. 'Officer Lindgren,' she says.

Loud, angry voices erupt from all sides, and Judge Rothstein has no choice but to finally go through with his threat. He clears the courtroom.

# Chapter Ninety-Eight

## Loco

Little Nikki puts on quite a show up on the witness stand. Who would have thought the slut had it in her? But after clever-girl Costello gets her to drop Lindgren's name and her arrest, all hell breaks loose, and Rothstein clears the courtroom and calls it a day.

Everyone spills out into the hot courtyard, and if not for two hundred cops, there would have been a riot then and there. The atmosphere is so messed up and ugly, Rothstein suspends proceedings for an additional twenty-four hours.

So it's not until Thursday morning that we all file back into the courtroom. Rothstein must think we're all basically children, because he gives us a stern lecture on the importance of orderly courts in a free society. What a crock, and most of us know it.

Then he turns to Ms Costello, who calls Marie Scott to the stand. *This should be good. Scott's a big witness for Dante, his beloved grandma.*

One look at Scott, I see she's one of those God-fearing, righteous women you always watch on the TV news after some tragedy happens. You know the type I mean, who somehow keep their shit together no matter what unspeakable thing has just happened.

She's no spring chicken but her back is straight as a plank. And the slow way she walks up to be sworn in, you'd think she's here to receive a special award from George Bush.

'What's your relationship to the defendant, Ms Scott?' asks Costello.

'I'm proud to say the young man is my grandson,' says Scott, hurling her big voice into the room.

'How long has Dante lived with you?'

'Five years. Ever since his mother began serving her sentence upstate. Dante's father had already passed by then.'

'So you've raised Dante since he was a young boy?'

'That's right, and until these false charges, he's never gotten into a bit of trouble. Not once.'

The question that always comes into my head when I see a woman like Marie is why, if her shit's so damn tight, did her kids all turn out so bad? Even if she did a great job with Dante, how come her daughter's in jail? That holier-than-thou attitude must drive them the other way.

'Where did he live in your place?' asks Costello.

'It's just the two of us. So he had his own bedroom.'

'Could you describe it for us, Marie?'

'Nothing fancy. He had a bed that was way too small for him, but a good-sized desk and bookshelves on the walls. We couldn't afford a computer, but he used one at school.'

'What was on those bookshelves?' asks Costello.

'On one wall were the things any high-schooler would have – books, CDs. The other shelf held his basketball stuff. He called it his Dream Wall because that space was dedicated to his dream of playing in the NBA. Of course, he never calls it that, he calls it "the League."'

*This is all highly fascinating, but where we going, Grandma?*

'What did that wall consist of, Marie?'

'There were five shelves. On the outside went his trophies from the all-star games and the summer camps and being named Suffolk County High School Player of the Year two years in a row.'

'And how about on the inside?'

'That was where he kept his basketball caps. He had all thirty, one for every team in the League. Because that's the moment he's living for, when they call out Dante Halleyville in that auditorium in New York City and he walks to the stage and puts one of those caps on.'

'Did he ever wear those hats outside of the house, Marie?' asks Costello.

'Never!' says Scott so loudly that the whole court-room feels the fury in it, and I don't need to look at Officer Lindgren to know he's sweating bullets now.

'He never wore those hats, period! Those hats weren't for wearing. They were for dreaming. He ordered them by mail, took them out of their box, and placed them on the shelf, but he never put them on. He was superstitious. He didn't want to put one on until they called him up on that stage and he knew which team he was playing for.'

I hate to admit it, but Lindgren was right. That bitch Costello has gotten too close.

'How long after the murders did the Suffolk County Homicide unit come to your home?'

'The next afternoon.'

'What did they do?'

'Searched Dante's room, photographed it, dusted for prints. Then they taped it off. I *still* can't go into my grandson's room. To this day.'

'Were they the first police to come to your house, Marie?'

'No. That morning an officer from the East Hampton Police Department came over by himself. He said he was looking for Dante and asked if he could take a look in his room.'

About now I get a bad feeling in the pit of my stomach.

'Did you let him in, Marie?'

'Yes, ma'am. I knew Dante wasn't involved in these crimes, so I didn't see the harm. In fact, I thought it would help the police see that he was innocent.'

'Did you go in Dante's room with the officer?'

'No, I let him in there alone. That's the way he wanted it.'

Now the crowd is rumbling so much that Rothstein holds up one black-robed arm. Not that it does much good.

'How long was the officer in there?'

'Not long,' says Marie. 'Not more than a couple minutes.'

'But long enough to take Dante's Miami Heat cap off the shelf?' says Costello.

Now three things happen at once – the crowd explodes; the DA shouts, 'Objection!' and Scott drills out, 'Yes, ma'am!' with everything she's got, which is plenty.

'Strike the last question and answer from the record,' Rothstein tells the stenographer, then turns to the smart-ass bitch. 'Ms Costello, consider yourself warned.'

'Marie, do you remember *which* police officer came to your house that morning?'

'Yes, I do. Of course I remember who it was.'

'What was his name?'

'Hugo Lindgren.'

'*Hugo Lindgren,*' says Costello as if she's stunned herself. 'The same officer who just happened to get the anonymous tip about the gun at the Princess Diner and the call from Nikki Robinson also spent several minutes unattended in Dante's room? Is that your sworn testimony, Ms Scott?'

'Yes,' says Scott. 'It most certainly is. Hugo Lindgren.'

By now the crowd, at least on my side, is ready to burn the courtroom down, no matter what Rothstein says about civic responsibility.

But it's Costello, not Rothstein, who gets them to shut up. Because this is where she blows everybody's mind, including mine.

'Marie Scott will be our only witness, Your Honor,' says Costello, twisting her gaze between the judge and the jury. 'Ms Scott said it all. The defense rests its case.'

Costello's announcement stuns both sides of the courtroom into silence, and as the lookyloos start to file out deflated and confused, it reminds me of a pay-per-view title fight that gets stopped way too early. But you know what else? That bitch is smart.

Maybe she just stole the fight.

# Chapter Ninety-Nine

## Tom

The next morning, when the crowd trudges back into the courtroom, you can read the tension on every face. It fills the room. After a very hot week and air-conditioning that's little more than a sound effect, this unventilated box reeks of dried sweat and body odor. As I walk to my seat alongside Kate, perspiration trickles down my back.

Deciding not to put Dante on the stand is a calculated risk, but putting a terrified teenager at the mercy of the prosecution seemed even riskier. Nevertheless, it places that much more pressure on my summation. I'm scribbling last-second notes when the bailiff crows, *'All rise!'*

Much too quickly, Judge Rothstein strides into the room, climbs onto his bench, and turns to me.

'Mr Dunleavy,' he says, and I rise to face the jury one last time.

'Ladies and gentlemen, when I stood before you at the start of this trial, my one request was that you accept nothing you hear until you've filtered it through your own judgment. I know you've done that because I sat and watched you do it, and because I can see the effect of that effort in your eyes. So, thank you.

'This morning we're going to examine the prosecution's case one final time and consider their so-called evidence piece by piece.'

Already, my face is dripping with sweat, and when I mop my brow and take a gulp of water, the only sound in the room is the drone of that useless AC.

'When I went to work for Dante, I thought this was a tragic case of an innocent teenager finding himself in the wrong place at the wrong time. Now I realize bad luck had nothing to do with Dante Halleyville and Michael Walker being at Smitty Wilson's estate the night Eric Feifer, Robert Walco, and Patrick Roche were murdered.

'Dante and Michael were deliberately lured to the scene so they could be framed for the murders. That's the *only* explanation that makes sense.

'How exactly did Dante and his best friend end up at Wilson's fifty-million-dollar estate that night? When Dante turned himself in, he told the police he got a call at about five p.m., and we know he's telling the truth because the records show he got a call eighty-three seconds long, exactly at five oh one. It came from a pay phone outside a seafood shack called the Clam Bar in Napeague.

'The caller identified himself as Eric Feifer. He invited Dante to come to the Wilson estate so they could clear the air and put this overblown incident behind them. Dante, being a good person who felt exactly the same way about that stupid fight – which the prosecution has shamelessly blown up into a mini race riot – immediately agreed to meet Feifer later that night. Also, apparently Michael Walker was looking to buy marijuana. Dante admitted as much.

'But the person who made that call, ladies and gentlemen, *wasn't* Eric Feifer. It was someone *impersonating* Eric Feifer.

'If Eric Feifer was the caller, he would have used his cell phone. He didn't need to go out of his way to make a call that couldn't be traced back to him, because he had nothing to hide. But the caller, who was setting up Dante and Michael for these murders, *did* have something to hide. So he used a pay phone.

'That call,' I say, pausing only long enough to swipe at my dripping face again, 'was only the first of several steps the actual murderers took to frame Dante, but it was the most important. It got Dante and Michael to the scene, and as soon as the murderers heard them arrive, they killed those three young men.

'Now the murderers had Dante and Walker at the scene, but that wasn't enough for them. They find out – possibly from a connection in the police department – where Michael Walker is hiding. They murder him with the same weapon used to kill Feifer, Walco, and Roche. After getting Walker's perfect prints on the weapon, they hang on to the gun until Dante turns himself in.

'As soon as they hear Dante stopped at the Princess Diner on his way back from the city that night, they drop the gun there. With another phony call, or so-called anonymous tip to Officer Hugo Lindgren, they reveal that the gun is in the Dumpster. How convenient.

'Ladies and gentlemen, *do any of you use pay phones anymore*? Do any of you not have cell phones? But in this case *two* crucial calls are made by pay phone. And both are made for the same reason – so the caller can't be traced.

'Think hard about what the prosecution has been telling you. It doesn't make sense. If Dante had killed those three young men, then used the same gun to kill his best friend, he had plenty of time to get rid of the murder weapon. If, as the prosecution maintains, he traveled alone from the Lower East Side to Brooklyn, killed Walker, and then returned to Lower Manhattan, he could have tossed the gun anywhere along the way. Instead, according to the prosecution anyway, he hangs on to it until the last minute. Then he recklessly discards it in a public place.

'And Michael Walker's *prints* on the gun. That fails the smell test too. If Dante killed Walker he would have wiped all the prints off before discarding the weapon. He wouldn't have carefully removed his prints and left Walker's.

'Now let's talk about the Miami Heat cap – because this is where the actual murderers slipped up in a couple of important ways. Since the killers couldn't get Dante's print on the gun, they decided to leave one of his caps at the scene. But how could the killers know that the hats on Dante's shelves were purely symbolic, that they were never worn, that Dante thought it was bad luck to put any of those hats on before the NBA draft? They couldn't.

'That's why they left a cap that had no trace of Dante's sweat or hair oil on the band. They left a hat at the crime scene that *had never been worn.* If Dante had gone off that night to kill his best friend, would he pick the brightest, reddest cap in his collection? And in a year, the prosecution hasn't been able to find one person, not one, who saw a nearly seven-foot man in a bright-red cap on the streets of New York City that night. Of course they didn't. He wasn't on the street that night.

'So what really happened? Who are the killers?

'Someone or some group of people connected to the drug trade that was conducted so brazenly at Mr Wilson's estate last summer killed those three young men. They opportunistically framed Dante Halley-ville. They killed Michael Walker too, but in the process they made serious mistakes. Killers almost always do.

'A hat that Dante had never worn at a crime scene. A gun planted in a Dumpster in a way that makes no sense. And then, the biggest blunder – leaning way too heavily on one crooked cop.'

At that, the whole room squirms, particularly the men in blue standing shoulder to shoulder along all four walls.

'Are we really expected to believe it's a *coincidence* that the same cop who received the so-called anonymous tip about the gun in the Dumpster also got the call from Nikki Robinson when she came up with her ridiculous fabrication of rape? And this is the same cop who arrested her for possession? And the same cop who was left alone in Dante's bedroom with those hats? *Please.*

'But for all the mistakes the killers made, one calculation proved to be spot on – which is that the police would be quick to believe that a black teenager, even one with no history of violence and the prospect of being a top selection in the NBA draft, would throw it all away because he lost a meaningless pickup basketball game and got hit by a harmless punch. Why? Because that's what black teenagers do, right? They go off for no reason.

'From the beginning of this trial, the prosecution has gone out of its way to talk about race. They told you about a basketball game in which, God forbid, one team was made up of black players and the other white players. They made sure you heard about a scared teenage kid who said, "*This ain't over, white boy.*" That's because at the core of the prosecution's case is the assumption that black teenagers are so fragile and insecure that anything can set them off on a murderous rampage.

'I know Dante Halleyville, and there's nothing fragile about his personality or character. When his older brother veered into crime, he stayed in school and worked on his game. When his mother lost her battle with drug addiction, he stayed in school and worked on his game, and now he's stood up to almost a year in a maximum-security jail for a crime he didn't commit.

'In this case, as in so many others, race is nothing but a smokescreen. I know you're not going to be distracted or misled. You're going to see the prosecution's case for what it is. Because there is not one piece of credible evidence connecting Dante to these murders, you are going to come to the only conclusion you can – which is that the prosecution has *proved nothing* beyond a reasonable doubt.

'And then your foreman is going to say the two words that Dante Halleyville has been waiting to hear for a year – *Not Guilty.*

'If you don't do that, you will be helping the murderers get away with *a fifth* murder, the murder of a remarkable young man, a very good friend of mine named Dante Halleyville.'

# Chapter One Hundred

## Kate

Tom collapses in his chair, and the jurors stare at him stone-faced. Five of the jurors are African Americans and eight are women, but talking about race is a risk, particularly to a jury that's mostly white.

Howard can't wait to make us pay for it. 'Ladies and gentlemen, my name is Melvin Howard. I'm fifty-two years of age, and to the best of my knowledge, I've been black the whole time.

'In Alabama, where my people are from, my grandparents were the grandchildren of slaves, and when my parents were coming up, black people couldn't use the same bathrooms as white folks or eat at the same restaurants. But none of that disgraceful history has one iota to do with Dante Halleyville or this trial, and Mr Dunleavy knows it.'

Tom didn't say it did. In fact, he was saying the opposite, but Howard is twisting it anyway, doing whatever he thinks will work. But all that matters is how it plays to the twelve folks in the good seats, and when I look in their eyes I can't read a thing. I'm proud of what Tom has done, but I'm nervous too.

'Race and police corruption?' asks Howard sarcastically. 'Sounds familiar, doesn't it? Now where have I heard that before?' And then he looks at the end of the press row where Ronnie Montgomery is sitting and holds his mock stare.

'Oh, now I remember. It was from the tabloid trial of the century, the murder trial of Lorenzo Lewis. About the only thing missing is a snappy little slogan, like "If the hat's too red, their case is dead."

'But how many people still think Lorenzo's innocent today? Not even his golfing buddies in Arizona. So don't let yourself be conned like that jury, ladies and gentlemen, unless you want to be remembered the same way.

'Now is the time for you to see through the nonsense and the imaginative conspiracy theories and focus on the evidence. For starters, we got a murder weapon with Michael Walker's prints all over it, recovered at a Southampton diner three hours after Dante Halleyville stops there. Although the defense tried very hard to put words in his mouth, Dr Ewald Olson, one of the nation's top forensic scientists, has testified those prints could only belong to Michael Walker, and that gun killed all four of those young men.

'Now let me say something about a highly decorated East Hampton police officer named Hugo Lindgren.' In Riverhead, every other family has a relative who's a cop or corrections officer, and Howard is about to appeal directly to their defensive loyalties.

'By irresponsibly dragging his reputation through the mud, they have not only impugned an officer who has earned seventeen commendations in his nine years on the force, but by extension all policemen and corrections officers who risk their lives every day so that we can go about our business in safety.

'According to the defense, it's evidence of a conspiracy that one cop should be so involved in every aspect of the biggest murder case in East Hampton in a hundred years. Good cops like Lindgren spend their whole career waiting for cases like this. It's only natural that he would become obsessed with it. And remember, the East Hampton PD is a small unit, so for one officer to be involved a couple of times over the course of an investigation is hardly suspicious. It's surprising to me *his name didn't come up more often.*

'The defense, in its desperation, has said a couple other things that are simply untrue and need to be corrected.

'One is that it's suspicious that the call about the gun came from the pay phone at the Princess Diner. Maybe most of us have cell phones now, but what if the caller was a busboy working the overnight shift at the restaurant that night for minimum wage? Not everyone can afford a cell phone. The second is the implication that the gun was found after the defendant told police he had been to the diner that night and that the defendant volunteered that information. Neither is true. Lindgren was nowhere near the room where the defendant was interviewed, and the police found out Halleyville had been at the diner *after* the gun was found.

'Bear in mind, also, that the one person who places that officer in Dante's room is Dante's grandmother, Marie Scott. Marie Scott may be a very good woman, and I'm sure she is, and she swore to tell this court the truth, the whole truth, and nothing but the truth so help her God. But she's also a human being, and who of us can say with any certainty exactly what they would do or say to save the life of their flesh and blood?'

Howard is sweating at least as much as Tom, but when he stops it's only for a drink of water.

'And there's an important part of this case that the defense hasn't even attempted to discredit or obscure, which is that on the morning before the murders, Michael Walker got a gun out of Dante's car, brought it onto T. Smitty Wilson's basketball court, and put it up against the head of one of the victims, Eric Feifer. As the witness told you, he didn't just aim the weapon at Eric Feifer, he put the tip of the barrel right up against his head, and you've seen those grisly photographs so you know how close the killer held the gun to the victims' heads when the shots were fired. And before Walker temporarily put that gun down, he announced, "This ain't over, white boy, not by a long shot." Before the actual murder, there was a dress rehearsal to which fourteen men and women were invited.

'Ladies and gentlemen, this is a pretty simple case. You've got two defendants at the murder scene; *you've got a murder weapon containing the fingerprints of one of them; you've got a hat with fingerprints that connects the defendant to the second murder scene.* And now, thanks to the courage of Nikki Robinson, you have a powerful motive – revenge for a brutal rape.

'I want to thank all of you for the focus and commitment you have shown already. And thanks in advance for the concentration you will bring to the work that is still left. You're almost home, ladies and gentlemen. Please, don't take your eye off the ball now. *Dante Halleyville is guilty of murder. If you value your safety and the safety of your loved ones, do not set him free.'*

# Chapter One Hundred and One

## Kate

For a couple of quiet minutes spectators linger in their seats like moviegoers reading the closing credits. 'We love you, Dante,' shouts Marie as two sheriffs approach the defense table to take him away. 'It's almost over, baby.'

'Yeah,' a guy in paint-splattered overalls calls from the door, 'and then you fry!'

Tom and I shake Dante's hand, which is still quivering; then the sheriffs put him back in handcuffs and lead him to the steel-cage elevator that will take him to the holding cell in the basement. On the opposite side of the room, another pair of sheriffs escorts the jury out a second door and walks them to a waiting bus. The bus will take them a quarter of a mile down the road to a Ramada Inn, where they'll spend the weekend on the eleventh floor, sequestered from one another and the rest of the world.

After the jury's bus pulls out, Tom and I slip out the same back door and hustle across the parking lot to where Clarence has left us his cab.

As we roll out the back exit in the yellow station wagon, TV reporters and other press are still waiting for us in front. By the time they realize what's happened, we're halfway to Sunrise Highway.

Neither of us says a whole lot during the drive home. Exhaustion is part of the reason, but mostly it's shyness, or something like that. Suddenly alone together again, we're not sure how to act. Actually, I'm thinking about the old days, when we were younger. During our senior year in high school, Tom and I saw each other just about every day – *beach bums forever.* It was pretty much the same way through college, and I went to almost all of Tom's home games when he was at St John's. That's why the breakup was such a shocker for me. I still don't know if I'm over the hurt.

Anyway, when Tom pulls into Macklin's driveway

and I quickly get out of the car, I can read the disappointment in his eyes.

I'm feeling it too, but I'm so bone tired I need to get to my room before I collapse. I unbutton my skirt before I reach the top of the steep stairs, pull the shades, and crawl into bed.

The relief at finding myself horizontal between clean white sheets lasts a minute. Then my mind hits Rewind and Play and the second-guessing starts. Did Tom have to mention race? Were we right not to put Dante on the stand? Why was I so easy on Nikki? I should have shredded her. How hard could we really have been trying if we didn't track down Loco? Who are we kidding – thinking we could win this case?

Then sleep, the loveliest gift a person ever gave herself, pulls the black curtain down.

When I sit up in bed again, awakened by what sounds like a woodpecker tapping against a pane of glass, it's three thirty in the morning. I've been asleep for more than nine hours.

There's another *click* on the glass, and then another *click*, and I climb out of bed and step groggily to the window.

I fumble for the shade, give one little tug, and it flies past my face up toward the ceiling.

Standing in the backyard, a bicycle lying at his feet, and about to throw another pebble at the window, is the only boy who's ever broken my heart.

When Tom's face breaks into a grin, I realize I'm naked.

# Chapter One Hundred and Two

## Tom

How can an ex-NBA player miss a target the size of a door less than fifteen feet away? The pebble bounces off the siding, hits the edge of the gutter, and lands in the grass near my feet.

I scoop another little piece of Mack's driveway out of my pocket and try again. This time I actually hit the window, and then I hit it again.

I'm wondering how many direct hits it's going to take when the shade flies up and Kate stands at the window, the moonlight shining on her freckled shoulders and full breasts. After a couple of interminable seconds, she lifts a finger to her lips and smiles, and I can breathe again, at least until the back door swings open and she steps outside barefoot in cutoff shorts and a Led Zeppelin T-shirt.

We tiptoe past the *National Enquirer* photographer asleep in his rented Toyota and walk down the middle of a sleeping Montauk street toward the beach. I leave my shoes under the bench behind the East Deck and we cut through the dunes.

The sand is damp and cool, and the moonlight looks like a white carpet rolling toward us on the light surf.

Before the beach narrows, I find a spot near the cliffs to lay out a blanket, and Kate pulls me to the center of it. She stares into my eyes. Her eyes, straight out of sleep, look so naked and beautiful, and the wind whips her red hair around her face.

'Who *are you*, Tom?'

'I thought court was adjourned.'

'Really, Tom,' says Kate, and she looks as if she's about to cry.

'A person who's changed. A person who's made mistakes. They're behind me now.'

'Why should I believe that?'

'Because this whole thing has been as much about you as Dante. Because I've been in love with you since I was fifteen, Kate.'

'Don't say things you don't mean, Tom. Please. I'm enough of a sucker to believe them. Twice. I still remember when you called me on the phone to tell me that you *didn't* love me. You were so cold. Maybe you don't remember.'

'Ahh, Kate, if there's no way I can ever win your trust again,' I say, a sickening desperation climbing into my throat, 'you got to tell me now because I don't know what else I can do. Back then, you know what it really was? *I didn't feel worthy of you.*'

Maybe it's the desperation in my voice that convinces her. I don't know, but she pulls down my neck and kisses me on the mouth.

'I'm warning you,' she whispers in my ear, 'screw up again and you'll answer to Macklin. You love me, Tom?'

'Kate, you know I do.'

She pulls her T-shirt over her head, and her shorts drop to her feet, and with her white freckled shoulders and red hair she looks more beautiful than the woman in that painting standing on the seashell. I reach out one hand, and when I touch the tiny silver ring cut through her left nipple, her mouth drops open and her head falls back with pleasure.

'When did you get the piercing?' I whisper, reaching for her again.

'Which one, Tom?'

# Chapter One Hundred and Three

## Kate

It feels awful to be this happy, even happy at all, while Dante sits in jail, his life in the hands of a fallible jury. But what can I do? I'm just a person, and people can't control the way they feel, and I feel happy. But I feel horrible about it too.

It's Sunday afternoon, and Tom and I are still on that beach blanket, but now it's spread out on his living-room floor, and I'm leaning back against the base of his couch with the *New York Times* on my lap, looking for articles I might have underestimated the first couple times.

Tom sits next to me doing the same thing, and Wingo lies between us, snoozing on his side. The three of us have been sitting like this for the last forty-eight hours, and even with the weight of the verdict hanging over us and the shades pulled tight against the photographers and camera crews camped out across the street, it feels as if we've been together for years, not just two days. But of course, in a way we have. I'm trying to keep the past out of this, but when it does bubble up, it's mostly the good stuff, not the breakup. The past ten years have humbled him, at least a little, and I like him more for it.

I get up to replace *Exile on Main Street* with *Let It Bleed*, while Tom puts the dishes in the sink and opens a tin for Wingo. While Wingo is engrossed, Tom sits back down and touches the bottom of my foot with the top of his. That's all it takes to get us groping between each other's legs and pulling off our clothes.

Like I said, we're just people, but it still feels wrong – and I'm relieved when we lead the press caravan back to Riverhead early Monday morning.

Tom and I are assigned a small room down the corridor from Judge Rothstein's chambers. We spend the day there, second-guessing, for the hundredth time, every strategic decision and line of questioning, each of us assuring the other without much effect that we did the right thing. We don't hear a word from the jury all day, and at 5:30 p.m. they are bused back to the Ramada Inn and we head back to Tom's living-room floor.

Tuesday is just as slow.

Same thing Wednesday.

But to be honest, I'm enjoying being with Tom.

Thursday morning our hopes soar when the jury requests transcripts of Marie's testimony, and then plummet in the afternoon when they ask for Nikki Robinson's. I'm rereading her transcripts when Rothstein's clerk sticks his bald head in the door.

'The jury has reached a verdict,' he says.

# Chapter One Hundred and Four

## Tom

The first to arrive are Macklin and Marie, Marie so hollowed out by five days of constant worry that she leans on poor Mack for support. Then come the parents of Feifer, Walco, and Roche, and their friends, who rush in like volunteer firefighters who have dropped whatever they were doing to answer the alarm.

For the trial itself, the courtroom was split down the middle, Dante's supporters and Montauk sympathizers, but because so many of Dante's people arrived from outside the area, today's crowd is made up of mostly Montauk people. Dante is represented by only a small, tight band of stalwarts – Clarence and Jeff, Sean in a FREE DANTE shirt, and a dozen or so of Dante's high school friends and teammates.

When the room is almost packed, the press pour in and fill their assigned rows up front.

The sketch artists have just set up their easels when Dante is led in one last time in handcuffs. He's so nervous he can barely meet our eyes, and when he sits between us and clasps our hands beneath the table, his hands are trembling and wet. Mine too.

'Hang in there, buddy,' I whisper. 'The truth is on our side.'

An hour ago, when they reached their verdict, the jurors asked to be taken back to their rooms to shower and change. Now they file into the courtroom in their Sunday best, the men in blazers and ties, the women in skirts and blouses. Soon after they take their seats, Steven Spielberg and George Clooney rush in fashionably late in their expensive yet casual clothes. Other than Shales, the screenwriter, A-list attendance had gotten spotty as the trial slogged on.

But no one wants to miss the last ten minutes.

# Chapter One Hundred and Five

## Tom

Suddenly it's all going down *too fast*. The bailiff cries, 'All rise.' Rothstein sweeps in and mounts his pedestal, and the jury forewoman, a tiny lady in her sixties with big plastic lenses, stands to face him.

'Has the jury reached a decision on all four charges?' asks Rothstein.

'We have, Your Honor.'

Dante looks straight ahead, his eyes focused on a secret spot inside himself, and his wet grip tightens. So does Kate's.

'And how do you find?' asks Rothstein.

I steal a glance at Marie's tortured face, and then, turning away from it, see the more composed features of Brooklyn detective Connie Raiborne, who is sitting right behind her. I guess he didn't want to miss the verdict either.

'In the charge of first-degree murder in the death of Eric Feifer,' says the elderly forewoman, her voice strong and clear, 'the jury finds the defendant, Dante Halleyville, *not guilty.*'

My hand inside Dante's feels like it's been caught in a machine, and behind us, anguished cries compete with hallelujahs and amens. Rothstein does his best to silence both with his gavel.

'And in the charge of first-degree murder in the death of Patrick Roche and Robert Walco,' says the forewoman, 'we find the defendant, Dante Halleyville, *not guilty.*'

The courtroom convulses, and the cops straighten their backs against the walls. Ten seconds stand between Dante and the rest of his life.

'And what is the jury's decision in the charge of first-degree murder in the death of Michael Walker?' asks Rothstein.

'The jury finds the defendant, Dante Halleyville, *not guilty.*'

The gray-haired woman says those final two resounding words with extra emphasis, but before the last syllable is all the way out, the room splits open. Marie and Clarence must feel as though they're watching Dante rise from the dead, and Feifer's mom, who lets out an awful wail, must feel as if she's seeing Eric get murdered again right in front of her eyes. The cheering and cursing, screaming and jubilation are way too close to each other, and the room teeters on the verge of violence.

But none of that means a thing to Dante. He springs out of the chair and pulls us up with him as he throws his huge fists into the air, tilts his head back, and roars. Kate gets the first hug. I get the second, and then we're at the center of a wet, hot mosh pit of pressed bodies; then the whole hot circle hops up and down and emits a chant.

'Halleyville! Halleyville! Halleyville!'

When Kate and I extricate ourselves enough to take in the rest of the room, it looks as spent as Times Square three hours after the ball drops on the New Year. Kate and I jump inside the phalanx of sheriffs who circle Dante, and as they usher us out a side door, my eyes lock with Spielberg's screenwriter, Alan Shales.

In this wild moment, Dante, Shales, and I are all

linked. Dante is free to play ball again; after my squandered decade, I have a career; and Shales's script is going to get made. If Dante had been convicted, there would have been no movie. But now, suddenly, all three of us have a future.

# Chapter One Hundred and Six

## Kate

Joyous neighbors and friends carrying food and drink show up at Marie's an hour after the verdict, but the celebration doesn't officially begin until Dante, a foaming bottle of champagne in one hand, scissors in the other, snips through the tangle of yellow police tape that sealed his bedroom for nearly a year. When the last sticky piece has been ripped away, he and his pals rush into the room like a liberating army.

'This is for my homeboy, Dunleavy,' says Dante, donning the black-and-blue cap of Tom's old team, the Minnesota T-wolves.

Then he tosses the other twenty-eight – the Miami Heat cap is still in a plastic bag in Riverhead somewhere – to his crew, and for the rest of the party, wherever I turn, brand-new gleaming caps bob jauntily above the fray.

As for me, I haven't been dry-eyed ten minutes since the verdict came down. All I have to do is see Marie gaze up at her grandson, or Tom and Jeff with their arms around each other, or the relief on Clarence's exhausted face for the tears to flow again. After a while, I don't even bother wiping them away.

Now Macklin bangs on the kitchen table and shouts, 'Order in the court! I said, order in the court!' And the room erupts in a riot of whistles, catcalls, and stomping feet.

'Anyone recognize this?' he says, waving a familiar wooden stick and sounding at least a couple drinks to the good. 'Let's just say that tight-ass Rothstein will have to find something else to beat on his poor pew. Because I wasn't leaving that courtroom without a souvenir.

'Goddamn it, Dante. I'm proud of you,' says Macklin. 'I don't know how you hung so tough, but based on what I see in your grandmother, I'm not surprised. I hope someday you can look back on this bullshit and feel you got something out of it. Anything. And now I want to hear from the brilliant and gorgeous Kate Costello.'

When the room twists toward me and cheers, I open my mouth to see what will fall out.

'To Dante!' I say, raising my champagne. 'And your long-overdue freedom! And to Marie! And *your* long-overdue freedom! I'm so relieved Tom and I didn't let you down. I love you both.' Then I lose it again as Dante and Marie rescue me in their arms.

'What my partner was trying to say, Dante,' says Tom, picking up my toast like a dropped baton, 'is you'll be getting our bill in the morning.'

The highly emotional toasts and festivities roll on without letting up. I go over and stand by Macklin and Marie while Tom steps outside to join the revelers dancing in the yard to Outkast, Nelly, James Brown, and Marvin Gaye. Half an hour later, a peal of thunder rips through the joyous din, and the clouds that have been swelling all afternoon spill open.

The downpour sends half the neighborhood running for cover back into Marie's six-hundred-square-foot trailer. Soon after that, Tom, his brow creased with worry, taps me on the shoulder.

'It's Sean. Seems my nephew just got dumped by

his girl. I didn't even know he had one, but I guess he did, because he's saying all kinds of crazy stuff.'

'You need to go talk to him?'

'I think so.'

'Well, give him a hug for me.'

'I will. And when I get back, I have a surprise.'

'I don't know if I can take any more surprises right now.'

'It's a good one. I promise,' says Tom, then gestures toward Mack and Marie. 'Am I hallucinating, or are those two holding hands?'

# Chapter One Hundred and Seven

## Loco

When Boy Wonder comes around the back of that shitty little trailer and walks across the muddy yard, he looks so different it sends a quick-silver shiver up my spine.

It's like I can barely recognize him, and I have this awful feeling that when he gets to Costello's car, where I have been waiting for forty-five minutes like he asked, he's not going to recognize me either. Or if he does, it's going to be like we're nothing but acquaintances and the last eight years never happened.

Boy Wonder is such a cunning bastard, that was

probably his plan from the beginning. I don't mean since this afternoon or last summer, I mean from the very beginning, eight years ago, when he came to the Village police station at three in the morning and bailed me out after the cops busted me for selling weed on the beach. I don't know what he did or how he did it, but somehow he got the chief of police to drop the whole thing and fixed it so completely even my folks never found out. But now that I think about it, I bet he set me up with the cops in the first place so he could come in and bail my ass out and I'd owe him from the start.

A week later, he took me to Nick and Tony's and picked out a three-hundred-dollar bottle of wine that he barely touched. He kept filling my glass though, and on the ride home, when I could barely sit up, he made what he called 'a modest little proposal.' I should leave the high school kids to the amateurs and instead help him take over the whole Hampton drug trade. 'It's nothing but funny money to these assholes,' he said. 'Besides, we've been staring at rich people our whole lives. It's time to join the country club.'

I was all of seventeen at the time, a high school junior. What did I know? But the Boy Wonder knew exactly what he was about, and with him doing the thinking and me the heavy lifting, it wasn't long before the money arrived in sacks.

Boy Wonder was smart about that too. Said that if we started living like pimps, the cops would be sniffing around us in months. So for eight years we lived like monks, nothing changing in our lives except the number in the bank accounts he'd opened in Antigua and Barbados.

Since then, it's just been a matter of hanging on to what we took, or what Boy Wonder calls 'our franchise.'

That's been no problem either. Ruthlessness is one of Boy Wonder's strong suits, right up there with cagey thinking, and I guess I'm no slouch in that department either. But I'll tell you, it's impossible to figure out what BW is thinking – always has been.

It's coming down in buckets now, but BW ambles through the rain like it's exactly what he needs to wash him clean. Maybe it is. I know better than anyone what he is capable of doing and living with. I stood next to him as he put a bullet in Feifer, Walco, and Rochie, them bawling for their moms until the last second.

And for what? Stealing a thousand dollars' worth of crack. Doing some small-time dealing. That's all it was. More of a prank than stealing, since the next day

Feif and Rochie came around with the cash, plus interest.

But BW wouldn't let me take the money. He said we had to send a message. A strong message. It was psycho but cunning too, because he waits until after that fight at Smitty's court where Walker pulls his piece on Feifer. That way we can pin the whole thing on the brothers, and I think, okay, maybe we can get away with this just like everything else.

But as Boy Wonder opens the door of the car, he seems so transformed and remote, his old name doesn't seem to fit anymore. And when he slides behind the wheel and gives me his chilly 'What's up?' I fall back on what I called him for fifteen years before he showed up that night at the police station.

'Hell if I know,' I say. 'What's up with you, Tom?'

That gets his attention. Never using real names is even stricter with us than not spending money, and before he can catch it, he flashes the same hard look he gave Feifer, Walco, and Rochie right before he shot them through the eyes. Then he covers it with a smile and asks, 'Why you calling me Tom, Sean?'

'Because the party's over, Uncle. We're done.'

# Chapter One Hundred and Eight

## Tom

'**M**aybe we can still figure a way out,'I say, starting up Kate's Jetta and carefully backing out of the muddy driveway. With every neighbor within miles celebrating at Marie's, the street is deserted, and in the heavy rain, it looks more desolate than usual. 'What makes you so sure it's over, Nephew? What happened?'

'*Raiborne* happened,' says Sean.'Soon as the verdict came down, I bolted out of there, but when I get to my car, Raiborne is standing right next to it. The son of a bitch is waiting for me. He must have sprinted to get there first, but if he was breathing hard, he didn't let me see it. He introduced himself. Said that as of three minutes ago the murder cases of Eric Feifer, Patrick Roche, Robert Walco, and Michael Walker were wide open again, along with the never-solved murder of Señor Manny Rodriguez. Then he smiles and says the only suspect he's got for all five is a psychopathic drug dealer named Loco.

'When I ask him why he's telling me, Raiborne looks at me cute and says, "Because I'm pretty sure you're him, Sean. You're Loco!"'

I'm on Route 41 now, but it's raining so hard, I'm doing less than thirty. I slow down even more when I see the boarded-up Citgo, and just past it, I turn off onto another depressed little street.

I look over at Sean – and I smile. 'Well, you don't have to worry about Detective Raiborne anymore.'

'Really?'

'Really. He came to see me too. This afternoon at my place, just after Clarence picked up Kate and took her to Marie's. He said he couldn't figure out how I knew so much about the murders – that the gun was a plant, the prints and the call from Feifer staged, that Lindgren was dirty. Then he realized I must have been involved too.'

'So what'd you do?'

'I was going to ask if he'd ever been to Antigua, any of the islands. Had he ever thought of taking early retirement? But I knew it would be a waste of my time.'

'So what'd you *do*?' asks Sean, looking away because he already knows the answer.

'What I had to. And I'll tell you, the guy's an easy two hundred thirty pounds. I barely got him in the trunk.'

'Now you're killing cops, Tom?'

'Didn't have much choice,' I say as we hear the siren of an East Hampton cruiser racing north on Route 41 toward Marie's place.

'How about letting Dante find his own lawyer? Or if you had to be the big star again, be in the spotlight with your girlfriend, how about letting him *lose*?'

The road, barely visible through the pounding rain, climbs past an abandoned trailer home.

'I guess you never heard of something called redemption, Nephew.'

'Guess not.'

'A chance to undo mistakes like mine comes once in a lifetime.'

'Isn't it a little late for that, Uncle?'

'What do you mean?'
'To undo the past? Start over?'
'Oh, it's never too late for redemption, Sean.'

# Chapter One Hundred and Nine

## Tom

Now it's raining so hard that even with the wipers flapping on the highest setting, I can hardly see the road. If I thought I could risk it, I'd pull over and wait for the rain to let up.

'So what are we doing with Raiborne?' asks Sean, trying not to look at me, the way I've seen people look away from born-agains.

'Bury him,' I say. 'At that old nigger cemetery up on the hill. Only seems right.'

The paved road becomes a dirt one. I know it well. Somehow I make out the half-grown-over opening in the bushes, and beside it what's left of a sign for the Heavenly Baptist Burial Grounds.

I push through the opening, the bushes flailing against the car windows, and up a dirt driveway. It's rutted and soft, but going real slow and avoiding the worst parts, I get the car to the top of the rise, where it opens on a clearing lined with dozens of modest limestone headstones and markers.

I park beside a rotting bench, nod to Sean, and we step reluctantly into the downpour. With the soggy mud sucking at our shoes, we walk to the rear of the car. Heavy drops ping off the roof and trunk as Sean pushes the chrome lock and then steps out of the way as the chipped blue lid slowly lifts open, but of course, the only thing inside is Kate's bald old spare and some gardening tools she uses around Macklin's place.

'What the fuck?' says Sean, turning toward me and quickly pinning my arms.

But by then my gun is tight against his side, and as he stares at me with the same shocked expression the mortician had to wipe off Feif, Walco, and Rochie, I shoot him.

I'll say one thing. Sean doesn't cry for his mother like those other boys did. He must think I'm his mom the way he reaches for me and says, 'Tom? What are you doing, Tom?'

I fire three more times, the barrel of the gun so tight against Sean's big chest it works like a flesh-and-blood silencer, and the sound of the muffled shots barely reaches the soggy woods. That shuts him up, but his eyes are still wide open and it feels as if they're staring at me. I feel Sean's eyes on me until I get a small shovel from the trunk and dig a shallow grave. Then I start throwing dirt over his face. I find another spot to bury the gun; then I get back into the car.

I love being in a parked car when the rain is tap-dancing on the roof, and for a while I just sit there and watch it wash the grime off the windshield, just like I washed Sean off of me. And you know what? I still feel redeemed.

# Chapter One Hundred and Ten

## Kate

Marie's tiny living room is so crowded it's kind of like swimming in the ocean. You go where the waves take you. One minute I'm listening to the very good-looking George Clooney rant about the American criminal justice system, the next I'm having an emotional heart-to-heart with Tom's brother, Jeff, who tells me he's been worried about Sean.

'He's not been himself since the trial started,' says Jeff. 'Anxious, depressed or something. And he never said a thing to me about a girl.'

'It's a tough age,' I say, and try to reassure him, but before I have much of a chance, I'm pulled away as if by an undertow to a spot in a corner beside Lucinda Walker, Michael Walker's mom. It's awful standing in such a jubilant crowd with the mother of a murdered child, but Lucinda takes my hand.

'God bless you, Miss Costello,' she says. 'You kept another innocent life from being destroyed. I never believed Dante killed my son or those others. Maybe now the police will concentrate on finding the real killers.'

As Lucinda talks about Dante and Marie, the front door opens and Tom wedges himself back into the packed party, and when he smiles at me across the room, my heart flies out to him. It scares me to think how close I came to not giving him a second chance. If not for this case, I might never have talked to him again.

'I feel like a salmon fighting its way upriver to spawn,' says Tom, sweat dripping off his nose.

'Hold that thought. How's Sean?'

'More down than I've ever seen him. It's sad, but I gave him my spiel and your hug. How about you, Kate? How's my girl?'

'I had no idea being happy could be this exhausting.'

'What do you say the two of us get lost for a little while?'

'You got a place in mind?'

'Actually, I do. But that's the surprise I told you about before.'

He leads me across the room toward Mack and Marie, and Marie hugs me so tight I laugh.

'Look at you two,' she says, her eyes dancing with joy. 'You showed everyone. *E-ver-y-one!* The whole world!'

'Us? How about you two?' says Tom, and clinks his beer bottle against Mack's glass.

'To twos,' says Macklin, putting his arm around Marie.

'Well, this couple's heading home,' says Tom. 'It's been a great day but a really long one. We can barely stand up.'

The guest of honor is in the kitchen surrounded by high school buddies who beam at him in awe. Although around the same age as Dante, they seem five years younger. Dante won't let us leave the house until he's introduced them all.

'This big fella,' says Dante, pointing to a heavyset kid on his left, 'is Charles Hall, C-H. These are the

Cutty brothers, and this is Buford, but we call him Boo. They're my boys.'

Tom and I give Dante one more hug, and then we're out of there. Actually, the more I think about it, I am in the mood for a surprise.

# Chapter One Hundred and Eleven

## Kate

Outside the house, where it's twenty degrees cooler, the rain feels like a warm, sweet shower. Tom puts an arm around me and leads me across the yard to my car. As I look down at the muddy tires, Tom pulls me to him hard and says, 'I just have to kiss you, Kate.'

'Works for me.'

We kiss in the rain, then climb soaked into the car. Tom buckles me in and heads for home, but at Route 27, he turns west instead of east, and if you grew up out here like us, that's not something you can do by accident no matter how hard it's raining or how tired you are. When I look over for an explanation, Tom responds with a shit-eating grin.

'I told you I had a surprise.'

'Let me guess,' I say, almost too exhausted to care. 'A weekend at the Peninsula?'

'Way better.'

'Really. You sure you can't tell me? That way I'll just be surprised *now.*'

'Kate, have we been working our butts off for like *decades*?' asks Tom, still smiling as he peers through the driving rain.

'Approximately.'

'Have we done well by our client?'

'You could say that.'

'And do you trust me?'

'You know I do,' I say, touching Tom's shoulder and suddenly overcome by such warm feelings, I'm choking up for the umpteenth time today.

'Then sit back and relax. You've earned it, Counselor.'

Like a good girl, I do as I'm told, and after a while I even manage to doze off. When I open my eyes, Tom's turned off 495 and is driving down a dark side road past overgrown lots and boarded-up houses.

Where are we now? I'm disoriented and lost.

Then I see the sign for Kennedy Airport.

'Tom?'

Tom offers nothing but that same silly smile as he swerves into the lane for international departures and pulls up in front of the Air France terminal.

'Ever been to Paris, Kate?'

'No.'

'Me neither.'

I'm feeling so many different things, but all I can say is, 'Who's taking care of Wingo?'

'Macklin,' he says. 'How do you think I got this?' And he hands me my passport with an e-ticket inside.

'I'm going to drop off the car,' says Tom, as if it's the most normal thing in the world. 'I'll meet you at the gate.' But I can't move or stop looking at him because it's as though I'm seeing him for the first time.

# Chapter One Hundred and Twelve

## Tom

T he overnight Air France flight touches down at 1:00 p.m. local time, and we hustle through the chaos of Charles de Gaulle Airport. With no luggage to wait for, we're first in line at immigration and pass effortlessly through Customs. I've never felt so free and easy in my life.

Eleven hours ago, I was driving through Queens. Now we're in the back of a black Fiat speeding past French road signs. We leave the drab motorway for the tree-lined postcard streets of Paris proper. The cab pulls off a grand boulevard, chatters briefly over cobblestones, and stops in front of the small hotel on the Left Bank I booked online this afternoon.

Our room isn't ready yet, so we walk two doors down to a coffeeshop. We order lattes and watch the bustling streets.

'Where are we, Tom?' asks Kate, licking the foam off her lips.

'Paris.'

'Just checking.'

Five minutes after we pay for our coffees, we're leaning against a stone balustrade and looking out over the muddy Seine. Elegant limestone buildings, none of which are much more than five stories tall or less than five hundred years old, line the far side of the river. The best part though is the light in Kate's eyes.

We cross le Pont-Neuf and follow the concierge's directions to the nearest department store. 'I could get used to this,' says Kate.

Inside the Galeries Lafayette, we allot ourselves a thousand euros each and split up to buy stuff. I get two pairs of pants, three shirts, a cashmere sweater, and loafers, all more adult than anything I've ever worn. Then again, I'm not the same person I was a year ago or even twenty-four hours ago, so why should I dress the same?

'No suitcases?' asks the well-dressed woman in a gray pantsuit behind the desk at our hotel.

'Traveling light,' says Kate, holding her own purchases in one shopping bag.

An elevator the size of a phone booth takes us to the third floor, where our antiques-filled room overlooks a tiny triangular square called La Place de Léon.

I tip the porter way too much, lock the door, and turn around in time to catch Kate skipping naked into my arms.

# Chapter One Hundred
and Thirteen

## Kate

T ry not to hate us, but here's our Parisian routine.
Tom gets up at eight, buys the *International Herald
Tribune,* and heads to the café. I come down an hour
later and help him finish off what's left of the croissants and crossword puzzle. Then Tom closes his eyes,
cracks open our guide, and lets fate pick the day's
destination.

Monday it was the Musée National Picasso in a
neighborhood of cozy winding streets called the
Marais. Tuesday we climbed the steep streets to the
top of Montmartre. This morning we're walking to an

eighteenth-century hotel converted into a museum for the French sculptor Rodin.

We see the powerful black-granite figure of the writer Balzac and, mounted on a podium, the famous, hulking *Thinker*, who looks awfully buff for an intellectual.

And behind them both, in a corner, is the epic *Gates of Hell*, on which Rodin spent the last thirty-seven years of his life. It consists of two massive black doors crawling with more than two hundred writhing figures, each living out his excruciating eternal punishment, and for some reason, Tom can't take his eyes off it.

He's so transfixed, I leave him to stroll the garden's stone pathways, which are lined with as many varieties of rosebushes as, I suppose, hell has sinners. There's an empty bench in the sun, and I'm watching a young mother breastfeed her infant when Tom finds me.

'So how many of the deadly ones have you committed, Tom?'

'All of them.'

'Busy boy.'

We have a sandwich and glass of wine in the garden café, then wander into the surrounding neighborhoods, many of whose stately homes have been converted to foreign embassies, with armed sentries posted out front. As beautiful and new as everything is, the wine and muscled, writhing sinners at the *Gates* have gone to my head, and I drag Tom back to our little room.

Actually, I can barely wait that long. As Tom fumbles with the key, I stick my tongue in his ear and tell him how hot I am, and as soon as we're inside the door, I pull him into the bathroom and undress him in front of the long mirror. I get on my knees between his legs and watch his face in the mirror as I suck his perfect cock.

'Is this a sin, Tom?'

'I don't think so.'

'Really? Am I doing it wrong then?'

'No, you're not doing anything wrong. You're doing everything just right.'

'Don't look at me, Tom. Look at us in the mirror.'

A couple hours later in our bed, Tom moans in a different way, then mumbles, 'No blood, no blood.'

I shake him, gently at first, then harder, and his terrified eyes blink open.

'You're having a nightmare, Tom.'

'What did I say?'

'You were talking about blood, Tom.'

'Whose blood? What blood?'

'You didn't say.'

'Did I say anything else?' asks Tom, his eyes still full of panic.

'No,' I tell him, and he smiles so sweetly that I need him inside me again.

# Chapter One Hundred and Fourteen

## Tom

I don't dare fall asleep again, but Kate does.

By the time she wakes, we've missed our reservation for dinner, so we head out into the night to see what we can find. As we pass various brightly lit windows, Kate seems unusually quiet, and I can't stop thinking about my nightmare and what I might have said in my sleep.

We leave crowded St Germaine for the quieter, darker streets along the Seine. The whole time Kate is clinging to my arm and not saying a word.

If something truly incriminating – about Sean or the others – had slipped out of my big mouth, she wouldn't have fucked me again like that, would she? But if I didn't say anything, why is she acting so squirrelly and tense?

We're both starving, but Kate rejects one promising-looking restaurant after another.

'Too touristy.'

'Too trendy.'

'Too empty.'

She's not herself. Whether I want to or not, I can't ignore the mind-numbing possibility that I've given myself away.

And if I have, how can I clean up my mess in a city I barely know?

We finally stop at a simple bistro packed with natives. The swarthy maître d' leads us to a red banquette in back, but even here Kate won't look me in the eye. Then, staring at her hands on her lap, and in a cracking voice, she says, 'Tom, there's something I need to talk to you about.'

*Not here. Not in front of everyone – where there's nothing I can do.*

'There's something I've been meaning to say too,'

I say. 'But my head feels like it's going to explode in here. Too noisy. Can we go someplace quieter, where it will be easier to talk?'

Apologizing to the maître d', we step back onto the curb and walk toward the Jardins du Luxembourg.

But even at 11:00 p.m., it's jammed with tourists. Every twenty yards or so there's another street musician strumming a Beatles song, or a juggler tossing burning sticks, and the benches that are empty are too visible from the pathways.

Finally, I spot an empty bench in the shadow of some tall trees. After a quick check to make sure we can't be seen, I pull her onto my lap. Still not quite believing that it's come to this, I look into Kate's eyes and put one hand at the bottom of her thin neck.

'Tom?'

'What is it, Kate?'

My heart is pounding so loud I can barely hear my words, and I look quickly over her shoulder to make sure no one is coming from the main path.

All night, Kate could barely look at me. Now her eyes are like lasers, and she won't take them off me, as if she's studying my eyes to read my reaction to what she's about to say.

'What, Kate? What's the matter?' I ask, and bring my other hand to her throat.

'I want to have a baby, Tom,' she says, 'I want to have your baby.'

I don't know whether to laugh or cry, but Kate, desperate for an answer, stares at me like a deer caught in headlights.

'Only one?' I whisper, kissing the tears on her cheek and lowering my trembling hands to her waist. 'I was hoping for three or four.'

# Chapter One Hundred and Fifteen

## Tom

Hours after our first baby-making session, I lie calmly on my side and watch Kate sleep, the desperation of a few hours ago just about swept away by euphoria. I used to hate to think about the future. I'd boxed myself into such a tight corner I didn't have much of one. Now I'm sitting prettier than the asshole who graduates first in his class at Harvard Law School.

Kate and I just won the biggest murder trial in the last ten years. We could live or work anywhere in the world, be partners at any law firm in the country, make a couple million a year between us without breaking a sweat. Or maybe, if we're not quite ready to jump back into the harness, we just hang in Paris for a while. Stretch our trip from a week to a couple of months. Rent an apartment in the Marais. Soak up the culture. Learn about wine.

A happy woman is such a lovely sight, and Kate looks so content, even in her sleep. If she's determined to start a family, why not do it? I'm not getting any younger. Maybe she can go to work, and I'll be the stay-at-home dad, teach the little ginks the fundamentals before it's too late, have them dribbling with both hands by the time they're in preschool.

The alarm clock on the nightstand clicks, and the digital readout flips over to 6:03. I carefully slide out of bed, and with that old Joni Mitchell tune – 'He was a free man in Paris' – lodged in my head, and willing the ancient floorboards not to creak, tiptoe to the bathroom.

I take a long, hot shower and shave. Slip on my new slacks and unwrap a shirt just back from the hotel laundry. Free and easy.

Of all the things I love about Paris, I love the mornings the most. I can't wait to step onto the wet streets and buy my *Tribune*. I can already taste the flaky croissants and rich, muddy coffee.

At the door, I take one last look at Kate, lost in her

unfathomable maternal dreams, and as I very gently close the door behind me, the cold steel barrel of a revolver presses into the back of my neck and the hammer is cocked back and catches in my ear.

Before I hear Raiborne's voice say, 'Thanks for bringing me to Paris, Dunleavy,' I smell his cheap aftershave. Then he kicks my loafers out from under me and throws me facedown onto the floor, pulls my wrists behind my back, and cuffs me. You could be a tough guy too if you had six gendarmes with guns drawn behind you.

I still haven't said a word because I don't want to wake up Kate. I want her sweet dream to live a little longer. Fucked up as it may sound, I was starting to believe in it too, and if Raiborne or someone else hadn't caught up with me, I might have gone through with it. It's all just acting, right? If I could act like a good enough lawyer to save Dante's ass, acting like a father and husband would have been a piece of cake.

But Raiborne doesn't care about that.

'Your nephew knows you better than you think, tough guy.'

'He was wearing a vest, wasn't he?' I whisper, still trying not to make any noise.

'How'd you know?'

'Because he's a little bitch,' I say, but really I know the reason – *because there was no blood. No blood!*

'Three days after he crawls out of his grave, he turns himself in. Doesn't even try to cop a plea. Just wants to share everything he knows about his uncle Tommy – which happens to be a whole lot.'

Why won't he shut up? Doesn't he know Kate's sleeping? For all we know, she's already sleeping for two. But it's too late.

The door opens and Kate steps into the hallway in her Led Zeppelin T-shirt. Her bare feet are six inches from my face, but it might as well be six miles – because I know I'll never touch her again.

# EPILOGUE

---

# AFTER THE FALL

# Chapter One Hundred and Sixteen

## Tom

The heavy boots of the day guard echo off the oppressive cinder-block walls that are all around me. A minute later there's a rattle of keys and a clanging of bolts, and when the footsteps resume I hop off the twenty-four-inch-wide metal cot. When the guard turns the last corner to my cell, I'm already standing by the door.

In the seven months I've been locked up in Riverhead – I'm on the same floor where Dante did his time – I haven't had a visitor, and the only letters I've received are from Detective Connie P. Raiborne, Brooklyn

Homicide. If Connie wants to pick my criminal brain, I say, pick away.

Since his letters are all I get in the way of human interaction, I do my best to keep him interested, even if I have to make shit up, which, if you haven't noticed, I'm very good at.

The guard leads me to a fenced-in courtyard for my federally mandated twenty minutes of outdoor exercise a week, unlocking my wrists through a slit in the barbed wire once I'm safely inside.

Across the way, the brothers run up and down the one court they got here, their black skin glistening with sweat even in the anemic December sun.

I still have more than enough game to school those fellas, but no one's going to let me play hoops in this joint. All I've got of freedom is the *pock* of the bouncing ball and the sun on the back of my neck. As I do my best to enjoy those, there's a commotion at the far end of the cage, and some inmates are shoved inside.

I'm in solitary, isolated from all the other inmates, since I fucked up that guy in the shower, messed him up so bad they're still feeding him through a tube. So right away I know what's happening and so does the whole courtyard, because the basketball stops bouncing and the place goes stone silent. For these sick bastards, this is better than HBO.

I almost feel the same way. I'm scared as hell, but excited-scared. No one ever learns the whole truth about himself, but in a place like this, you find out what you miss, and more than Kate's skin or smile or the daydream she kept alive, I miss *the action,* the rush of shaking the dice and letting them roll, and right now they're bouncing across the caged cement of this prison courtyard.

I stand up and, making a point of taking my time about it, move to the corner near the fence. That way no one can get behind me, and only one of them can get at me at a time.

They sent three people to do the job. There's a pasty-looking white guy with a full sleeve of green tats on both arms, plus two thickly built black guys.

But I never take my eyes off the white guy, because I know the one in the middle is holding the blade.

They're halfway across the lot now and closing fast, but I don't move a muscle, not even in my face. I let them get close, and then everything changes in an instant. I bring my right foot up hard into the kneecap of the brother on the right. There's a crunch and a scream of pain, and now, despite the four-leaf clover

417

carved on his bicep, Irish boy is not feeling nearly as lucky, is he?

But he's up next, and he's got no choice. He pulls his right hand from behind his thigh and lunges at me with the knife.

Like a slow punch, I see it coming all the way. I've got all the time I need to turn and grab his wrist and throw him up against the second brother. Now I'm beating the shit out of Shamrock at the same time I'm using his body to shield me from the brother. When he goes limp, I snatch the homemade blade out of his hand, and with the courtyard mob stomping their feet like this is a prizefight, I turn it on the one guy left standing, who, big as he is, freezes, suddenly in no hurry to get closer.

They already got me for three homicides; one more isn't going to make any difference, but something makes me hesitate – maybe the fact that there's a little bit of Raiborne in his eyes – and that's when a *fourth* guy, the one I never saw because he's standing outside the cage, sticks his arms in through the mesh. He slices my throat from behind.

'That's from Macklin,' says the voice behind me.

Once the hot wet comes flooding down my neck, I know it's over.

I drop to my knees and then onto my back, wondering, what's the last thought I'll have, the last thing I'll see? I don't need a priest or anybody else to hold my hand. I saw Kate stand naked on the beach in the moonlight. I played hoops in the NBA. I got to Paris.

The sun gets brighter and brighter and breaks into a thousand white dots before the dots dissolve and a huge black rectangle fills the sky. From behind it comes a horrifying clamor of metal rubbing against metal, and then the rectangle splits in half and becomes those two huge doors, the Gates of Hell. Then, as the last drops of blood drain out of me, the doors screech open and welcome me home.

# Chapter One Hundred and Seventeen

## Kate

I park just off Beach Road, and as soon as I open the door, Wingo bolts out of the car and sprints onto the vast white beach. His entire canine being is beaming with happiness. The empty expanse of water and sand make me feel better too. That's why I'm still coming out here every day, even on a mid-December afternoon like this with the temperature barely in the forties.

I walk half a mile down the beach until I find a flat, sunny patch against the cliffs, somewhat protected from the biting wind, and I stretch out my blanket.

The rhythmic collapse of the breaking waves calms

me down and helps me concentrate, and I need all the help I can get. It's been months since I got back from Paris, but it feels like yesterday, and I still don't have a clue about what I'm going to do to start up my life again.

An exhausted Wingo curls up beside me, and I take out my radio and tune in to the end of the Miami Heat–Boston Celtics game. After winning a special lottery at the end of the summer, the Celtics signed Dante to a twelve-million-dollar, three-year rookie contract, and he rewards them with twenty-two points, eleven rebounds, and four blocked shots. For his all-around performance this afternoon he is interviewed live at courtside, and even Wingo's ears prick up as Dante's excited voice comes out of my tinny little transistor.

'I just want to give a shout-out to my grandmom Marie,' says Dante. 'And to my homegirl, lawyer, and agent, Kate Costello. I love you both, and I'll see you soon.'

'You hear that, Wingo? I just got my first shout-out from the FleetCenter,' I say, and then I nuzzle my sweet, faithful dog.

In the distance, a couple steps onto the sand and starts to walk toward us along the tide line. They move slowly, leaning into the wind, and when they get closer, I see it's Macklin and Marie.

Wingo and I get up to welcome them, but something's wrong and Marie's face is streaked with tears.

'What's wrong?' I ask before they even get up to me.

'Tom's dead,' she says. 'He was murdered in jail this morning, Kate. Mack doesn't understand why I'm crying, but maybe you will.'

I'm not sure I understand it either, but suddenly I'm crying too, hard, as if someone threw a switch, and as Marie and I cling to each other, Macklin looks at the sea and stamps the sand uncomfortably.

'What's with you two? The guy was a lying, drug-dealing piece of scum, and a cold-blooded killer. He had it coming ten times over.'

'I know that,' says Marie, staring straight into my own crying eyes and dabbing at my tears with her handkerchief. 'But still. He helped Dante. He did one good thing.'

'Right, after he framed him,' says Mack, but no one's listening.

Marie invites me to her place, but I need to be alone. Despite my tears, a heavy weight is suddenly gone, and for the first time in months, I can think clearly about the future.

Wingo and I sit back down on the blanket in the sun, and by the time we get up and trudge back to the car, I think I know what I'm going to do.

I'm going to move to Portland or Seattle, where no one knows or cares who I am. I'm going to buy a little house with a porch in front, and maybe a stream running through the backyard, and I'm going to put a satellite dish on the roof so I can watch all of Dante's games.

And then, when Wingo and I are settled into our new neighborhood and I have the place set up just like I want it, everything warm and cozy, I'm going to get my name on a list to adopt a baby. I don't care if it's white, black, brown, or yellow, or if it's from Albania, Chile, Korea, or Los Angeles, but there's going to be one stipulation that's not negotiable. The baby has to be a girl. Because even though I know that Tom Dunleavy wasn't an example of anything other than his own twisted self, Wingo and I have about had it with human men.

'Isn't that right, Wingo?'

Turn the page for a preview of another compelling
thriller from master of suspense James Patterson

# JAMES
# PATTERSON
# LIFEGUARD

AND
# ANDREW
# GROSS

# PART ONE

# THE PERFECT SCORE

# Chapter One

'Don't move,' I said to Tess, sweaty and out of breath. 'Don't even blink. If you so much as breathe, I know I'm gonna wake up and I'll be back lugging chaise-longues at pool-side, imagining this gorgeous girl that I know something incredible could happen with. This will all have been a dream.'

Tess McAuliffe smiled, and in those deep blue eyes I saw what I found so irresistible about her. It wasn't just that she was the proverbial ten and a half. She was more than beautiful. She was lean and athletic with thick, auburn hair plaited into a long French braid, and had a laugh that made you want to laugh too. We liked the same movies: *Memento, The Royal Tenenbaums, Casablanca*.

We pretty much laughed at the same jokes. Since I'd met her I'd been unable to think about anything else.

Sympathy appeared in Tess's eyes. 'Sorry about the fantasy, Ned, but we'll have to take that chance. You're crushing my arm.'

She pushed me, and I rolled onto my back. The sleek cotton sheets in her fancy hotel suite were tousled and wet. My jeans, her leopard-print sarong, and a black bikini bottom were somewhere on the floor. Only half an hour earlier, we had been sitting across from each other at Palm Beach's tiny Café Boulud, picking at DB burgers – thirty dollars apiece – ground sirloin stuffed with foie gras and truffles.

At some point her leg brushed against mine. We just made it to the bed.

'Aahhh,' Tess sighed, rolling up onto her elbow, 'that feels better.' Three gold Cartier bracelets jangled loosely on her wrist. 'And look who's still here.'

I took a breath. I patted the sheets around me. I slapped at my chest and legs, as if to make sure. 'Yeah,' I said, grinning.

The afternoon sun slanted across the Bogart Suite at the Brazilian Court hotel, a place I could barely have afforded a drink at, forget about the two lavishly appointed rooms overlooking the courtyard that Tess had rented for the past two months.

'I hope you know, Ned, this sort of thing doesn't happen very often,' Tess said, a little embarrassed, her chin resting on my chest.

'What sort of thing is that?' I stared into those blue eyes of hers.

'Oh, whatever could I mean? Agreeing to meet someone I'd seen just twice on the beach, for lunch. Coming here with him in the middle of the day.'

'Oh, that . . .' I shrugged. 'Seems to happen to me at least once a week.'

'It does, huh?' She dug her chin sharply into my ribs.

We kissed, and I felt *something* between us begin to rise again. The sweat was warm on Tess's breasts, and delicious, and my palm traveled up her long, smooth legs and over her bottom. Something magical was happening here. I couldn't stop touching Tess. I'd almost forgotten what it was like to feel this way.

*Split aces*, they call it, back where I'm from. South of Boston. Brockton, actually. Taking a doubleheader from the Yankees. Finding a forgotten hundred-dollar bill in an old pair of jeans. Hitting the lottery.

The perfect score.

'You're smiling.' Tess looked at me, propped up on an elbow. 'Want to let me in on it?'

'It's nothing. Just being here with *you*. You know what they say – for a while now, the only luck I've had has been bad luck.'

Tess rocked her hips ever so slightly, and as if we had done this countless times, I found myself smoothly inside her again. I just stared into those baby blues for a second, in this posh suite, in the middle of the day, with this incredible woman who only a few days before hadn't been conceivable in my life.

'Well, congratulations, Ned Kelly.' Tess put a finger to my lips. 'I think your luck's beginning to change.'

# Chapter Two

---

I had met Tess four days before, on a beautiful white sand beach along Palm Beach's North Ocean Boulevard.

'Ned Kelly' is how I always introduced myself. *Like the outlaw.* Sounds good at a bar, with a rowdy bunch crowded around. Except no one but a couple of beer-drinking Aussies and a few Brits really knew whom I was talking about.

That Tuesday, I was sitting on the beach wall after cleaning up the cabana and pool at the estate house where I worked. I was the part-time pool guy, part-time errand runner for Mr Sol Roth – Sollie to his friends. He has one of those sprawling Florida-style homes you can see from the beach north of the Breakers and maybe wonder, *Whoa, who owns that?*

I cleared the pool, polished up his collection of vintage cars from Ragtops, picked up mysteries specially selected for him by his buddies Cheryl and Julie at the Classic bookshop, even sometimes played a few games of gin with him around the pool at the end of the day. He rented me a room in the carriage house above the garage. Sollie and I met at Ta-boó, where I waited tables on weekend nights. At the time I was also a part-time lifeguard at Midtown Beach. Sollie, as he joked, made me an offer I couldn't refuse.

Once upon a time, I went to college. Tried 'real life.' Even taught school for a while back up north, until that fell apart. It would probably shock my pals here that I was once thinking of doing a Master's. In Social Education at Boston University. 'A Master's in *what*?' they'd probably go. 'Beach Management?'

So I was sitting on the beach wall that beautiful day. I shot a wave to Miriam, who lived in the large Mediterranean next door and was walking her Yorkies, Nicholas and Alexandra, on the beach. Another of Sollie's neighbors, Melanie Butschere, the famous biographer, was out with her sons Michael and Peter. The boys are

Fescoes – their father owns the Red Sox – but Melanie kept the name she's always written under. A couple of kids were surfing about a hundred yards offshore. I was thinking I'd do a run-swim-run. Jog about a mile up the beach, swim back, then run *hard* up and back. All the while – watching the ocean.

Then like some dream – there she was.

In a great blue bikini, ankle-deep in surf. Her long, reddish-brown hair knotted up in a twist with a flutter of tendrils.

Right away, it was as if there was something sad about her, though. She was staring vacantly at the horizon. I thought she was dabbing her eyes.

I had this flash – the beach, the waves, the pretty, lovelorn girl – like she was going to do something crazy!

On my beach.

So I jogged down to her in the surf. 'Hey . . .'

I shielded my eyes and squinted into that gorgeous face. 'If you're thinking what I think you are, I wouldn't advise it.'

'Thinking what?' She looked up at me, surprised.

'I don't know. I see a beautiful girl on a beach, dabbing her eyes, staring forlornly out to sea. Wasn't there some kind of movie like that?'

She smiled. That's when I could see for sure she'd been crying. 'You mean, where the girl goes in for an afternoon swim on a hot afternoon?'

'Yeah,' I said with a shrug, suddenly a little embarrassed, 'that's the one.'

She had a thin gold chain around her neck, and a perfect tan. An accent – maybe English. God, she was a knockout.

'Guess I was just being cautious. Didn't want any accidents on my beach.'

'*Your* beach?' she said, glancing up at Sollie's. 'Your house, too, I guess?' She smiled, clearly toying with me.

'Sure. You see the window above the garage? Here, you can see it,' I shifted her, 'through the palms. If you lean this way . . .'

Like an answer to my prayers, I got her to laugh.

'Ned Kelly.' I stuck out my hand.

'Ned Kelly . . . ? Like the outlaw?'

I did a double take. No one had ever said that to me. I just stood there with a dumb-ass, star-struck grin. Don't think I even let go of her hand.

'Sydney. New South Wales,' she said, displaying her Aussie 'Strine,' her accent.

'Boston,' I grinned back.

And that was how it started. We chatted a little more, about how she'd been living here for a couple of months and how she'd take long walks on the beach. She said she might come back this way the next day. And I said there was a chance I might be here, too. As I watched her walk away, I figured she was probably laughing at me behind those four-hundred-dollar Chanel sunglasses.

'By the way,' she said, suddenly turning, 'there *was* a movie. *Humoresque*. With Joan Crawford. You should check it out.'

I rented *Humoresque* that night, and it ended with the beautiful heroine drowning herself by walking into the sea.

And on Wednesday Tess came back. Looking even hotter, in this black one-piece suit and a straw hat. She didn't seem sad. We took a swim and I told her I would teach her how to bodysurf and for a while she went along. Then as I let her go she hopped the right wave and crested in like a pro. She laughed at me from the shore. 'I'm from Australia, silly. We have our Palm Beach, too. Just past Whale Beach, north of Sydney.'

We made a 'date' for lunch at the Brazilian Court in two days. That's where she was staying, one of the most fashionable places in town, a few blocks off Worth Avenue.

Those two days were like an eternity for me. Every ring of my cell phone I figured was her canceling. But she didn't. We met in Café Boulud, where you have to make a reservation a month in advance unless you're Rod Stewart or someone. I was as nervous as a kid going out on his first date. She was already sitting at the table in a sexy off-the-shoulder dress. I couldn't take my eyes off of her. We never even made it to dessert.